THE DISCARDED

By Louis van Schalkwyk

KINGSLEY
PUBLISHERS

First published in South Africa by Kingsley Publishers, 2022
Copyright © Louis van Schalkwyk, 2022

The right of Louis van Schalkwyk to be identified as author of
this work has been asserted.

Kingsley Publishers
Pretoria, South Africa
www.kingsleypublishers.com

A catalogue copy of this book will be available from the National
Library of South Africa
Paperback ISBN: 978-0-620-99689-1
eBook ISBN: 978-0-620-99690-7

For Courtney

CHAPTER 1

"Can you two keep it down out there?!" Stephen shouted into the night sky. He slammed the sliding window above the kitchen sink shut, causing it to shudder violently in its frame. It was late and his two Rottweilers were driving him insane. They were usually the first ones planted on the couch after dinner, but in an out-of-character twist the two had insisted on being let outside tonight. They had squealed and scratched at the back door: there was no choice but to set them free or risk having to do extensive repairs in the morning. Since then, the pair had been barking incessantly and the sound was beginning to reverberate in Stephen's skull. Through the glass, he could see the animals' faded outlines. They were running around like rabid beasts. He wondered what had gotten into normally docile and lazy pair.

What Stephen was also unaware of was the fact that, before the night was through, he would be dead.

He looked down at his hands. His palms felt leathery and coarse after a good twenty minutes battling the crusted, burnt edges of tonight's lasagna dish in the soapy water. A few lackluster scrubs later, he decided to dump it back in to let it soak overnight and commenced feeling around the bottom of the sink for cutlery – his absolute nemesis in the process of washing up. He cursed under his breath and a chill of disgust ran through him as morsels of food and grease brushed past his fingers, like little creatures lurking in the deep. There was a time when he had more patience for performing mundane tasks at the end of a long day, but lately his twenty-eight-year haul of swinging the courtroom gavel had begun to feel like it was deliberately dragging his exhausted soul to the depths of perdition. And it was showing. Patience wasn't only a virtue – it was also a critically endangered species in the wilderness that was Judge Stephen Thatcher's mind. Retirement was only three months away but for a man at the end of his professional rope, it might as well have been three years. It was all he thought of and it couldn't come soon enough.

"They're probably just after that squirrel again." Stella's velvety voice came from the living room around the corner. She was perched on the sofa where she could habitually be found after supper, hidden behind her horn-rimmed glasses and a Dean Koontz novel. "It's bother, hun," she continued. "Why don't you come and sit down?"

She had always been the coolant to his fire, ever since that fateful summer day when their paths crossed on Harvard University's main campus. They had been close to graduating and were astounded that they had never met before. Both were natives of the same suburb in Toronto and had traversed the grounds of Harvard in a parallel fashion for at least three years. They had walked through corresponding hallways, sat through identical lectures, and frequented the same cafeteria, all without fate ever arranging even a glance between them. That was until they reached for the same empty seat in the Widener Library just across from the Tercentenary Theatre early one Wednesday morning. The connection had been instant, and the pair ended up spending all afternoon and most of that night comparing notes and discussing politics, the law and love in a coffee shop across the road. Several dates in quick succession ensued and here they were, forty-one years, three children and six grandchildren later. They had accomplished much together, both personally and career-wise, and were looking forward to easing into a version of their lives that they had built from the ground up and could now enjoy to the very fullest.

Stephen gladly accepted his wife's offer and dried his hands on the towel hanging from the edge of the sink. Just then, a flicker of movement caught his eye through the kitchen window. He peered through, almost pressing his face up to the glass. His eyes squinted as he saw what appeared to be a round, red shape floating next to the Silver Maple tree in the distance. The lighting outside was dim and hazy, so he reached for the exterior light switch, flicked it and returned his gaze towards the window, studying the scene.

Nothing.

Must've been one of the mutts, he thought as he snuffed the light and strolled into the living room. He gave Stella a peck on the cheek and flopped into his chocolate brown La-Z-Boy recliner, making it creak and moan. It was worn out and almost as old as he was, but he refused to give it up, much to his wife's protestation. She had the record player on and was humming along to Bill Withers paying tribute to "Grandma's Hands" in his smooth baritone. The judge unfolded the newspaper next to his steaming coffee mug and scanned the front-page articles. A famous tech magnate was getting divorced and the Russian President was unleashing yet another feeble attempt at PR work. Neither of these stories surprised him. Stephen grunted and flipped to the sports pages.

*****

One a murky night in an affluent neighborhood a white van pulled up to the corner of a quiet street. It had blacked out windows and the faded decal on the sides read *Frank's Motor Repairs*. The van's engine and headlights were turned off, abruptly ending the flow of steam exiting the exhaust. Then the driver's side door opened and a male figure wearing dark clothing and a red ski mask exited. He mounted the sidewalk, crossed the front lawn of a large Swiss-style house and hopped over the six-foot perimeter wall that divided the front and backyards without making a single sound. He skirted his way around the house then advanced through the back garden, negotiating a scattering of toys on the perfectly manicured grass: a girl's pink bicycle with white ribbons bursting from the handlebars, several dolls dressed in the same purple cheerleader outfits and a plastic replica of an M-16 Assault rifle with a bright red muzzle that had a sticker attached reading *RAMBO: FIRST BLOOD*. Frost had begun to form on the abandoned playthings giving them an odd glistening appearance in the faint moonlight.

The figure made his way to the rear of the lawn and approached the wall that bordered the backyard of the adjoining property. He could hear dogs barking and howling. Big ones and by the sounds of their footfall, they were getting closer. He boosted himself off a small nearby chair, mounted the wall and drew a handgun and a silencer from his pocket. He then proceeded to join the two together with the fluency of an expert hand. The dogs were right below him now, growling and snarling with strings of saliva flying from their exposed teeth. They jumped up repeatedly, snapping at the dark figure on the wall, but he was just out of reach.

Then, four muffled sounds rang into the night. The two canines went quiet.

The figure glanced around to see if the abrupt end to the noise had drawn interest. When he was satisfied that it hadn't, he dropped down onto the soft soil next to his kills. Twenty meters ahead of him was a sizable colonial style house with wooden shutters, a deck crowded with outdoor furniture and a flat, round barbeque pit made from cast iron. A weathered tire swing was hanging from the lowest branch of a nearby tree, gently ebbing and flowing in the cool winter breeze.

In the center of the stately home was a large window, revealing an older man elbow deep in the kitchen sink. The dark-clad figure cocked his weapon and stepped forward through the garden, crushing bright yellow dahlias under his boot heels.

*****

Stephen stood in front of the bathroom mirror carefully

attempting to remove one of his contact lenses when a blood-curdling scream came from the kitchen.

"Stella!" he yelled as he ran down the hallway in his boxer shorts, his gown flowing behind him like a cape. As he made the turn into the kitchen doorway, he caught a glimpse of the butt of a gun smashing into his face. The blow shorted out his eyesight and sent a sharp pain from the bridge of his nose to the back of his head. The judge went down, crashing straight through a scanty two-seater table in the middle of the room where he'd had this breakfast nearly every morning for the last twenty years. His ears rang as he moaned and rubbed his eyes to get a semblance of vision back. Footsteps approached from an unknown direction. Trying to get a look at his attacker, Stephen swung his head from side to side. Warm blood ran into his eyes from a gash right between his eyebrows. He blinked ferociously and wiped at his face but only muddled images of a dark figure standing next to him came through.

"Where is she?!" Stephen screamed and blood-tinged saliva sprayed from his mouth.

The figure loomed over him, grabbed his hair, jerked his head backwards and landed a punch on his right cheek. Stephen heard a cracking noise coming from inside his head and he caught a whiff of the leather glove the figure was wearing. It smelled of sweat and damp animal hide. A few seconds passed before he partially regained his sight. He spotted a paring knife on the floor that used to reside on the destroyed breakfast table. Gathering all his might, he lunged for it. The knife found its way into his left hand and he spun around on the floor, landing flat on his back. The figure brought a heavy foot down onto Stephen's shoulder in an effort to stop him from using the knife, but his arm sprung free, and he reached up, jamming the small blade squarely into the attacker's upper thigh.

A stifled cry came from the figure's ski mask, and he recoiled backwards, losing his footing and landing with his back against the refrigerator door. Stephen jumped up and ran at full tilt, heading towards the cabinet behind the mahogany cocktail bar in the corner of the living room. It was where his Remington was kept. His heart was pounding through his chest, and he could hear his lungs heaving and throat wheezing from swallowing blood. Once ducked behind the bar he flung the small door open to reveal a black gun safe with an electronic keypad. His hands trembled uncontrollably, and after a third attempt the little red light next to the numbers went green and the safe door clicked ajar, opening just enough to see the gleam from the barrel of the revolver inside. He wiped blood from his face, retrieved the gun and checked if it was loaded. The back of six unspent bullet casings greeted him and he felt a miniscule sense of control return to his psyche.

The house was silent aside from his own breathing and the monotonous tick-tick-tick coming from the antique grandfather clock in the hallway. With the gun in a tremoring death grip, Stephen slowly emerged from behind the countertop. The room was dark and through his blood-misted vision he could barely discern anything beyond the outlines of the objects he was looking at. Across the living room was a beam of light emanating from the kitchen doorway. Stephen stayed low and forced himself to put one foot in front of the other. He knew he had to find Stella. She hadn't been in the kitchen during the half-a-second glimpse he got before he was sucker-punched.

Maybe she got out already, ran across the road to Richard and Deedee's and called the cops, he thought. *Fuckin' better be.*

Stephen moved toward the kitchen entrance. He leaned around the corner and saw the smashed table, blood on the floor and a large dent in the bottom door of the fridge where the attacker had landed. There was no sign of Stella or the dark figure. He turned left and headed back down the hallway toward the bedrooms, planting his feet as lightly as possible on the thick, wool carpet. On a small dressing table which usually housed their keys and cell phones, his fingers fumbled around on the surface, hoping and praying to all manner of deities that he would find either his or Stella's phone. His prayers went unanswered – the man in the mask must have taken them.

"Stephen!" Stella, from the main bedroom. Her voice was shrill and it raised the hair on the back of his neck. "Run, Stephen! Don't come in here pl—"

He heard the sound of something hard connecting with a soft object and it chilled the judge's veins as his wife was silenced by force. A combination of panic and rage that he had never felt before gripped his insides and twisted them into a barbed entanglement of horror. He held the Remington at arm's length and charged into the bedroom but was stopped in his tracks by the sight before him. Stella was lying down on the bed, shivering, with tears streaming down her bruised face which was contorted in fear. The dark figure with the red ski mask stood next to her, facing Stephen with the silencer of his firearm pressed closely to Stella's temple. For a moment, they just stood there, staring at each other. Stephen's quivering hand was sweating around the revolver's handle, but he knew there was nothing he could do. The dark figure reached out to the judge with his free hand, palm upwards and flicked his fingers in a "hand it over" gesture. The judge grit his teeth and pulled the hammer back on his gun. But the figure shoved the front end of his weapon harder onto Stella's temple, making her head bob unnaturally. She let out a desperate sob. "Just go, Stephen!" she screamed through her tears.

But he couldn't. The message was clear.

The figure walked over and snatched the gun from his hand. After securing it to his waistband, he shoved the judge onto the bed next to his wife. They embraced, crying and exchanging repeated "I love you's". The figure walked over to the foot of the bed and stared at the couple in silence. Stephen looked up at him, raised a pleading hand and said, "Please ... *Please* ... Just let her go."

The dark figure raised his weapon and pulled the trigger six times.

CHAPTER 2

Ellis Neill rolled over and stuffed his face back into the pillow in an attempt to escape the daylight cascading through his bedroom window in sporadic beams. He slowly opened one eye then the other and stared at the clock radio's red, digital numbers on his bedside table: 6:31a.m. From the kitchen downstairs he heard the coffee machine being fired up. It whirred and spluttered like the old pipes in a very tiny house. Ellis turned his head to check if it was Cynthia rustling up the java and smiled when he saw her still asleep next to him, her rhythmic breathing almost inaudible. Long, jet-black locks were still settled peacefully in a frame around her face making her appear like she had been professionally organized by a set designer on a photo shoot. Even in slumber she gave the impression of being ready for anything, but she was rarely up and about this early especially now that she was working from home.

Shortly after COVID-19 struck its initial blow, many of her colleagues got the boot but through sheer will, hard work and determination she had proved to the suits that she was invaluable to their business, and they had been enthusiastic about keeping her on the payroll. Ellis was grateful. Every bit helped, particularly after their impromptu move from Edmonton to Toronto six months earlier. It hadn't been an easy decision by any means. He had to take a lower paying job, but the hours were good, and it was peaceful: a sharp contrast to his career preceding this move. The determining factor in his decision had been the survival of his marriage and avoiding the uncoupling of his family unit. Money had to take a backseat for now and Cynthia had been all too happy to fill the financial gap. Sacrifices had been made all around in a joint effort to rectify the family dynamic.

Ellis kissed his wife's forehead, got out from under the sheets and made his way downstairs. Rose's skinny frame, hidden by her oversized school dress, which was engulfed in a wide red belt, was sprinkling sweetener into a glass mug filled with black coffee.

"Morning, darling."

"Hey, Dad," she said while stirring.

"A bit young for the hard stuff, aren't you?" he asked as he yawned and inspected the label on the coffee packaging that read *100% Insomnia Blend*. Ellis wondered how that brand name was passed in a marketing meeting.

"Uh, I'm ten," came Rose's reply, drenched with the sass that Ellis had come to accept as part of his daughter's spirited demeanor. "I've been drinking this since I was six. Hellooo."

"Of course. Far be it from me to tell you what to do, I'm just your dad." He winked at her. She smiled and hugged him tight. Her radiant blue eyes looked up at him. Ellis could see more of her mother in them every day. Rose was wise beyond her years;

she had somehow grown up with the street smarts of a seasoned private detective, even though she had a fairly sheltered and controlled opening few years to life.

"Is Mom up yet?" She sipped her coffee and let out a sigh of satisfaction.

"Nope. She had a pretty late meeting last night so try to keep it down, okay?" Ellis glanced at the kitchen wall clock. "Why are you shakin' so early?"

"Nelly and I are going to the library before school. She needs help with her homework which is due today." She shook her head with disdain, then added in a TV-infomercial tone, "Failing to plan is planning to fail."

"You're not doing the homework *for* her, are you?" Ellis said and saw the corner of a paperback novel peeking from inside Rose's bag. He slid it out a bit further and read the title: *The Edible Woman* by Margaret Atwood. He smiled when he saw that he had predicted the author correctly.

"Not without payment, no!" Rose flashed him a you-should-know-better look and grabbed her backpack from underneath his hand. It looked more like an adult's briefcase than the usual pop star-inspired collage that graced the bag of a typical female fifth grader. "Relax, Dad. I promise I'll only ever break the law to spring you or Mom from the clutches of an evil madman," she said and kissed him on the cheek. "I'm out! See you later!"

"Did you take your meds?" Ellis' tone was slightly sterner than he had intended.

"Yes, Master," she said with her palms clasped together while bowing, followed by a playful eye roll.

Her generous helping of auburn hair, tied up in a high ponytail today, bobbed gingerly as she made her way out. Ellis stood staring at the door as if his daughter were still there. He often marveled at how far she had come since drawing her first few breaths at the Gray Nuns hospital on a crisp evening in October. Minutes after uttering her rudimentary cries the doctor had rushed the newborn out of the delivery room. A blue tinge had encroached her face and limbs, accompanied by an unnatural gasp from her tiny lips. The perplexed and agitated new parents were reeling when they hadn't received any solid answers until three torturous hours later. Rose had gone into cardiac arrest upon birth and was hurried into emergency surgery to restore circulation. Against all odds she had pulled through and was diagnosed with a congenital heart defect, similar to the condition that had plagued and eventually ended the life of Ellis' mother. Countless visits and consultations with an innumerable number of specialists later, the doctors settled on a medication that gave Rose the best possible quality of life going forward. Strenuous exercise and any form of athletic achievements had been cut from her future endeavors, however the academic gods had come through and bestowed upon her a mind which rivalled that of a genius in the making. She was smart, thoughtful and caring.

Ellis was relieved that their relationship was heading in the right direction following a strained few years when she was filled with resentment towards him. Frequent traveling for work had left a hole in the home where he was supposed to be and this had translated into an emotional canyon between father and daughter. Both he and Cynthia had hoped that their recent move would remedy that, and Ellis quietly celebrated any small indication that he had begun to regain his daughter's trust.

He made two cups of coffee but not from Rose's stash. One was black and the other had milk and two teaspoons of sugar added for Cynthia. When he got back into the bedroom his wife was already in the shower.

"Hey, babe. Did Rosey leave already?" Her voice echoed off the tiles through the sound of rushing water. He could see her outline through the frosted glass door and stopped to have another look. Clouds of steam rose from above the glass and were slowly sinking down from the ceiling onto the carpeted floor.

"Yup. Off to conquer the world. How about the other woman in my life?"

"I can't believe I missed her again." The disappointment in her voice was palpable. "This woman is a bit worse for wear today, but she'll live."

"How was the meeting?" he said and placed Cynthia's coffee on her bedside table.

"How much time do you have?" she scoffed. "I might bore you to death halfway through with all the eloquent and riveting jargon I have to filter through to make it understandable. I swear the corporate world has its own damn language."

"That good, huh?" Ellis conceded to his better judgment. Cynthia didn't enjoy talking shop first thing in the morning.

"Was great!" she said with obvious mockery.

Ellis took chewing gum from a pack that read *Nicotine-No* and popped it into his mouth. Ten seconds later he grimaced, spat it into his palm and dropped it next to his coffee mug.

He settled into an armchair in front of the window. It was late November and most of the trees were already bare. Only a few still had their final specks of brown and yellow leaves that were clinging on to witness the first snowfall of the coming winter. A light fog was lingering just above the tree line which made the scene outside look like something out of a fairy tale. Or a horror movie, depending on the beholder.

"My parents are arriving tomorrow. Have you fixed the heater in the spare room yet?" Cynthia said from under a towel draped over her head as she entered the bedroom. "I won't have time to remind you today. It's Ruth's birthday and she wants all the girls over for breakfast." She picked up the hair dryer, considered it, then dropped it again and went with a black hair tie she spotted on the dresser instead.

"Getting on it after this, dear." Ellis raised his coffee mug. "I'm only on from one until five at the workshop today so I'll take care of it before I go."

"You're a doll," she said and ran her fingers through his hair as she walked past him towards the closet.

"Have they said how long they are staying?"

"No, but they're not doing well. Mom said two weeks but you never know. Ralph is drinking again and he doesn't know that she is fully aware of it. That probably means they'll be here until after Christmas, possibly New Year's as well." Cynthia let out a sigh as she browsed for an outfit and began to lay options onto the bed.

"Could that be an issue, him being drunk in the house? For Rose, I mean. She isn't used to that kind of thing," Ellis said, replaying the highlights of the catastrophe that was last Christmas in his mind. As it always played out, everyone was quite merry around the table but Ralph took it a few steps too far. The pinnacle of his performance for last year's gathering was to stand up on his chair in the middle of Christmas lunch, unzip his pants and urinate all over the table while shouting "Crop Circles" at the top of his voice. Not a single plate went unscathed and lunch ended quite abruptly with the frenzied packing of suitcases and the slamming of car doors as ninety percent of the family and friends made a hasty exit. Ralph couldn't understand what all the fuss was about. Until the next morning.

"I'm more worried about what'll come out of *her* mouth. You know what she's like with that no-filter wit of hers. She could send him straight into a full-on bender." Cynthia smirked, pulled on a pair of jeans from the bed and paired it with a white sweater and beige flats.

"Shall we book our daughter into a hotel then?" Ellis knew his words were questionable as she shot him a fiery glance in response. He rephrased: "I'll have a talk with her when I get back from saving humanity tonight."

Cynthia grabbed her coffee, bent down and kissed him. "I love you. I know this isn't the perfect job and you'd rather be running around shooting at bad guys but we're both proud as hell. Remember that, Mr. Neill. I'll see you later." The soles of her shoes clicked on the wooden floor and intensified as she descended the stairs.

"Have fun!" Ellis smiled and turned his gaze back to the unfolding morning beyond his window.

*****

The rolling storm clouds appeared ominous in the rear-view mirror as the battered, old Dodge Ram cruised down the Gardiner Expressway en route to the West Don Lands in Old Toronto. Ellis took the Lakeshore Boulevard East exit and swung left onto Mill Street, driving past the Soulpepper Theatre where he and Cynthia spent most of their bi-weekly date nights. She had always been a sucker for musicals and plays. On the corner of Mill and Trinity streets he turned onto a gravel driveway that led to a lot strewn with old cars and trucks. He parked the Ram and walked over to a lofty brick warehouse with steel-framed windows and two large roller doors fitted side by side that stood open. Several mechanics could be seen cranking away at a variety of old and new vehicles as the high-pitched whirring of power tools and chatter echoed off the walls. The place smelled of gasoline and burnt rubber which always took Ellis straight back to his first tour of Iraq.

He was an unsteady apprentice in the world of vehicle mechanics as well as gunfire and violence back then. He often wondered how different his dreams would be if he had chosen another direction for his life instead of enlisting. Yes, he was only sent to the desert to keep the Hummers and tanks running but on the odd occasion he was forced to pick up a rifle and help defend his unit as best he could. Most of the jarheads bragged about the number of notches carved onto their helmets and the ceremony of attaining a new one was deemed honorable and sacred. Ellis had one notch. And nobody wanted to talk about it afterwards – least of all him.

A few of the other wrench wranglers nodded in greeting as he crossed the workshop floor towards the neatly organized shelf of staff timecards in the office. Underneath the door was a rusted sign that read: *Frank's Motor Repairs*. Inside, a stocky man in his late forties with a thick, wild mustache was sitting behind a metal desk scattered with papers and fast-food containers. A tightly spanned Blue Jays T-shirt was battling to contain his bulging gut. On the front end of the table among grease-stained stationery was a modest black plaque that read: *Reynold Pope, MANAGER* in faded, white letters.

"How we doin' on that Fairlane?" came Pope's gruff, tobacco-altered voice from across the desk. The Louisiana native turned Canuck wasn't ever a man for chit-chat and today was no different.

"Hey, Pope. The transmission is almost done, then it's a quick oil change and she's good to go," Ellis said and regarded the man across from him whose eyes were still fixed on today's newspaper.

"Good. I want that old geezer off my ass about it. If he calls again, I'm makin' *you* talk to him."

"She'll be done by four," Ellis said and thought it would probably be closer to three, but with Pope it was better to under-promise and over-deliver.

"Not with you standin' around here it won't," Pope barked and lit a half-smoked Cuban cigar as he shifted his gaze from the paper to Ellis. "And give Gary a hand with that F-150 when you're done, will you? That fucking idiot's about as green as they come."

"Will do."

Ellis clocked in, grabbed his tool belt from the communal locker, swung it over his shoulder and shut the door behind him. He strode toward a row of beaters in need of care that were hoisted up on car lifts and stopped at a sky blue 1972 Ford Fairlane. He secured the tool belt around his waist and pulled a socket wrench from one of the belt loops.

"On your knees! Right now!" a voice boomed without warning from behind him. Ellis swung around and a jolt ran through him as he saw several automatic weapons and handguns aimed straight at him from across the warehouse floor. The varieties of guns were manned by masked and goggled cops in full SWAT gear. Ellis counted eight of them. In the middle of the group was a man in a suit, pistol drawn and held to his side with a megaphone in front of his face. "This is your last warning!" the forceful voice said again. "On your knees! Now!"

"What in the hell?" Ellis blurted out and one of the SWAT cops racked his shotgun and they all took a step closer in unison. "All right! All right!" Ellis yelled and his heart leapt into his throat. Ellis dropped to his knees. He could feel a thin film of icy sweat break out all over his body. As he raised his hands the wrench he was holding hit the floor with a resounding clatter. The entire workshop was silent. Everyone was frozen in place, eyes wide and mouths hanging open while their eyes shifted between the cops and Ellis as if watching a tennis match. Pope barged out of his office and one of the SWAT cops took aim at him which made him stop dead in his tracks, palms raised.

"Both hands behind your head! Fingers interlocked! Slowly!" the suited voice continued. Ellis complied and four of the SWAT members cantered over and pushed him to the ground onto his chest. The side of his face hit the concrete hard enough to make his head bounce off the unforgiving surface. He felt two knees mount his back right under the shoulder blades and another set of hands yanked his arms backwards. The tight pinch and clicking sound of handcuffs locking was unmistakable. The suited man walked over and Ellis strained to look up at him.

"Comfy, motherfucker?" He smiled as he stared at Ellis. "I hope you don't have dinner plans, because you'll be missing them."

CHAPTER 3

The drive from the workshop to Police Headquarters on Grenville Street felt like it was taking hours to Ellis, when in fact it was a mere twenty-minute journey. He was in the back of a large police van with thick, black bars in front of the small windows mounted high up on the side panels. Through the ungenerous portal to the outside world, nothing more than cloudy skies and the top halves of glistening skyscrapers were visible.

Seated on the dented steel bench, Ellis had a SWAT cop on either side of him and another right across – a young, three hundred pounder with a buzz cut and goatee. He kept his gray eyes fixed on the man in handcuffs, almost without blinking. Between him and the other cops involved in this arrest Ellis definitely picked up an undercurrent of rage and forcefulness. Not at all like the arrests he was used to seeing on reality TV. Unfortunately, that was the only benchmark he had to compare it to. That and the military police he had contact with in the desert. They had more of a neutral touch to their procedures. This contrast in styles planted a seed in Ellis' mind: whatever these men thought he had done, it was pretty bad. Their glares told a story of personal offence and he had enough common sense to know that was very grim news.

Ellis tried to move his feet to brace himself as the van tore through the streets of downtown but the ankle chains limited his range of movement, bouncing him off the officers on either side as the vehicle made what felt like several thousand turns. The prisoner compartment smelled of sweat and rust and he suddenly realized the odor came from his own body. His shirt was drenched and it clung to his chest and back as if it were glued on.

In the back of his mind, he replayed the last twenty minutes. *Did the guy in the suit say I was arrested for murder?* he thought. *Yes, he had said murder.* Ellis tried to remember everything that had been said. There was a lot of shouting, warnings and questions to which he just recalled nodding at while he was being shoved into the van. His head began to spin and he tried to think of ten things at once: Had they followed him to work that morning? They got there about five minutes after he clocked in so they must have been watching him or waiting for him to arrive. Where would Cynthia be now? Still at her birthday breakfast, probably. He needed to get in touch with her. Would he need a lawyer? Who the hell would that be? Ellis had always considered attorneys as something you never think of until the need arises. Unless you're of the Pablo Escobar graduate class, then you'd probably have one permanently living in your house.

Ellis tried to harness his thoughts. His mind began to attempt logical scenarios. *This was just a mistake,* he thought. *It'll all be taken care of once I can sit down, talk to them, and straighten this whole thing out, whatever it is.*

"Do I get a phone call?" Ellis asked the cop next to him.

"Be quiet, sir." The officer gave a sharp answer.

"I just need …"

"He said shut up!" the massive SWAT cop across from Ellis barked and tightened the grip on his rifle. Ellis' mouth slammed shut instinctively and he sank back into his seat.

The van made one final gut-wrenching turn and came to a stop. There was muffled conversation coming from the cockpit, which was divided from the back section of the van by a solid steel wall with a small, square sliding window in the center. It was only wide enough to see the eyes and brow of whoever opened it to check if their prisoner was still intact. The engine rumbled again and the van was parked. Without warning the back doors flew open and Ellis saw the suited man and two other plain-clothes officers staring at him as if he were the newest addition to the traveling freak show in town.

"Let's go," the suited man snapped. Ellis' two chaperones hoisted him up by his arms and escorted him out of the vehicle towards a large building with a steel door that gleamed in the sunlight. The third SWAT cop was directly behind Ellis, rifle at the ready. Suit guy buzzed the door and it clicked open. They walked through a long corridor with gray walls and even grayer floors. A white line divided the passageway into two halves. The left lane, which they were walking in, had the words "KEEP LEFT" painted on it in intervals and the right lane had the same but printed upside down.

At the end of the passage there was a gate with a security guard behind it who straightened his posture when he laid eyes on suit guy. He said something over a two-way radio and the gate buzzed open. The guard collected their weapons and only Ellis and suit guy passed through, with the SWAT cops staying behind. Ellis could feel their stares burning a hole into his back and he grew increasingly worried. They passed doors numbered in sequence until they reached one that had a number 9 printed onto a sheet of paper and taped to it. Ellis was pushed through the entrance and firmly planted onto a small chair. His cuffs were secured to a thick metal loop which was welded onto the adjoining steel table. Suit guy exited without saying a word and shut the door behind him.

The room was lit up with several fluorescent lights. It was brighter than the daylight outside and he had to squint for the first few minutes until his eyes adjusted. Chipped green paint lined the walls and there were scratch marks and dents in the table. The place was windowless except for a large, mirrored pane of glass to Ellis' left. He wondered how many sets of eyes were on him from behind it and what were they thinking. In the far-left corner of the room was a ceiling mounted camera with a red light blinking above the lens. The door opened and a young officer in uniform popped her head in through a gap. She had a youthful appearance with red locks of hair protruding from under her hat.

"Coffee? Water?" the officer offered in a disinterested tone. Ellis shook his head and the door shut again. Once the echo from the slamming door faded, the only sound he could hear was the faint buzzing of the lights above. That and his heart which was still pounding as if it were trying to claw its way through his ribs, out of his chest and make a run for it. His legs shook and he tried his best to get them to keep still.

A few minutes passed slowly. Ellis closed his eyes, took several deep breaths, and opened them again.

The door swung open and suit guy walked in carrying a brown folder. He dropped it on the table in front of Ellis and sat down in the chair on the opposite end. He was in his mid-forties with patches of gray that stained his dark hair and continued in his beard. Knowing brown eyes peered at Ellis like those of a leopard about to pounce on its prey. The man produced a pack of Marlboros from his jacket pocket, lit one and offered Ellis another, which he accepted. He then placed the box and cigarette lighter on the table. His hand moved to the folder and drew it closer to his chest. There was a long pause where the two men sat in silence, each trying to get a read of the other. The buzzing of the overhead lights seemed to get louder. Finally, suit guy spoke up.

"My name is William Black. Would you like to tell me why you're here, Mr. Neill?" Black's voice was calm and low. He placed his elbows on the table and interlocked his fingers in front of his jaw.

"I don't know why I'm here." Ellis shook his head.

"Okay. Why do you *think* you're here?"

"I know the reason you gave me when I was arrested." Ellis' tone was flat but he was still shaking inside.

"And what was that?"

"Don't I get a phone call?" Ellis frowned as he asked.

"I see you're familiar with this process." Black smiled and opened the brown folder. "No, Mr. Neill, you don't. Not right now, anyway. I am under no obligation to have your lawyer present during questioning."

"When do I get to do that then?" Ellis came back.

"We'll get to that. How long have you worked at Frank's Motor Repairs?"

"About six months."

"And how did you get that job?"

"It was listed in a newspaper," Ellis answered, figuring he could help himself by being upfront.

"Which one?"

"What?"

"Which newspaper?" Black returned.

"*Edmonton Journal*."

"Edmonton?" Black looked confused. The expression appeared foreign to the detective's confident demeanor.

"I moved here from Edmonton when I got the job."

"I see." Black took a notebook from his jacket's inner pocket. "Do you own a firearm, Mr. Neill?"

"No."

"Officers are searching your house right now and it would be better for you if you were honest."

"I am being honest. I want this over with." Ellis spoke in a calm and firm manner. He didn't want to sound like he was pleading as it could be construed as a sign of presumed guilt.

"Ever killed anyone before?"

"Um, no." Ellis was surprised at the sudden shift in questioning.

"You're sure?" Black's stare intensified like that of a poker player who knew he was sitting on a winning hand and was completely inept at hiding it.

"Yes, I think I'd remember that happening," Ellis said and watched the detective pull a sheet of paper from the folder on the table and hold it up.

"August 2007. Your unit was camped ten miles outside of Karbala, Iraq in support of US forces in the area. In this incident report from your C.O., it says—"

"Those records are sealed." Ellis' words were barely out when Black slammed his fist onto the steel table hard enough to add another dent to the collection.

"Don't interrupt me!" Black barked. Beads of sweat were on his forehead which weren't there a second ago. "They're not sealed anymore, Mr. Neill. Shall I continue?"

Ellis stared blankly ahead, not quite sure how to respond.

"Thank you." Black turned his eyes back to the sheet and read: "The men were eating and drinking around a fire as they had the night off. A scuffle ensued, shots were fired and Master Corporal Neill – that's you – discharged his weapon killing a member of his platoon." Black looked up at Ellis and shrugged his shoulders.

"There's more to the story than that. I was court-martialed and found not guilty."

"Mm-hmm," Black replied, still reading the report.

"What does this have to do with why I'm here, Detective?" Ellis felt his fear temporarily being replaced by frustration.

"A lot, Mr. Neill. It tells me that you are a killer by nature." Black dropped the paper on the table and sat back in his chair.

"Can you at least tell me who I've supposedly killed this time?"

"Okay, I'll play your game," Black said and produced an A4 sized photograph from the folder and slid it across the table. It was of a couple in their sixties, locked in an embrace and covered in blood on a bed. Ellis could see several gunshot wounds to their upper bodies and heads and severe bruising on their faces like they'd both gone a few rounds with Tyson.

"Who is this?" Ellis asked as he studied the picture.

"Don't recognize your own handiwork?" Black scoffed. "I'll tell you this – Judge Thatcher over here was a mentor to the current District Attorney and a close personal friend to the entire law enforcement community. Do you know what that means? Do you know how fucked you are?" Black leaned forward. "If you think I came in here to squeeze a confession out of you, you're dead wrong because I don't *need* it. You've probably killed a lot more people than these two." Black tapped his index finger on the photograph. "But this time you were sloppy. Real sloppy, and you can tell your friends I'm coming after them next."

"What?! What friends?! Who in God's name do you think I am, exactly?!" Ellis' voice cracked. Black got up off his chair, picked the folder up and started for the door. He grabbed the handle, paused, then spoke over his shoulder.

"You know what the difference is between you and me? I

wear my colors. Some criminals wear their colors too. They don't lurk in the shadows like cowards and I can respect that, as fucked up as it sounds. At least they know they've made a choice and there will be consequences. But *you*. You wolves in sheep's clothing who slink around and prey on the innocent and defenseless. *You* are the worst of the worst."

Black exited and the door locked behind him.

*****

The holding cells at Police Headquarters consisted of several steel cages lined up in a row, separated by ten centimeter concrete walls which prevented any form of physical contact between inmates. Ellis was placed right at the end of the row and his cell had a thicker, tiled wall on one side which indicated the end of the building. Inside the enclosure was an aluminum toilet bolted to the floor and a single bed with a thin mattress covered in dark blue waterproof upholstery. He was sitting on the bed with his head in his hands, thinking about the phone call he had with Cynthia an hour earlier. She had been hysterical, something Ellis didn't associate with his wife. She'd cried and kept asking how this could've happened, what they would do next and what this would do to Rose. He eventually got her calm enough to devise a plan. She was to call her mother and ask if she knew of a decent attorney. It could be anyone, as long as they were loyal and he could avoid being assigned a court-appointed lawyer. When Ellis was forced to hang up by a guard standing watch next to the payphone, Cynthia was sobbing again. The officer grabbed the phone and flung it onto the hook. That had torn Ellis' heart out. There was no comforting her and it ate at him.

The lock on his cell door buzzed and a stately looking man in a dark blue suit was let in. He was in his late fifties and had soft blue eyes behind wire framed glasses. The door closed behind him as he sat down on the bed.

"Mr. Neill?" he said while opening a slim, black briefcase.

"Yes?"

"My name is Victor Redpath. Your wife sent me." Redpath handed Ellis a business card that read: *Victor J. Redpath, Attorney at Law.* "How are you holding up?"

"Not great. Is Cynthia here?"

"She's outside. They won't let her in until you're officially awaiting trial."

"And Rose? Is she with her? Is she okay?" Ellis began to shake at the thought of how scared his daughter must be. She was tough but this was uncharted territory for all of them.

"Mr. Neill, I understand your concerns, but we really need to focus on *you* right now. What have the police told you?"

Redpath took notes as Ellis replayed the entire day for him, from the time he left for work that afternoon until the attorney showed up at his cell door a few minutes ago. Redpath sat in silence for a few seconds, lightly chewing on the ends of his glasses. He took a deep breath before he spoke.

"Okay. Here's what we know so far. The police are quite open about sharing information on this which isn't usually a good sign. It means they think their case is watertight. The victims in this double homicide are Stephen Thatcher and his wife Stella. Stephen was a highly decorated Justice of the Crown and almost exclusively dealt with high-profile crimes. Murder, armed robbery, organized crime, that sort of thing. He was straight as an arrow and absolutely incorruptible. The good news is they don't have a motive. The bad news? Your fingerprints are on a Glock 9 which was found at the bottom of a neighbor's pool. They're still doing ballistics on it, so we don't know anything about that yet. A witness said that they saw you driving around the area at 11p.m. the night of the murder in a workshop van. Pointed you out in a photograph. And then …" Redpath paused, and Ellis could see the doubt and disappointment on his face. "They searched your house," he continued, "and found DNA on one of your jackets and hair samples from both victims under a pair of your trainers. The shoe prints found in the judge's garden also match your shoes. Same pattern, same size." Redpath put his notebook on the bed and shifted so he could squarely face his client. "Can you explain *any* of this to me? I need to hear something from you."

"I don't know what to tell you except that I didn't do any of this," Ellis said, closing his eyes and kneading at his temples with the heels of his hands. "I've been trying to put this together since they picked me up and I'm at a loss, Mr. Redpath."

"Do you own a firearm, Mr. Neill?"

"Yes, but it's locked in a safe. I haven't taken it out or fired it in months," Ellis replied.

"Yes, they've taken the safe from your house and are in the process of opening it."

"Can they do that? Legally, I mean."

"Yup, they've got all the necessary paperwork signed off." Redpath put his glasses back on, shifting the base onto the bridge of his nose with an index finger. "Here's what I think – the evidence is stacked sky-high, so we're in a bit of trouble here. On the other hand, your mother-in-law vouches for you and I've known her for forty years. So, if she says you're not a stone-cold killer then I'll believe it. Besides, if you were a killer, you'd be a really dumb one, leaving all of that behind for the cops to find and Cheryl also said you're definitely not a dumpling so same goes. Here's what's going to happen. You'll be put in front of a judge tomorrow morning and moved to a holding cell in a local jail. We'll shoot for bail but it's going to be expensive, if we get it at all. Do you own your house?"

"No, I don't. We're renting for now."

"Anything substantial in the bank?" Redpath came back.

"Some, but not much," Ellis said and thought of the college fund they were slowly assembling for Rose. He didn't want to touch that at all.

"Okay. I'll handle that. All you need to do is keep your mouth shut. Don't even look at anyone else. I need a list of everyone you've ever known and how to get a hold of them. Can your wife provide that?"

"Yes." Ellis nodded. It felt like there was something gnawing at his stomach.

"Good." Redpath put a hand on Ellis' shoulder and let out a deep sigh. "Try to get some rest, Mr. Neill. We can't have you looking like death-warmed-up in court tomorrow," he said as a guard appeared at the door, tapping his watch and eyeballing the pair. The lock buzzed and Redpath was escorted down the corridor. Ellis' eyes followed him until he vanished through the green, iron door that led to the police station's reception area.

A sense of abandonment accompanied by severe nausea flushed over him and he lay down on the scant mattress, covering his eyes with his forearm.

*****

The arraignment the next day went about as well as the Hiroshima bombing went for the island of Japan during World War II, as Redpath put it afterwards. The Assistant Prosecutor kicked off with a gun-less safe found in the defendant's home, as well as records showing that the Glock found swimming in the neighboring pool two days ago was registered to an Ellis J. Neill. Bail was denied outright by Judge Reiner, who looked like he wanted to spit fire at Ellis during the entire procedure and a trial date was set for just over a month away. Ellis' attorney had thrown everything he had, including the proverbial kitchen sink, at the bail application, but it all fell on deaf ears and at one stage the irate judge had threatened to hold him in contempt for "antagonizing the court and the prosecution". Later that night during a phone call to his mother Redpath would confess that he hadn't been steamrolled like that in a courtroom since his rookie days back in eighty-seven.

Six weeks later the trial commenced with every news outlet in the greater Toronto area vying for seats in the overcrowded

courthouse. On TV the heading used was *The Trial of a Killer.*
Ellis was led in wearing a green prison-issue jumpsuit, which
bore *INMATE 01487, D.O.C. TORONTO* in bright white decals
on the left breast pocket and just below the collar on the back.
Redpath's request to have his client in a suit and tie during the
trial was summarily dismissed without impetus. This would be
an early indication of the direction the trial was headed in.

The prosecution, led by District Attorney for the Crown John
Layfield, battered the defense from the get-go. They came in hard
and fast, and it soon became glaringly obvious to Redpath that
they wanted to please the crowd that was baying for blood – and
do it swiftly. Cynthia sat in the galley, day in and day out, coming
in with renewed hope each morning only to have it shattered by
the end of each day's proceedings. Ellis and his attorney would
take one step forward, then get obliterated soon thereafter by
the undisputable, seemingly endless supply of evidence in the
governmental arsenal. Cynthia kept up appearances as far as
her courage could take her. Redpath said that she was just as
important from a jury's perspective as Ellis was, so she needed
to be steadfast and supportive without ever showing any doubt
or negative emotion of any kind. This plan had worn thin after
day two and she was losing control fast. She looked gaunt, her
eyes sunken in like that of a victim of dehydration. At home,
she wandered the halls and garden aimlessly at night, crying
and drinking. Lots of drinking. If it weren't for her mother being
there, the household would've come to a complete standstill.

The whole affair took only five days and by the end Redpath
had exhausted all his options. His witnesses were able to provide

no more than good character references. Even Ellis' alibi was snuffed as soon as it was launched. The prosecution argued that Mrs. Neill was no more credible in her testimony than her murderous husband. And Rose ... Much to Ellis' protest, both Redpath and Cynthia had agreed to put her on the stand in a last-ditch effort to prove that the defendant couldn't possibly be in two places at once. The earnest testimony of a young girl had never been quite so feebly cast aside in the eyes of the jury and press. During cross-examination, Layfield had Rose confused, shaken and distressed and Ellis had to utilize all his willpower not to leap across the table and defend his daughter. The look in her eyes as she stared at her father while being led off the stand was that of utter devastation and regret. She kept looking back at him through a waterfall of tears. He clenched the armrests of the wooden chair behind the defendant's table and kept repeating "I love you, it's okay" to her over and over again until she was escorted out of the room, his own tears making it hard to focus on his daughter's face that was ravaged with sorrow.

Closing arguments ensued the following day and twenty-four hours later the jury was adjourned for deliberation. The press swarmed the steps of the courthouse, elbow to elbow, making their own predictions and speculating on the details of the sentencing. Forty-five minutes later, the jury had made their decision.

Ellis Neill was found guilty on all counts and twenty minutes later Judge Reiner sentenced him to life imprisonment without any possibility of parole.

As if a switch had been flicked, Cynthia's knees caved in, and she collapsed. Her parents' screams for a medic were muddled out by the deafening applause from the crowd and the relentless fall of the gavel.

CHAPTER 4

Warden Andrew Blakeway hit the brakes on his Jeep Cherokee, swerved to the left then navigated his way through the snow-covered tarmac and back to the right-hand side of the desolate road. In the rear view mirror, he could see that the fox he'd just come within inches of hitting had turned back and was staring at the passing SUV in an accusatory manner.

"Goddammit!" Blakeway hissed as he hit the horn a few times and watched the animal scurry away. Its snow-white coat blended seamlessly into the similarly colored surroundings. With his left hand on the steering wheel, the other hand searched in between the two front seats for the hip flask he had dropped when the animal decided to leap in front of his car. Nothing. He averted his eyes off the road for a second, spotted the bottle next to the brake pedal and grabbed it. He took a large swig, screwed the metal cap shut and returned it to its usual abode – the inside pocket of his coat. His hands were still shaking, but not as bad as they were earlier that morning when he rolled out of bed. At least the swamp that was the inside of his head was slowly becoming unstuck. The four beers he had chugged in the shower only provided enough clarity to get him dressed and out of the house. After one unintentional glance at himself in the driver side window of his car, he knew that a lot more of the sap would be needed before he arrived at work. The skin on his cheeks was blotchy and red, and the dark circles under his eyes looked like they had been drawn on by a three-year-old with a black crayon. Before getting in the car, he recalled that he had left his coat in the backseat the night before and breathed a sigh of relief when he felt the familiar shape of the flask as he slipped the thick garment over his shoulders. It was about half full. Not nearly enough, but it would have to do until he could get to the locked bottom drawer of his office desk. He was sure there was another bottle of bourbon in there. Maybe even two. He felt the last gulp that he greedily forced down a minute ago slowly claw its way back up his throat and swallowed hard to keep it from returning to his mouth. His stomach was churning and his tongue felt thick and woolen, like the clothes he was wearing.

After many mornings like these during his almost thirty years on the bottle Blakeway knew he just had to push through, get another fifth in him and he'd be right as rain and ready to face the day. Or at least, appear to be so. His staff had never mentioned anything about catching fumes of his boozy breath or his near constant crooked stride, so according to the warden, his charges were none the wiser. Or maybe they knew and either didn't give a shit or were too terrified to speak up for fear of retaliation.

He was knocking them back even more now that Martha was gone and out of the house for good. She had complained incessantly about his drinking, until one day around a year or so ago she had finally had enough and packed her bags. Thirty years of marriage, over in one day. He didn't fret too much. Yes, he missed her but deep down he had always known that she was better off without him. She hadn't told him where she'd gone and he hadn't tried to find out.

His memory shifted from his wife to last night's events. It started to come back to him in fragmented flashes. He remembered his record player blaring Don Williams. Then seeing the rope. The cold feeling of it around his neck. Then the sound of something snapping and everything went black. He had awoken a few hours later in the garage, where Martha's car used to spend nights, and had barely managed to crawl to his bed on his hands and knees. He dismissed the thoughts and focused on the road ahead.

Blakeway's car ploughed on through the snowpack. He passed a rusty, rectangular sign that read *DO NOT PICK UP HITCHHIKERS – YOU COULD BE AIDING AN ESCAPE!* in thick black lettering on a bright red background. He exited the main road and turned off onto a dirt pathway that was now an unnaturally colored mix of mud and snow. It led through a cluster of pine trees which were dusted with pure white from the first blizzards of winter that started two days ago and still hadn't let up. Ten kilometers further, he rounded a sharp turn, exited the forest and pulled up to an old wrought-iron gate where a lone guard sat in a small, fiberglass shed with large windows on all sides. Flanking the medieval-looking barred turnstile was a ten-foot-high fence with coils of razor wire mounted on top. As Blakeway's car stopped one of the shed's windows slid open and the guard leaned out. He was holding a mug of coffee in gloved hands and steam rose from the rim in thick wafts. A small television behind him was bellowing the morning newscast in crackled words and distorted images.

"Mornin' Warden," the guard said in a cheerful tone, his meaty cheeks and the tip of his nose glowing red from the cold. "Winter's here to kick our asses all over again, hey?"

"Morning, Leo. Yup, it sure is."

"Did you catch the game last night?! We gave those Jets-assholes a real spanking! First game of the season! It was fan-fucken-tastic!" He cackled and spilled a bit of coffee from his mug.

"No. No I didn't." Blakeway forced a smile that he reserved for uninteresting parties. Leo tried to make conversation with him every day and on the odd occasion Blakeway had accommodated him. Today was not one of those occasions. He needed to get to his office. "I've kind of lost touch with the hockey league."

"That's too bad, Chief. The guys are lookin' real good!"

"Yeah." The Warden eyed the giant switch that opened the gate just inside the shed window and he felt the tremors return to his hands, this time accompanied by a Lars Ulrich drum solo kicking off inside his head. The guard noticed the warden's bloodshot eyes darting between the control panel and the gate and his face went sullen.

"Well!" Leo was still grinning as he hit the button with his gloved palm and the gate crept open with a sluggish moan. "I'll let you be on your way then. Have a good one, boss."

Blakeway gave half a wave, rolled his window back up and sped through the entrance. The Jeep fishtailed from side to side as it carved a path through the snow. Another kilometer down the road he pulled up to a sign built into a six-foot high, freestanding rock wall that read *Stone Hill Penitentiary* and parked in front of it.

The administration building was separate from the main facility which was behind another ten-foot-high fence, this one sporting twenty thousand volts of current just begging to annihilate any would-be Houdini. The warden stumbled out of the car and hunched over as he walked up the hill, clutching his midriff and doing his best to walk in a straight line against the force of the freezing wind. His stomach churned again and a sharp pain flashed through his sides as he got to the outer gate. He slid his access card over the sensor and it buzzed open. Once through, he headed for a door which opened in the same manner and he went inside. A middle-aged woman with pristine curls in her shoulder length hair was startled by the sudden clunking sound of the door opening. The thick heels on her court shoes echoed in the sparsely furnished reception area as she jumped to her feet.

"Morning, sir!"

"Hi, Thelma." Blakeway avoided looking her in the eyes while pretending to find the correct pocket for his card.

"I have some messages for you." Thelma began to round the desk with several yellow post-it notes in her outstretched hand when she was stopped by Blakeway's raised palm.

"Not now. I need you to clear my schedule for the next forty-five minutes," he replied in a mumble. Her mouth opened to respond then froze as the warden continued. "I mean it. No calls." The warden's office was on the second floor and there was no elevator in the building. He brushed past the stunned receptionist and gingerly made his way up the stairs, gripping the handrail to stop himself from falling backwards. Just beyond the landing he entered through a door marked *A. Blakeway – WARDEN* and closed it behind him.

The tremble in his hands was incessant now and it was impossible to get the key into the lock of his makeshift drinks cabinet that was disguised as a desk drawer. After pausing for a deep breath, the key slid in, and it unlocked. Blakeway lifted half a bottle of bourbon out, unscrewed the cap and took four large mouthfuls. He closed his eyes, sank backwards against the wall with the bottle close to his chest. Almost immediately his stomach began to settle and the fog in his brain showed the first inclinations of lifting. He took two more swigs and a nearly inaudible noise akin to that of water trickling in the distance passed from the base of his skull down into his spine. The gentle fingers of alcohol enveloped his brain which caressed away the pain and throbbing from his mind. His eyes opened and his vision was clearer than he had ever experienced. Or at least to him it was. A smile teased the corners of his mouth as he took the final drops from the bottle and spotted another unopened bourbon container peeking out from under a folder inside the open drawer. Pure bliss was coursing through his veins and his smile broadened into the grin similar to that of the devious cat who tricked Alice.

The phone on his desk rang and he jerked, dropping the empty bourbon bottle on the carpet beside him. His fingers fumbled for the phone, snatched the receiver from the table and brought it to his ear.

"I said no calls!" the Warden barked, droplets of bourbon mixed with saliva spewed from his cracked lips onto the receiver.

"Hi, Andy. It's been a long time."

The voice on the other end of the line transformed the warm, comforting buzz in Blakeway's mind into a multitude of frosted, piercing daggers.

*****

A blizzard had broken out and the wind and snow was cutting cold streaks of frost across the open area. Ellis clasped his hands together and blew warm air into them to generate heat but it provided no relief. The prisoner who he was cuffed to on his left yanked the chain back down and gave a grunt in response. There were fifteen of them in total, lined up like school kids on the edge of the runway. Two correctional officers were standing watch and another was speaking into a two-way radio when a CC-115 Buffalo model aircraft pulled up from behind and came to a stop a hundred yards ahead. The plane was a mustard yellow color with red trimming around some of the edges and had *RESCUE – SAUVETAGE* printed on the sides. The two propellers from the twin engines kicked up more snow and blew a cloud of chalky powder into the air as it swung around and the back door slowly slid open. The guard on the two-radio waved to his partners and in response they grabbed the leader of the chain gang and marched him towards the open plane door with the rest of the prisoners in tow. Once inside the aircraft, the guards unchained their quarry and secured them individually to steel loops on the left-hand armrests of their seats.

Ellis was grateful to be out of the cold and even more so when he noticed the seat next to him was left vacant. Radio-Guard was about to close the door when an unmarked van pulled up and the driver hopped out, seemingly startled by the ongoing snowstorm.

"One more!" the driver shouted towards the plane's door. A short, slender man with cropped gray hair and a thick, dark gray beard exited the van accompanied by yet another prison guard. He was led onto the plane by his handcuffs and unceremoniously dumped in the seat next to Ellis.

"You have fun in the freezer now, old man." The guard grinned as he chained the slender man to his seat and walked off. From the corner of his eye Ellis surveyed his neighbor. A dark bruise circled his left eye and continued across the crooked bridge of his nose, ending right below a swollen cheek. The knuckles on both of his hands were also bruised and distended, and a small scab was forming on a superficial cut to his left hand. Ellis' attention was shifted briefly by the sound of the aircraft's door being closed. It rattled, got stuck on its tracks and the guards had to pull it shut as the struggling mechanical door winch seemed to be several years older than the aircraft itself. Flying didn't come naturally to Ellis and witnessing that fiasco didn't make him feel any better about it. The plane rolled forward, made a left turn and he was pushed back into his seat as the pilot gunned the throttle for take-off. What felt like an eternity later, the aircraft's nose finally tilted upwards and they lifted off with every possible surface in the cabin rattling as if everything was attached with paper glue. The plane climbed at a steep angle and soon nothing could be seen from outside the window except for thick, rolling storm clouds.

A voice came from the man next to him: "You're not gonna puke on me, are ya?"

"Excuse me?"

"I saw you eyeing that door like this is your first time on a plane. If you need to hurl, go ahead. Just not on me. I've got a weak stomach."

"I'll be fine," Ellis said.

"Ask one of these fine gentlemen if you need a bag." The man pointed to the three guards who were now sitting neatly buckled into their seats opposite the front row of seated prisoners.

"Thanks."

"So," the slender man continued while studying Ellis' face intently, "are you a cop?"

"What makes you say that?"

"You look like a cop," was the reply. Ellis never thought he looked like a cop, but he supposed that compared to the crew on this flight he may as well have been the police commissioner.

The slender man stuck out his hand that wasn't chained to the seat. "Robert, but you can call me Bobby."

"Ellis." He shook Bobby's hand briefly. During the pre-flight briefing, the guards had forbidden any physical contact between prisoners. That and spitting, shouting and pissing on the floor would get you a nightstick across the knees. Ellis wasn't sure if that was the official version of the pre-flight announcements the guards had been taught, but it was the one that was handed out.

"You ever need anything, you let me know. There are only two blocks on Stone Hill and I supply them both. If I ain't got it, I can get it," Bobby declared while jamming a thumb into his chest.

"You've been there before? This prison, I mean." Ellis felt his guts twist as the plane hit an air pocket, plunged for two seconds then recovered. It brought on a stifled jeer from the other inmates which was quickly silenced by the rapping of a truncheon on the floor of the plane.

"Oh yeah." Bobby smiled. "It's my home away from home. The ol' Hotel California." His smile turned to a grin. "You can check out anytime you want …" Bobby pointed a finger at Ellis, his eyes gleaming in anticipation.

"But you can never leave," he eventually replied and Bobby broke into a restrained laugh. Ellis couldn't help but smile at the old man's exuberance and realized he hadn't done that since the day he was arrested. Not much reason to smile, he guessed. With that thought, his mind returned home.

In the week that passed between his sentencing and his arrival on this flight, a lot had transpired. He hadn't been allowed any visitors but they did let him make two phone calls. The first of which was on Wednesday, two days after the conclusion of court proceedings. Cheryl had told him that Rose was okay, but that Cynthia had been admitted to hospital for observation. She'd received a diagnosis of severe fatigue and mental distress after she collapsed in court. During the second phone call, on Friday,

Cheryl was once again his source of information and gave him the news that Cynthia had been released from hospital and that she and Rose would be accompanying them back to Edmonton for the time being. Just so they could re-group and his wife and daughter could have twenty-four-hour support around them. Ellis then briefly spoke to Rose. She sounded exhausted and defeated. Her tone was flat and she kept crying and asking him when she would see him again. He had no answers for her. There had been even fewer answers the next morning when a group of guards stormed his cell and told him he was being transferred. Ellis wasn't given a chance to ask questions or even speak to Redpath. He was dumped into the back of a van and driven to a private airfield, where he was chained to fourteen other prisoners awaiting a flight to God-knows-where. And now, here he was, quoting song lyrics with a man he had met five minutes ago. He considered pinching himself, just in case.

"You look like a good egg, Ellis," Bobby said while tapping his index finger to his temple. "And I know. Been around the block enough times, I can sniff out the psychos. Hell, Toronto PD should put me on their payroll if they knew what was good for them."

"Got any advice for a new guy at this Stone Hill place we're off to?"

"Brother!" Bobby smiled. "Is it your lucky day or what?"

Ellis listened with intent as Bobby laid out all the details over the next two hours. The facility had only been running for two years. It had previously served as a log processing factory which had been bought by the state and transformed into a jail using new technology mixed with traditional fixtures. Stone Hill's PR slogan preached fairness, safety and above all, good governance. The cold hard reality, Bobby said, couldn't be further from that. The inmate capacity was two hundred but on any given day the population count was around three hundred. Double-cells often had an additional inmate who bunked on the floor which added tensions outside of the already volatile general population areas. Add an intermittent water-shortage and generally poor food quality to the mix and you had the perfect recipe for unpredictable behavior. Most of which materialized in the forms of riots and the burning of mattresses until demands were met.

There were two rampant gangs at Stone Hill and between them nothing happened inside the prison walls without their knowledge or approval. The first, and slightly larger in numbers, were known as the Aces. This was your run of the mill white supremacist group. They took what they wanted and who they wanted. Made up of Caucasian members only, they were a low-key version of a Neo-Nazi prison gang, but smarter. They ran booze, cigarettes and weed through the prison's arteries. The second group was called Purgatory or Purgs for short. This gang's racial demographic was much more varied – except membership was banned if you were white, obviously. Their specialties were heroin, cocaine, meth, and women. Many of the Purgs were from the area, meaning the majority of their numbers were from the local Inuit and Metis community. According to Bobby, the Aces would almost certainly attempt to recruit Ellis, being a strong and relatively young man at thirty-seven with a military background. They were always on the lookout to add depth to their muscle department.

"But where exactly are we going?" Ellis asked. "I felt the

plane turn north, maybe northwest but I couldn't be sure."

"Close. Ever heard of a town called Fort Resolution?" Bobby replied and Ellis shook his head. "Yup, didn't think so. It's pretty much the Arctic. The jail is about thirty miles from the town. Long-timers call it the Ice Box. Whenever the gangs get out of hand, the warden likes to kill the heating and let everyone freeze their balls off until the fight is sorted out. But he mostly bends to whichever gang leader has the most influence at the time. You watch out for that one, by the way. Warden Blakeway is a man who doesn't hesitate to dish out hurt."

 "Sounds a bit lawless up there," Ellis commented, feeling even more apprehensive about his destination, if that were even possible.

"You bet your ass," Bobby said and lightly rubbed the bruise on his eye. "But there are worse places."

"All right ladies!" one of the guards yelled, got up and started down the passage between the seated inmates. "Ten minutes to touch down!"

Ellis had a look out of the small window to his right and saw a few faint streetlights strewn down a long road. Several small houses were on either side of the street and a few larger buildings which looked like they could make up the town center were nestled at the end. The plane made a sharp turn to the left and Ellis could see running lights indicating a very short runway. A yellow school bus was parked to the left of the airfield. The snow was still falling but much more gently now, as if it had taken a breath in anticipation for the arrival of its new imports.

"What about these guys?" Ellis motioned to the guards.

Bobby looked up from his seat belt buckle.

"Crooked as a barrel of snakes, the lot of them," he said in a hushed tone. "But they're loyal to the warden. Most of 'em anyway."

Ellis felt the plane descend rapidly. It hopped once as it made contact with the tarmac, then bonded to it when the wheels connected again. Shortly after, they came to a stop and two of the guards moved in among the inmates, securing all of them back to the single, twenty-foot-long chain. The third was opening the plane door and the cold night air took Ellis' breath away as it streamed into the cabin.

"Let's go!" the front guard shouted and the gathering of fresh prisoners shuffled along, each yanking the chain when the amount of slack they wanted wasn't provided. They made their way across the storm drain beside the runway and approached the waiting bus with *N.T. CORRECTIONAL SERVICE OF CANADA* printed on the side. A few of the windows were cracked behind outward mounted bars and the wheels already had their snow chains fitted. The inmates ascended the steps like a row of penguins carefully hopping onto slippery ice and were each allocated individual seats. The driver tugged a lever next to the steering wheel and the doors folded shut. Ellis surveyed the world outside – not much apart from wilderness, trees and the white blanket of snow that was getting thicker by the minute. The bus growled to life and clawed its way over the narrow shoulder and onto the main road, headed for Stone Hill and whatever lay in wait within its walls, deep inside the boreal forest.

*****

Cynthia Neill jolted upright in bed, breathless. She felt cold and was surprised to find warm beads of sweat as she ran her palm across her forehead. Her heart was racing and memories of the dream she'd just woken from resurfaced in fractured remnants, like pieces of an obscure puzzle. It was the same one she had been having almost every night since the final day of Ellis' trial.

In it she, Ellis and Rose were having a pizza and movie night as they did every Friday. They were watching one of Rose's favorites – the tale of the princess that froze everything she touched. Ellis was being his usual comical self during these occasions. He enjoyed adding commentary to whatever film was on, much to Rose's dismay. The girl always objected profusely to it but Cynthia knew deep down that Rose found her father to be quite hilarious and it wasn't long until the pair of them were rolling on the floor and laughing at each other's lame one-liners. It was always at this point that the atmosphere of the dream shifted and transformed into a terrifying nightmare.

The front door blew off of its hinges and a four-legged creature with glowing red eyes and tufts of greasy, rancid hair hanging over its contorted face stormed into the living room. The color of the dream turned from a soft white to a murky purplish-green. Ellis would always run towards the thing while she and Rose would back away, taking shelter behind a sofa as Rose let out a series of deafening screeches. The thing would grab Ellis by the throat, rip his chest open and take huge bites from him. Thick red blood would spray over his family's faces as they watched their father and husband being consumed alive. Rose would try to crawl to him on her hands and knees in a feeble attempt to help but Cynthia would grab her by the ankle and drag her back to safety, only to have the thing drop Ellis' lifeless corpse and charge at the girl. Then, all of a sudden, it would be gone, as abruptly as it had appeared. Rose would turn to Cynthia, her face still dripping with her father's blood, pleading for answers and asking questions in an incoherent rambling. The dream would end when the thing rose up slowly behind her daughter, then lunged and sank its rotten, yellow teeth into Rose's neck, her face twisting and writhing in pain until her eyes rolled backwards. It was always the same, except in tonight's version Ellis was standing behind the monster as it ravaged the girl. He was in that awful, green jumpsuit that he wore in court and he kept moving his lips but no words could be heard.

Cynthia let out a sigh and looked over to Rose who was sleeping soundly next to her. She felt envious and grateful at the same time. Grateful that her Rosey was somehow able to keep functioning through this ordeal and envious that she wasn't able to show the same strength her daughter displayed. Of course, having her grandmother there was a huge help. She found comfort in her Nana's tranquil nature and soothing voice.

She swung her legs off the bed and stood up, careful not to wake Rose, who muttered something in her sleep that her mother couldn't quite make sense of. Cell phone in hand she crossed the hallway into the living room, then onwards past the wall that was adorned with their family photos and into the kitchen. Bright streaks of moonlight carved square formations onto the terrazzo floor tiles through the bow-window. Her mother's house in West Edmonton was crammed with these reading nooks as they offered ample sunshine in winter. Cynthia checked the water level in the kettle and switched it on while fishing for the instant coffee in an overhead cupboard. Her fingertips had barely touched the metal container when a rhythmic vibration came from her phone on the counter. She checked the screen and it read *Victor Redpath – Ellis Attorney.* She slid the green *Answer* icon on the screen to the right.

"Hello? Victor?"

"Hi Cynthia. Sorry to call so late." Redpath sounded out of breath.

"Is everything okay? Have you spoken to Ellis?"

"Uh, no. I just left the Police Station. It looks like they've moved him."

"What? When?"

"Yesterday, around 5 p.m." Redpath's voice was almost drowned out by a police siren passing by.

"Where did they move him to? Surely they have to tell us before it happens, right?" Cynthia could feel a chill run through her as the image of the thing from the dream popped into her head again, then promptly faded.

"Yeah, usually, but the paperwork is vague so I'm guessing it was a last-minute move. I've contacted CSC to see if I can track him down."

"CSC?" Cynthia asked.

"Prison services. They should be able to tell us but probably only tomorrow. Look, I just wanted to let you know because I was going to see Ellis tonight anyway. I'll do some more digging on my end and keep you posted."

"Victor." She paused. "That doesn't sound right. I'm worried." Cynthia's voice cracked and she tried to hide the panic welling up in her chest.

"I'm sure everything's fine, Cynthia. This sort of thing does happen, just not very often."

"None of this is fine, Victor!" she snapped. "This whole thing is one big fucking disaster! The way the cops handled it, the trial, it's all wrong! Jesus, he could be dead for all we know!" Cynthia turned around and jumped when saw Rose standing in the doorway, rubbing one eye with the heel of her hand.

"I know, but—" Redpath was mid-sentence when she cut him off.

"I have to go. I'm sorry, I'll call you tomorrow." She hung up and walked over to her daughter.

"Mom. Was that Dad?" Rose said, still rising from sleep. Cynthia wondered how much of the conversation she had heard.

"No, sweetie. What are you doing out of bed?" She wrapped her arms around Rose and picked her up.

"I heard you talking. What's going on?"

"It was just work, honey. Why don't you go back to bed?" She hated lying to Rose, but she felt like these days, and under these circumstances, it was justified.

"You're lying. You're doing that thing with your lip. You only do that when you're lying." Rose was staring up and straight through her mother's eyes. "Besides, it's 3 a.m. You never work *that* late."

"What are you talking about?" Cynthia forced a laugh, but it sounded more like a badly impersonated hyena cackle.

"Mom!" Rose's tone demanded an honest response and Cynthia knew she couldn't avoid it this time.

"All right, all right." She took a deep breath. "Your dad's been moved to another jail. We don't quite know where he is yet but Mr. Redpath is going to find out tomorrow."

"Will he call first thing?" Rose looked both puzzled and uneasy and Cynthia could almost hear the cogs in the girl's mind turning. She needed to be careful with what she said next.

"Yes, honey, he promised."

"Mom." A single tear welled up in Rose's left eye. "I'm scared. For Dad. I've been reading up about what happens in prisons on social media and ..."

"Hold on now, missy." Cynthia's tone was soft and endearing. "What have I told you about the things you read there? C'mon, what did I say?"

"It's nothing more than a tabloid," Rose replied, not happy about having to admit defeat.

"Exactly." Cynthia stroked her hair. "I'm scared too, honey. It's okay to be scared. But we have to keep believing. Without that, we have nothing."

"It just makes me so sad that we can't even talk to him." Rose was sobbing faintly now and Cynthia wiped the tears away with the sleeve of her gown and held her daughter's face in both palms, the tips of their noses almost touching.

"Do you remember when you were little, about three or four

years old, and Daddy went away for work all the time?

"Yes. Yes, I remember."

"You thought that you would never see him again, you'd cry and cry. But what did your Dad do then?"

"He came back."

"Well, this is almost the same as that. He *will* come back to us. I promise you, Rose." Cynthia felt Rose's embrace soften a little at hearing that and Cynthia found herself wishing that she believed those words as well.

*****

The intake procedure for new arrivals at Stone Hill wasn't overly dissimilar to other maximum security correctional facilities. All new inmates were subjected to a routine physical examination and body inspection, followed by showers and the issuing of prison attire, toothbrushes, towels and digital wristbands that provided the names and inmate-registry numbers of all new prisoners. The only practice that was in any way out of the ordinary was the mandatory COVID-19 tests. It was a simple, streamlined operation. Ellis and his fourteen companions, all seated two meters apart on steel chairs, were instructed to provide a deep throat saliva sample and deposit said sample into a small, plastic tube which contained a preservative solution. Each tube was labelled according to the owner of its contents and electronically synchronized with the depositor's wristband details. They all spent the night in a hermetically sealed room the size of a school hall, just north of the main prison complex. It was barren, apart from thin mattresses for each of the new intakes which were carefully placed according to social distancing requirements. The makeshift beds hugged the four walls which were a brighter shade of white than the snow outside. In the middle of the room a lone prison guard sat watch, sporting an unusual new set of equipment in the form of a surgical mask and face shield to accompany his usual stun gun and truncheon.

The following morning, after confirming negative test results for the whole group, the men were each assigned a case officer who handed out inmate handbooks and talked them through a ten-minute orientation video. Work detail was compulsory and the labor options during winter were positions in the bakery, woodshop, the carpentry room (which also handled upholstery repairs) facility maintenance or kitchen duties. Ellis signed his name under carpentry and maintenance. The case officer, a portly man with a countable number of hair strands glued to his lustrous dome, noted that all new inmates would be informed of their stations in the next forty-eight hours. They were all handed daily routine schedules and it seemed fairly simple, although they were informed that spontaneous head counts were on the cards at any time.

- 06:45 – Inmate count
- 07:00 – Breakfast
- 08:00 – Go to program, work or back to the cell or room
- 11:45 – Return to cell or room for inmate count and lunch
- 13:00 – Go to program, work or back to cell or room
- 16:30 – Return to cell or room for inmate count and then

supper
- 18:00 – Go to recreation, cultural events, self-help groups, etc.
- 22:30 – Night inmate count
- 23:00 – Lock-up and lights out

Ellis folded the booklet and slid it into his pocket as a guard took him by the arm and led him to his cell. They entered the main housing block and the sheer size of the place was immense. Ellis' eyes scanned the area from top to bottom. A single guard tower stood ten meters high in the middle of an open concrete floor where several steel table and chair combinations were bolted to the floor in an octagonal formation. There were three floors of cells on either side of the complex, each cell connected to the other by a separating wall about eight inches thick. Everything was the same color – a dull gray which amplified the contrast created by the orange jumpsuits worn by the inmates seated on the tables and dangling from their cell doors. The droning of chatter subsided as the new arrivals walked in. Ellis felt several hundred sets of eyes survey him for a few seconds, then turn back to their checkers and chess games and the chatter resumed. Only one of them didn't follow suit.

An older man in his early sixties with long silver hair and a goatee was staring intently at Ellis from the third-floor walkway railing. He only broke eye contact when the prison guard led Ellis up the stairs to the second floor and stopped at cell door 7B. The guard mumbled something over his radio and the barred gate slid open. Ellis was uncuffed and placed on the lower bunk bed. The bed above him was vacant and pristinely made, a blue woolen blanket folded neatly over the thin mattress and single, gray pillow. He placed his belongings next to him on the bed and assessed the room as the guard departed, leaving the cell door open. Both beds were mounted onto the left wall and the brackets were almost brand new. Same went for the paint job, which was a continuation of the prison's textbook shade of gray, however the cells were flowered up with two sets of bright orange circles on the wall opposite the bunk beds and two more sets of circles were painted on the floor beneath them. Stenciled above the wall-circles were the words: "PLACE HANDS AND FEET HERE WHEN ALARM SOUNDS". There was a single window, if you could call it that, fitted just below the next floor level. It measured around thirty centimeters in height and width, and had wide bars crisscrossed on the inside. The glass was thick and stained brown from exposure to the elements. Ellis noted a faint odor in the room, like that of rust mixed with acetone. He couldn't quite figure out where it came from but he detected it as soon as he entered.

A shadow fell over the floor and Ellis turned to see a man standing in the doorway. He was young, probably in his late twenties with lanky arms and legs and a shaved head. There was an ace of spades playing card tattooed on the skin over his throat underneath a grin that revealed a set of brown-stained teeth. His blank stare was fixed on the man sitting on the bed.

"Help you?" Ellis said.

"Just wanted to say, welcome to the neighborhood," the gangly man said. His voice was surprisingly high pitched.

"Thanks. Are you the welcome wagon?"

"Nope. Just here to get my extra cover." Gangly Man nodded towards the blanket Ellis had been issued minutes ago. He was still grinning, running his tongue over the top row of his gnashers.

"Why don't you try next door?" Ellis smiled and scoffed. "There's nothing for you here."

"You sure about that?!" Gangly Man yelled in his soprano tone. The veins stood out on his neck as he slid his left hand behind his back. The prison behind him fell silent. Ellis grabbed his toothbrush and snapped the head off with his thumb. A sharp edge now protruded from the handle and he held it in front of him while staring at the wall ahead. Gangly Man straightened up and took a step back.

"Make your move then." Ellis could see him from the corner of his eye. Gangly Man looked like he had been caught off guard and kept glancing over his shoulder, seemingly waiting for a signal. Ellis' body tensed up, ready to lunge at a moment's notice. *This is bad,* he thought. *Not how I wanted to start my stay here.*

"Miles!" a voice said from down the passage. "Get your skinny, white ass out of my cell or no more sissy porn for you. I'll cut your supply, boy!" The whole block broke out in a chuckle and Ellis saw Bobby walk up and stand next to Gangly Man, now known as Miles. "Go on now! *Get!*"

"I'll be gettin' that blanket," Miles said, and he turned his gaze towards the long-haired man who was still examining Ellis' cell from the third-floor railing. The spectator nodded at Miles who reluctantly proceeded to walk off, his glare shifting between Bobby and Ellis.

"You make friends real quick-like, don't you?" Bobby strode in and shooed Ellis to the top bunk. "My ass is too old to get up there."

"It's a gift, I guess," Ellis replied and Bobby laughed.

"Not if it attracts the likes of *that* dude. There are many various species of animals here at the Ice Box. Think of Miles as a … sewer rat … on meth. With an advanced case of Ebola. You don't want *nothin'* to do with that."

"How did this happen?" Ellis asked, gesturing between Bobby and the bottom bunk of his cell.

"They like to pair me with a new guy whenever I pop by. To show them the ropes and all that. The sooner a Chop falls in line, the less paperwork it is for the guards."

"Chop?" Ellis figured he knew where the term came from but confirmed anyway. "As in fresh meat?"

"That's right." Bobby grinned as he made his new bed, tucking the blanket carefully around the corners. "You catch on quick, you'll be alright."

A buzzer echoed through the vast structure and heavy footfalls landed on the steel grid walkways as all the inmates scrambled to their cells. Thirty seconds later all the doors slid shut simultaneously with a thunderous bang.

"We've got about two hours until dinner. Best get comfortable," Bobby said as he lay down on his bunk with his arms folded behind his head, and Ellis did the same. "So." There were a few seconds of silence before he spoke again. "You popped that judge and his wife, did you?"

"Would you believe me if I said no?" Ellis said after a long pause while studying the cracks in the concrete above his head. This section wasn't painted and had old damp stains crawling across it in between an array of graffiti carved out by former prisoners. *I miss Mom* and *Bundy was a pussy* were among those that stood out to Ellis' eye.

"Sure, I'm innocent too," Bobby replied, scoffing.

"Just a case of bad luck?"

"Well." Bobby sighed. "Guess you'll find out sooner or later, so it may as well be sooner."

Ellis listened as Bobby told him of how he had killed a man eighteen years ago. He had been divorced from his wife at the time, but as rare as these things are, they remained friends afterwards. Not because they had kids, but because the split had been a mutual decision; they both had realized shortly after getting married that they would never be any more than good friends. They lived in the same neighborhood and would often bump into each other on the street and attend the same birthday parties or other social events as their circles of friends often overlapped.

Around six months after the divorce Bobby was exiting a Seven Eleven a block away from his house when he saw her again, this time with a new boyfriend. They met and spoke briefly and the guy seemed alright. The next few times he saw them together she was often sporting bruises on her face or arms or walking with a limp. She wouldn't look Bobby in the eye and appeared nervous and jumpy. He knew exactly what was happening. Many attempts to speak to her about it went either unacknowledged or she would just deny it. One night, Bobby was at home watching TV when his phone rang. It was Shannon, his ex-wife. She was sobbing. He could hear screaming and glass breaking while a man was shouting incoherently. Bobby jumped in his car and sped over. After kicking the door in, he found the boyfriend in the midst of beating Shannon's legs with a pair of handcuffs wrapped around his fist. Bobby tackled him and they started fighting. At a stage during the scrimmage Bobby was on his back with the boyfriend on top of him. Bobby landed a solid kick to the man's midsection, sending him careening through the living room window. As he landed outside, a shard of broken glass slashed the man's jugular and he bled out before the ambulance could arrive. Turns out the boyfriend was a cop which all but sealed Bobby's fate.

"And that, my friend, is how I was cut from the fabric of society and discarded as if I were nothing. By saving someone's life."

"Jesus." Ellis ran his hands through his hair. "Didn't she testify on your behalf?"

"She did, but they didn't want to hear it. Red tape won the day. The prosecutor kept hammering on the fact that a police officer was dead and there was no evidence or reports filed about the abuse, so that was that. Cut and dried."

"I'll tell you one thing – if they want you, they'll get you. I've caught on to that really quickly over the last few weeks," Ellis said. "I'm not a saint, far from it, but I didn't lay a hand on those people. Fuck, I didn't even know them or know anything about them. Why would I kill a judge and his wife? Did they even stop to ask themselves that?"

"Do you have a family?" Bobby asked.

"Yes." Ellis tried to hold it back, but his eyes filled with tears at the thought of Cynthia and Rose and he laid his arm over his brow. "Wife and a daughter."

"It's harder on them, you know, us being in here. Their lives are now standing still, like someone pulled the plug on it."

"I don't know what I'm going to do, Bobby." Ellis' voice quivered, and the pit of his stomach rose up to his throat. He felt a deep and primal sense of fear engulf his mind, the likes of which he had never experienced before.

Bobby fell silent and the only sounds that could be heard were that of a howling wind swirling outside, and the distant whispers emanating from the darkened corners of the cell block.

CHAPTER 5

Cheryl Hawthorne's cozy, two-story house was neatly tucked away in a wide crescent along one of the numerous arches that stretched the length of Ormsby Lane. A soaring Balsam Poplar tree that stood in close proximity to the front entrance cast a welcome shadow over the living room area during summer, although in autumn and early winter the wide, heart-shaped leaves that fell from it tended to spread across the entire property. This resulted in Ralph spending most Sundays during the colder seasons up on the roof clearing the gutters blocked with pulpy yellow and brown masses. And of course, he would've had a few helpings of the clear stuff with the Russian name on the label before mustering the gusto to perform this arduous task.

This was the exact scenario playing itself out on this crisp and overcast Saturday morning as Cynthia gathered Rose's jacket and scarf from the coat stand at the foot of the stairs.

"Hurry up, Rose! We're going to be late!"

"I'm coming!" Rose's voice was muffled as it traveled from beyond the bathroom door on the second floor. She was usually ready quite early during her morning routine but today the timing had caught her off guard and the failure to set her alarm clock last night had contributed to the chaotic start to the day. She ran out of the bathroom, grabbed a sports bag which contained boots, a hockey stick and a mouth guard and rushed down the stairs, taking them two at a time.

Rose and her mother gave Ralph a quick "See you later" then hopped into Cynthia's bottle green Ford Taurus Station Wagon and set off down the road. Ralph's words of well wishes for the match followed them in the slipstream of the vehicle that shrunk into the distance.

"Are you excited?" Cynthia smiled at Rose who was still battling to get her seatbelt secured. Cynthia had signed her up to a sports club downtown a few days earlier. She figured it could lift Rose's spirit a bit after everything that had happened. The girl had also expressed frustration at being away from her friends and her home and Cynthia had taken note. She wasn't too keen to keep living in her mother's house for much longer either. The space was ample but as time went on it seemed to encroach on everyone like a slow-moving junkyard press and she knew things would soon boil over. As much as Cheryl adored her granddaughter, she wasn't used to having anyone under thirty in the house and Cynthia had noticed a toll being taken on the already strained Hawthorne household. On top of that, Ralph kept finding excuses to go outside and each time he returned, he staggered just a bit more. Cynthia was getting to the point where she couldn't control Rose's responses to that anymore.

"Yeah, I guess." Rose cracked half a smile.

"It'll be fun. I bet you'll make at least two new friends today." Cynthia placed a hand on her daughter's lap and flashed her best infomercial smile.

"Statistically, that would be a waste of time, Mom. We don't live here. When would I see these new friends you keep touting?"

"You never know, some of them might have family in Toronto and they'll swing by for a chat when they come down to visit. Stranger things have happened," Cynthia said as she made the turn into the sports complex. Several girls of Rose's age were doing warm up laps on the pitch straight ahead of them.

"Can we talk about going home, please?" Rose asked. "I know I keep bringing it up but it's only because we haven't had a proper conversation about it." Rose had an earnestness in her voice that tugged at her mother's heart strings.

"Tell you what. Promise me you'll do your best to have fun and talk to some of the other girls today and if you still feel the same way afterwards we can go for breakfast and weigh up our options. Deal?" Cynthia held her hand out. She knew that Rose had a knack for charming people and hoped the encounter with new faces today would distract her from the desire to go back to Toronto, even if it was only for a short while.

"Deal." Rose smiled and sealed it with a handshake. She snatched her bag, kissed her mom on the cheek and sprinted towards the field, where the match was about to start. Cynthia got out of the car and strolled over to a small coffee stand. She got a cappuccino and walked over to the seating area next to the sidelines, being mindful not to get too close to where the other parents were milling about while chatting and cheering their offspring on. *I'm such a hypocrite,* she thought to herself.

Cynthia pulled her phone from the handbag and texted

Victor Redpath. The coffee warmed her as she watched the pre-teens scurrying around on the dark green grass which had been cleared of snowfall earlier that day in a studious manner. It wasn't long before her thoughts returned to Ellis. It had been six excruciating days since she'd last heard anything regarding her husband. She knew Victor was working tirelessly to find him but he wasn't making much progress. Somehow, all the doors had been slammed in their faces and bolted down. Even her own daily, sometimes hourly, phone calls to the Police and Prison Services departments had been met with false promises of a return call from whoever was in charge, or in some cases the call was summarily dropped as soon as she mentioned her name. To Cynthia it began to feel like her husband had simply been erased off the face of the earth and in the authorities' version of events, his family was just expected to let go and get on with it.

During a previous phone call, Redpath had said he'd spent this week challenging the legality of the stonewalling they were getting. He was supposed to call Cynthia last night with an update but he insisted they meet in person, even if it meant he had to make the drive up to Edmonton on a weekend. Cynthia was touched by his dedication but she had a feeling that it wouldn't be good news. The attorney had been vague on the phone and there was something unsettling in his tone of voice.

Her eyes caught a glimpse of a white Toyota Camry pulling into the parking area and coming to a halt in between a large truck and a Prius. Redpath exited and walked briskly between the other cars and trucks until he reached Cynthia.

"Hi. Were you followed?" His head swiveled around as he sat down beside her.

"Um." Cynthia looked around briefly. "I don't think so."

"Okay." Redpath lit a cigarette and offered her one.

"Since when do you smoke?" Cynthia asked and declined the offer with a raised palm.

"You know what they say, nobody ever *really* quits." Redpath gave a wry smile. The hand holding the butt had a faint tremble to it.

"What's going on, Victor? What's with all the cloak-and-dagger?"

"We can't be too careful." Redpath looked tattered and nervous. His hair, which was usually pristinely sculpted, was frayed and he looked pale, like he hadn't slept in a few days. "We can't talk on the phone anymore. Okay? Emails only from now on."

"Okay, sure." Cynthia was now fidgeting as well, as if Redpath's anxious condition was contagious.

"Look, I can't stay long. I'm catching a flight in two hours." Redpath's eyes scanned the surrounding area again then turned to Cynthia. "I don't know where Ellis is. The cops aren't telling me anything and after a week of trying, no judge will grant me an order to get information from them." He paused and rubbed his forehead. "Also, somebody broke into my office two days ago and trashed the place. They took my computer as well, and I don't use any online backup systems so everything's toast. And then there was this." Redpath unlocked his phone and pressed play on a video clip. In it, an old woman was being filmed from behind. She was sitting on a large sofa in an overly-decorated living room with Gerry Dee flinging questions at the contestants of *Family Feud* on the television set in the background. Then, the person behind the camera raised a handgun and aimed it straight at the woman's head. She was blissfully unaware of the barrel that was mere inches from the back of her skull. The video ended and Redpath dropped the phone in his lap. "That's my mother. I got it via text message last night. I called her straight away and she answered, thank God. I'm going there now."

"Oh … oh my god," Cynthia stuttered, her mind racing.

"Listen to me." Redpath took her by the arm and she turned to him. "I don't know who these people are but the message they're trying to send is loud and clear. You need to be careful, Cynthia. You *and* Rose. They're probably watching you as well."

"Right. Right, yes," Cynthia muttered. Panic threatened to take full control of her as the shock took hold and she could feel herself slipping into a cloud of confusion and fear.

"If I were you, I'd disappear for a while," Redpath continued, raising a shaking hand to his mouth and drawing on the cigarette. "Just get out of here. I'll contact you in a few days. I need time to think about what we're going to do next. Is there a place where nobody can find you, somewhere no one else knows about?"

"Yes, I know a place." Cynthia felt dazed, like she was in a dream and hearing everything from a faraway distance.

"Good. Go there, today. Don't talk to anyone. Don't even tell your parents where you're going." Redpath glanced at his watch and got up. "I've got to go. Be careful." He touched her shoulder and walked off. Cynthia watched the attorney dash to his car, get in and disappear down the street, tires screeching. She got up, negotiated the stairs down the stand towards the pitch and waved to Rose until the girl noticed her and walked off with her palms turned skyward and a grimace on her face.

"Mom! The game is still on!"

"We have to go! Now!" Cynthia shouted, slightly louder than she meant to and a group of parents looked over at her. She smiled and raised a hand in greeting.

"What is it?" Rose asked, visibly unsure of her mother.

"Get your things. Quickly. We're leaving." Cynthia picked the sports bag up and took Rose's hand. The hockey coach, a tall man with shoulder length hair and a scanty beard, walked over.

"Hi. It's Mrs. Neill, right?" the coach asked, smiling. "I'm Dave King. I don't believe we've met." He held out a hand.

"I'm so sorry Mr. King, we really have to get going. C'mon Rose." Cynthia was tugging at Rose's arm.

"But it's still the first half …"

"Yes, I know. I'm terribly sorry." Cynthia let out an unconvincing giggle. "I'm sure Rose will be here for the next one. Nice to meet you," she said to the coach while almost dragging Rose towards the car. She bundled the bag along with her daughter into the front seat and closed the door. The stunned coach was still staring at them in disbelief.

"Mom! What the …"

"Sweetie," Cynthia cut her off. "I'm going to need you to trust me right now, okay? I'll tell you everything once we're on the road." She started the car, swung out through the entrance and onto the main street.

"Are we going home?" The excitement and surprise may as well have been written on Rose's face, it was that obvious.

"Yes, darling," Cynthia said and depressed the accelerator deeper, making the Ford's engine growl as the panic in her turned to determination. "We're going home."

*****

Detective William Black's Crown Victoria hummed a rhythmic tune as it cruised the streets of downtown Toronto. The clock on the dashboard read 6:47 a.m. The morning was darker than usual for this time of year. Heavy cloud cover stagnated in the sky like an enormous blanket enveloping the city. He made a left turn and rolled through Broken Alley, as it was christened by those who inhabited it. Most of the street was covered by a wide bridge that made it appear as if it were an elongated tunnel. Old oil drums were reincarnated as makeshift fire pits which lighted the small groups surrounding them, casting eerily long shadow people onto the glistening walls where melting snow spawned miniscule waterfalls from the roads above. The city's homeless tended to congregate here during winter since a lot of the soup kitchens began rolling out food trucks to the area in the hope of reaching those who weren't willing or able to report to the food halls in person. The mayor had approved it and invested millions in taxpayer dollars in these as part of his re-election campaign. Those less fortunate were only too content to benefit from it, whether it was a glaringly obvious publicity stunt or not.

Black slowed down to let the foot traffic cross and his eye

caught a young girl, probably no older than fourteen, being accosted by three men in hoodies approximately a hundred meters ahead. She was attempting to create space between herself and them by using a stack of pallets towards the mouth of the tunnel. Black sped up until he reached them, flashed the single red light on his roof and flicked the siren switch to "YELP", sending a short *whoop-whoop* sound echoing through the space. The three men scattered faster than a gang of cockroaches on a kitchen floor caught off guard by the eruption of fluorescent lighting. This was a regular occurrence and the detective always rued the day that he would not be there in time to stop these maniacs. It was one of the many things that kept him up at night.

Black rolled the window down. The girl looked up at him, picked up her plastic bag with three servings of soup in sealed, polystyrene containers and a few bread rolls packed inside and walked shakily over to the car.

"Morning, Abby."

"Morning, Mister Black."

"You by yourself today?"

"Yessir. Momma and Nathan are still in bed." She fidgeted with the slim handles of her bag. She was staring at the ground and Black could see a fresh bruise on her forehead, unsuccessfully hidden beneath her torn and faded pink beanie. A cartoon unicorn missing an eye was on the front of her red sweater which looked several years older than she was.

"Get in. I'll take you home."

"It's okay, sir, I don't want to be a bother."

"No bother at all." The detective gave her a warm smile and she returned it as she hopped into the back seat. The car filled with the aromas of chicken soup and rough living.

Black had met Abby about a year ago during a domestic dispute call and liked to check in on her now and then, as she has no one looking out for her aside from herself.

He eased his foot onto the accelerator as her eyes stayed fixed on him in the rear-view mirror. They had gotten to know each other quite well over time but she was still wary of any man due to the grisly experiences in her life so far. Black guessed that she would always be that way. *Scarred for life by a world filled with evil,* he thought. Four blocks to the north they pulled up to a compact house with a porch the size of a bathtub. Two wooden chairs and a cracked fiberglass table were leaning against the rickety railing. The front lawn was overgrown with weeds and one of the living room windows was shattered with shards of glass sticking from the corners of the frame like long, sharp fingers. The paint had begun to peel off of the blue and white structure to the point where it was hard to tell what color it had originally been.

"Thank you, Mister Black," came Abby's timid voice as she opened the car door.

"Won't you ask Nathan to come and talk to me for a second?"

"I … I don't think he will," she muttered, visibly terrified by the detective's request. He turned around to face her.

"It'll be alright, darling. Tell him Mister Black is waiting for him outside."

She nodded, exited the car, skipped up the three porch steps and disappeared behind the front door of the house. Black got out and leaned against the hood of his car, stared at the gray sky, then dropped his gaze to the humble abode as he heard a man shouting from inside. One of the curtains in the top floor window moved to the side and ten seconds later the front door swung open. A man in his mid-thirties with wild, shoulder-length hair and a cigarette hanging from his mouth stood in the doorway. He was shirtless and the only items of clothing on him were a pair of severely worn-out jeans and a belt with a copper buckle in the shape of a bison. He scoffed at the cop then made his way down the steps until he stood in front of Black.

"You here to tell me that child services are on their way, detective?"

"No," Black said in a low, calm tone. "Something much simpler."

"You gonna have me arrested? Again?" Nathan laughed and the cigarette fell from his lips. He bent down to pick it up and as he grabbed it, Black slammed the heel of his shoe onto Nathan's hand, making him cough and gasp for air. He jerked back up and grabbed his palm with the other hand. Black took a step closer. He could smell booze and an array of chemicals on the man. Fresh track marks on his arms told a tale all their own.

"Listen to me very carefully. Your time is up. You touch that girl again and I won't arrest you. I'll fold you into a barrel and dump you in the ocean. You got me?" Black hissed.

"Fuck you, you're a cop. You can't do that!" Nathan laughed, still gripping his hand which had begun to show swelling and the initial signs of a bruise.

"Can't I? Have you thought about it? I mean *really* considered it?" Black said, and the gleam in his eyes made Nathan go quiet. "If you see my car pull up here again you better fucking run." Black stood a moment, fixing his eyes on Abby's stepfather to let the words really sink in. "Do you understand me?"

"Yes," Nathan murmured.

"I can't hear you."

"Yes, fuck, I got it," he said, rubbing his hand with his eyes on the ground.

"Okay." Black got back into his car and reversed out of the terse driveway. Nathan's eyes, wide with surprise, followed him until he disappeared around the corner.

At 7:15 a.m. Black arrived at the homicide office, switched his computer on, checked his Inbox and then went about setting his priorities for the day. A day planner his daughter had given him for Christmas assisted in labelling cases or queries according to priority. Black wondered how he ever got anything done before receiving this gift which helped him deal with everything coming across his desk in a much more efficient manner. Charlene was only eight years old but she was consistently voted the "most thoughtful gift-giver" in the family every Christmas.

First order of business for the day was a report from a marked unit: the body of a male, twenty-five to thirty years of age, had been picked up last night at 1:15 a.m. He was propped up against a tree in Dufferin Grove Park. Initial reports claimed a possible drug overdose, however, upon closer inspection the officers discovered a hole the size of a golf ball in the back of the victim's head. The body was currently over at the coroner's office undergoing an autopsy and Black would receive a report from both him and the forensic entomologist the following day, as was the standard.

His computer beeped. A bold-print number one appeared in brackets next to the word "Inbox". He clicked on it and saw it was from Sergeant Harry Stamp at the Forensic Crime Scene Unit. Since joining the unit he had become Black's go-to guy for scene processing and follow ups as his eye for detail was second to none. The email's heading read *Similarity to Judge Thatcher Crime Scene*. Black scanned it and opened the attachments which contained several photographs of the Thatcher scene and another set labelled "Anthony Sturgess Murder – 2007". He was about to scroll through the pictures when his mobile rang. It was Stamp.

"Did you get my message?" Stamp asked. Black could hear what sounded like a crowd of people in the background.

"Looking at it now. Where are you?"

"Train station. Bessie died on me again." Stamp's voice had a tone of defeat.

"I hope this time it's convinced you to get rid of the damn thing," Black said and wondered why Stamp had such a hard time getting rid of his old Volvo. He supposed it had a fair amount of sentimental value to the young man.

"That's exactly what my wife said."

"She's a smart woman. What am I looking at here?" Black knew that Stamp was aware of how he loathed reading through detailed reports, as time was a commodity every detective in the unit was short on. And Stamp didn't mind summarizing it for him.

"I know this is all after the fact and the process has run its course on this case but something about it haggled me since the judge was gunned down."

"Okay." Black was apprehensive. His intuition told him that he already knew where this was going. Stamp had a manageable case of OCD which meant that if something wasn't quite right in his world he would obsess over it until he found the answer, come hell or high water.

"I've cropped the images side-by-side. Open the one marked C dash twenty-two."

"Got it." Black opened the image. In the photograph on the left Stephen Thatcher and his wife were in their final embrace on the bed and on the right Sturgess and his daughter were in the same position on the girl's single bed. Focusing on the right image, Black shuddered as he noted how the red blood of the victims contrasted against the light pink hues of the girl's bedding. *This is something that no cop ever gets used to, no matter how tough they proclaim to be,* he thought to himself.

In both cases, the gunshot total was six. Each victim received two in the chest and one in the head. Black studied both pictures intently even though he had laid eyes on them many times before. He knew what Stamp wanted him to say but he took a few moments to absorb what he was looking at. He wondered how this detail never managed to leap out at him as it was doing now. He'd worked both cases, however, during the time of the Sturgess murders his personal life was in a similar state to that of a hurricane-aftermath. Not that it was an acceptable excuse. Upon further reflection, he decided that he needed more information on this new development before mentally beating himself up.

"Well?" came Stamp's excited tone. "I don't know about you, boss, but this looks like a whole lot of fastballs to me." In Stamp's world, fastballs represented really tough questions.

"Do you have anything else?"

"Of course. Open C dash forty-eight," Stamp answered and Black did as he was told. This image exhibited two similar looking shoeprints, both in turf-like soil. One was labelled "THATCHER" and the other "STURGESS" with their respective case numbers beneath the headings. They were the same size and pattern, all displayed in high definition. It didn't take a genius or a microscopic examination to reveal that these were made by the same shoe.

"A case could be made for an exceptional series of coincidences here." Black uttered after a long pause. "These cases are fourteen years apart. If it's a serial, the creep gives a whole new meaning to the term 'going dark'."

"Suppose it's possible," Stamp replied. "There's more, but I'll tell you when I get in." Stamp disconnected the call and Black sat back in his chair, crossed his arms and went into deep thought. He tilted his head back and stared at the sign that read "HOMICIDE" hanging above his desk.

He had been sitting in the exact same position with his eyes fixed on the exact same sign when the call had come through late on that cold, November night in 2007. Uniformed officers had responded to a report from a concerned neighbor who mentioned sounds of a scuffle and screaming coming from the house next door. Upon arrival the officers reported that the living room had been ransacked and that the bodies of two victims had been found in the girl's bedroom. When Black arrived on the scene they had already been identified as Anthony Sturgess, forty-six, who was an in-house accountant for a shipping company and his daughter, Lisa Sturgess, twelve. The mother, named as Rebecca Sturgess, forty-one, had passed away a year earlier from colon cancer.

Black could still recall walking the crime scene as if it had happened five minutes ago. There was blood spatter on the living room sofa, which was where the confrontation had started, and on the hallway carpet and walls. Several bullet holes graced the wall and some of the bedroom furniture, which indicated that Mr. Sturgess put up quite the fight before his demise. Before Black could enter the room where the bodies lay, his phone rang. It was a nurse from the emergency center at Mount Sinai hospital in downtown, who said that they had received a patient named Christopher Black. He had sustained multiple gunshot wounds and Detective William Black was listed as his next of kin. Black's blood had frozen in his arteries upon hearing his son's name. Chris' eighteenth birthday had been only a week prior and he had been scheduled to depart for Spain to commence his studies in linguistics that very next day. Black raced from the crime scene without a moment's hesitation.

At the hospital the frantic father was forced to wait three hours as a team of surgeons attempted to save his son's life. Eventually, at 1:37 a.m. a doctor emerged from behind the surgery doors to inform the detective that they had failed to repair the extensive damage to his son's lungs and liver, and that the boy had passed away.

Devastation encompassed the detective's household for a long time afterwards. He had refused to take time off until the authorities forced him to do so, citing a loss of focus on his work. Black and his entire family had undergone several months of group counseling, without which his marriage would've surely ended. His entire demeanor towards violent crime changed on that single night. His son had been an innocent bystander to a gang-war, mistaken for a member and shot down without rhyme or reason. The gunman was never found, as is often the case with gang-related incidents – witnesses are too afraid to come forward and won't consider testifying even if their lives depend on it. To Black every case following his son's death was, in his eyes, a chance at retribution – a chance to obtain a distorted version of justice for his own slain child.

Upon his return to the Homicide unit, the Sturgess case was still open and the leads were few and far between. A year later it had been passed to the cold case unit and had remained unsolved to this day.

"Have a look at that," Stamp said, and his voice jolted Black back to the present moment. He dropped a folder on Black's desk. The detective leaned forward and studied it. The cover read "Canadian Armed Forces Service Record - Ellis J. Neill".

*****

"The number you have dialed does not exist. Please try an

alternative number or—"

Ellis slammed the receiver down on the wall-mounted payphone causing some of the inmates in the line behind him to jump while others merely gave him a sideways glance. The guard patrolling this section of the facility let out a bark, rapped his truncheon on the wall and pointed at him with the business end. Ellis took a few deep breaths and sat down at a vacant steel table. Across from him, two inmates were nearing the end of a chess game. Black was the clear winner with most of his arsenal still intact, in contrast to the solitary white king now fleeing for his life while under constant threat of attack. Ellis couldn't help but sympathize and somehow feel a connection to the inanimate object. At that moment it appeared that they had much in common.

He hadn't been able to reach Cynthia or his attorney since he landed at Stone Hill and it was beginning to be a cause for serious concern. With the passing of each day, he felt further away from his family and the world he knew. It was as if the plane they boarded in Toronto two weeks ago had touched down on another planet altogether. Perhaps even a different galaxy. Among all the elements swirling in his mind, one stood out as particularly worrying: *why* was it that he had seemingly been cast back into a bygone era where prisoners were locked up and instantly forgotten about, even by those they knew and loved? He wondered if Cynthia had tried to contact or see him at all. She was the very first of two people he had added to his visitor card upon intake and he had sent her numerous emails over the past fortnight. One per day was allowed and only to vetted and monitored addresses through the "Email an Inmate" program.

The only response he had received as yet was the deafening silence that countered his repeated clicks of the *Send* icon.

None of it made sense to him. He refused to entertain the suggestion that they had all simply moved on with their lives. However, as much as he affirmed this resolve, it was still something that haunted him in the small hours of the night when the only thing keeping him company was Bobby's steady breathing. In the deep recesses of his mind, Ellis knew that his fears of being abandoned by his family weren't even remotely close to the truth but occasionally, in moments of doubt, he would fall victim to thoughts that didn't seem to be his own. They tended to enter his mind when the chips were truly down and he was desperately trying to claw his way toward a solution in this maelstrom that had become his life.

"Hello, Friend." A low, raspy voice came from behind Ellis. He turned and saw the long-haired, silver goateed man who had eyed him out on the day of his arrival. He was sitting at a table with two meaty guys with shaved heads, one on either side. "Not gettin' through?"

"Come again?" Ellis said, frowning.

"On the phone." He pointed towards the wall with the three payphones using a crooked index finger.

Ellis shook his head.

"I might be able to help." Silver goatee man smiled, and for a second Ellis thought he looked almost trustworthy, like a ragged version of your neighborhood mailman. Just for a second, though. Behind his eyes there lurked something else entirely.

"Yeah? How's that?" Ellis asked and wondered why he was

even considering engaging in this conversation.

"Where are my manners?" The inmate got up and his two meatsacks stood up with him. "Name's Elroy Leonard." He reached a hand out and Ellis shook it briefly.

"I know who you are," Ellis said. "One of your friends paid me a visit on my first day here. Said something about a blanket. I can't quite recall the specifics."

"Yes." Elroy gave a soft chuckle. "You'll have to forgive Miles. The elevator doesn't always go all the way to the top, if you know what I mean. Anyway ..." One of the meatsacks handed Elroy a cigarette from a square tin that had red, flowery decals on it. He lit it with a gold-plated zippo and blew clouds of blue, rolling smoke into the air. Cigarettes, or *silver* as they were known inside these walls, were considered contraband and Ellis knew Elroy was trying to assert himself with this open display of power and influence. The three guards on duty in the common area didn't bat a single eyelid. "There are alternative options," Elroy continued and tapped at something square shaped in his chest pocket.

"At a price, right?" Ellis scoffed.

"Have you ever gotten *anything* for free, Mr. Neill?" The way Elroy Leonard spoke reminded Ellis of Jack Nicholson's Joker. It was slow but methodical.

"I guess not. Is there something wrong with the phones here?" Ellis strongly suspected that this leader of the "Hitler Youth" was feeding him bullshit, but he decided to test him out anyway. It wasn't like he had somewhere else to be.

"Well." Elroy exhaled another smoke cloud and flicked the

lid on the lighter open and shut. It made a *click-clack* sound that was somehow louder than any of the ambient noise in the hall. "Let's just say that, if the Warden doesn't want you to talk to the land of the living, then it won't happen. Emails not working either?"

"I didn't say that."

Click-clack.

"You didn't have to. Your mug said it all."

Something sparked in Ellis' mind as he considered Elroy's words. He did find it strange that he hadn't been able to make *one* phone call or establish any communication with the outside world, while the majority of the other inmates had no trouble at all. If he wasn't a desperate man, he would've told this guy to take a walk. But he was, so he pressed on to see what was on offer.

"So how much do you want?" Ellis asked, knowing he didn't have much in the line of commissary.

"I've got all the money I need, Mr. Neill. I was thinking more of a service rather than currency." Elroy's ingenuine smile made an unwelcome comeback.

Click-clack.

"I'm not sucking your cock," Ellis said and the man across from him burst out laughing with his two meatsacks chuckling in support.

"Don't flatter yourself buddy!" Elroy managed in between fits. "I got my lady coming in on the regular for that."

"Alright. What do you want?" Ellis was getting impatient

and annoyed at the extent of this conversation. Elroy nodded to his meatsacks. They left the table and stood against the wall where the phones were now abandoned. The old guy leaned in.

"There's this hooker in eighteen-B that's been having a lot to say about yours truly. His name's Alfonso. Black as night and twice as ugly. You throw him a beating and you can call anyone you want from this phone." Elroy tapped the object in his pocket again.

"Forget about it," Ellis said as he started to get up.

Click-clack.

"Don't let that moral compass of yours rob you of an opportunity here, Mr. Neill." Elroy sounded almost sincere.

"Don't you have henchmen or whatever you want to call them to do that for you?" Ellis didn't like the turn this chat was taking.

"I do. But this one can't circle back to me." Elroy dropped his cigarette on the floor and stepped on it. "So, it has to be *you*. Make it look like a fight or a deal gone bad, will you? Something that won't make the stiffs look too hard at it."

"I thought I made myself clear, Mr. Leonard." Ellis felt his temper fraying at the edges.

Click-clack.

"Oh, I heard you. But that was back when you were under the impression that you had a choice." Elroy sat back in his seat and regarded Ellis with a cocked head. "You're quite friendly with that geezer in your cell, right? Bobby, is it? Yeah, that's his name. Be a shame if ol' Bobby had a fall down some stairs or woke up with a blade sticking out of his neck one morning. Heck, they might even say that *you* did it." The two meatsacks were now standing directly behind Ellis and one of them put a heavy hand on his shoulder. "You have twenty-four hours," Elroy said, grinning. "Make 'em count." He put a finger to his lips then calmly got up off his chair and sauntered away with his bodyguards in tow.

On the walk back to his cell for the evening headcount, Ellis felt a dull kind of unease that he thought he'd left behind when he returned from the desert. It was like a shadow that spawned out of nowhere. It wouldn't leave him alone, consuming his energy and muddling his thoughts. Not only had he reached a dead end in trying to reach Cynthia, but now he had to contend with Elroy and his squad as well. He needed to do what he had to, for his own sake. But beating another man up for no reason? That was out of the question.

Maybe he could warn Bobby, tell him to watch his back and be extra careful for the next few days. But Elroy had said they could get to him *inside* the cell, so he wasn't sure what good that would do. Maybe the old racist was bluffing – about the phones, the warden *and* getting to Bobby. How far could his reach possibly go? The guards seemed to be turning a blind eye to his antics but that didn't mean he had the warden in his pocket. Problem was, there was no way to know for sure. Ellis knew that there were way too many balls in the air to convince himself that his rationalizations were anything more than wishful thinking. He couldn't risk it. Bobby had no way of defending himself against Elroy and his gang which, according to the rumors, was well over a hundred strong and present in every corner of this concrete and steel laced hellhole. But what was the solution? Could he really lay a beat down on someone he had never met or had no conflict with? Maybe he could just do a light one. A few punches with some bruising, draw a bit of blood without causing any real harm. Just for effect. Would that fly with Elroy, though? Ellis wasn't sure of anything now. All he knew was that he had to make a decision – and he had to do it fast.

The next morning, he got up at the stroke of 6:30 a.m. which was the scheduled time that all cell doors opened for the day. He hadn't gotten much sleep that night but that was nothing new and he was beginning to grow accustomed to it. Towel and toothbrush in hand he joined the small group of early risers on their way to the shower unit. The prison was strangely quiet for a change and Ellis wondered how many souls had traveled this route before him. Maximum security facilities were notorious for housing nefarious creatures, those who had no regard for human life or empathy for their fellow human beings, for whom this locale was the perfect solution. He had certainly come across a few of those since his relocation here. But there were also others. Men who were under pressure, who made one bad decision or had landed here because of events outside of their control, like himself. Ellis had no illusions and knew very well that not everyone in here that claimed innocence could be believed, however, it didn't seem fair for all of them to be measured with the same stick.

This was also true for the two men that Ellis worked with in the upholstery shop. Their purpose was to repair old and damaged mail delivery bags, the kinds that held air mail in the cargo holds of commercial aircraft. They were large enough to fit two average sized men inside and were made using a thick and dense nylon-type fabric, which made stitching them together by hand an arduous task. On his first week, every day after his shift, Ellis' hands would cramp up from the intense strain of the day. This dissipated in time and he later found it to be a good exercise to strengthen the gripping force in his hands. Ray and Bill had accepted and guided him from the first day he walked in and they were genuinely polite and agreeable people. Ellis didn't know either of their stories and he never asked, but he liked to think that he had a nose for pure evil and those two were *not* it.

"Morning, sweetheart." One of Elroy's meatsacks appeared from around a corner in the hallway and took Ellis by the arm. He felt the man-rhino pressing a sharp object against his back, right below his left kidney. "Just keep walking."

"I still have time," Ellis protested.

"No, you don't. This is happening now," Meatsack said, quickening their pace. Ellis could feel his pulse rising and the adrenaline that flooded his system made his entire body tense up.

"I don't even know what he looks like."

"That's why I'm here, fuckstick. I'm walking you right to him. Have you ever shanked anyone before? Go for the side of the neck or the liver."

"Wait! Elmore didn't say anything about that." Ellis' voice shook and he felt a wave of nausea wash over him.

"Plans have changed. The eight ball has to die," Meatsack said. Ellis looked down and could see a tattoo of a letter *A* imposed over a swastika on the hefty hand that was clamped with a vice-like grip over his elbow.

They reached the wash unit and Meatsack shoved him into one of the showers, then took a seat on a lone chair by the doorless entrance. For a moment Ellis stood frozen then commenced removing his jumpsuit and turned the water on. The place was freezing cold and it wasn't long before a veil of steam hung from the ceiling, transforming the entire room into a misty chamber. Then, Ellis heard two men walk in. Their conversion was in French, and he turned to see that they were both of a darker complexion. He looked over to Meatsack who pointed to the one on the left without raising his hand from his knee. The man that the behemoth pointed out was tall, over a hundred and ninety centimeters by Ellis' guess, slightly taller than himself. He was thin but athletic and had large, afro-style hair with fine features. Both men entered the same shower cubicle across from Ellis' and Meatsack slid a knife over the floor toward him until it came to a standstill next to his left foot. Ellis bent down, picked it up and held it behind his back. He took several slow steps within the walls of his shower until he stood at the threshold of the adjacent one where the two men were laughing and kissing. Alfonso, the target, looked over his partner's shoulder and smiled at Ellis.

"Hey, handsome. You want to get in on this?" Alfonso said. His partner turned around and faced Ellis.

"You need to get out of here," Ellis whispered, leaned across and turned the water all the way up to try and drown out the sound of their conversation.

"Sorry baby, I can't hear—" Alfonso said but Ellis cut him

off.

"Get out. Now," Ellis said once more and flashed the blade of the knife from behind his back. At the sight of this the couple grabbed their towels, covered themselves and headed for the entrance. Meatsack jumped to his feet and blocked them using his considerable bulk. He reached out, grabbed Alfonso by the hair and slammed a meaty fist into his jaw, sending the slender figure floating through the air and landing flat on his back.

"What the fuck are you doing?!" Meatsack roared at Ellis, then bent down to pick the now unconscious Alfonso up, no doubt to finish the job himself. Ellis built up a head of steam as he sprinted across the room and shoulder charged the mammoth, knocking him off his feet and onto his right side. In a flash Ellis was on top of him, landing repeated elbow strikes onto the giant's head. The knife slipped from his grip and slid across the wet floor in the direction of the entrance. Meatsack regained his composure and wrestled his attacker off him, pinning Ellis' shoulders to the ground with his chest. Ellis was surprised at the pure, brute strength of the man. He expected an excessive amount of force from him, but this was in another league altogether.

Alfonso's partner carried him to the entrance then stopped at the threshold and picked the knife up. He took several skittish steps towards the two grappling men on the ground and shoved the knife, handle first, into Ellis' left hand which was gripping his assailant's back.

"You're fucking dead!" Meatsack groaned while forcing an elbow into Ellis' face. Warm blood trickled down his throat after hearing a cracking sound from the bridge of his nose. Ellis clutched the knife tightly. He was unable to move and, realizing he was running out of time, he had only one option left. He raised the knife and stabbed the colossus on top of him. One, two, three, four, five times. Meatsack let out a howl like that of a dog whose paw had been stepped on. Thick, dark blood was now gushing onto the floor and Ellis could feel Meatsack's body losing tension. He managed to roll the monster off him and get to his feet. Meatsack was lying on his back, squirming and wailing loudly. Ellis placed a quivering hand over the mountainous man's mouth and slashed his neck from ear to ear. Twenty grueling seconds later, the behemoth stopped gargling and remained still. The light in his eyes went dim and he let out a final ragged breath.

Ellis' stomach did an impression of a tumble dryer and he fell to his knees, spewing out nothing but a murky, gray bile. Supporting himself on the wall, he got to his feet and saw that the shower unit was now completely abandoned. It would be mere minutes until the guards arrived and Ellis knew that he had to get the hell out of dodge. The shower he had been in was still running. He got in, washed the blood-cocktail made up of his own and Meatsack's off his chest and donned his jumpsuit, making sure not to leave any of his possessions behind.

The common area was still fairly quiet as he arrived back at his cell and hopped onto his bunk. Only a few inmates were milling about outside, trying to shake the sluggishness of sleep off. Bobby was still lights out with a faint snore accompanying his machine-like breathing in sharp contrast to what was happening in the bunk above him. Ellis kept closing his eyes, hoping against his better judgment that this was all a dream and he would soon wake up in his own bed next to his wife and Rose would come creeping in to tickle his nose as she so often did when she was up first. He longed for the peace and tranquility of home and made a pact with himself that he would do anything to achieve that, even if it killed him in the process.

In his mind, he replayed the incident over and over again. The fog that hung like a spirit in the showers. Alfonso's expression of pure terror when Ellis had shown him the blade. Meatsack dropping the slender man with one blow. And then there was Alfonso's partner who had saved Ellis' life. Surely the man-mountain could've killed him quite easily with his bare hands. Ellis could defend himself using the hand-to-hand combat techniques he had learned in the military, but against a man that size, and add to that the fact that Meatsack already had him pinned – that was only ever going to end one way. He *had* to do it.

But the blood... All that blood on the floor. It tinted the vision in Ellis' mind's eye to a light red, like a camera lens painted in streaks of crimson. He recalled the feeling of the blade going into the large man's body. Sometimes it was like butter, other times the handle of the knife vibrated in his hands as the serrated edge of the weapon scraped past Meatsack's ribs. He could still feel it where he lay in his bunk, could still hear the sound of the behemoth drowning in his own blood after he had slashed his neck.

"What the ...?" Bobby said, jerking from the bed as an alarm sounded and all the cell doors slid closed. From the ground level, a door opened and several guards in tactical gear bearing truncheons and pepper spray descended on those who didn't make it to the inside of their cells on time. They were soon overpowered, handcuffed and dragged back through the same door that the nameless, faceless guards had come from. Tear gas canisters were launched in every direction leaving arched bows of smoke hanging in the air.

"Cover your face!" Bobby yelled and dropped onto the floor with his towel over his mouth and nose. Ellis did the same and joined Bobby on the cold concrete. His eyes and throat burned as if he'd just swallowed a tablespoon of wasabi from his and Cynthia's favorite sushi place. All around them prisoners were letting out screams and purging whatever was contained within their stomachs. The overbearing sound of the guards' footfall on the steel grid walkways outside the cells drew closer. A cell door slid open and Ellis only realized that it was theirs when three sets of gloved hands grabbed him and began to drag him out of the room. Bobby got up and said something inaudible but the old man was met with a solid punch to the gut, doubling him over and sending him sprawling back onto the floor. The abductors yanked the towel from around Ellis' face and all he could see through the haze of smoke and tears were the gas masks that surrounded him.

They carried him down the stairs and strapped him to a wheelchair. He was carted out past the steel tables and chairs in the common area and rolled into the service elevator. Five seconds later the doors opened again and he was wheeled through a dark corridor with several doorways on either side. The doors had no windows and were made from solid steel with double deadbolts on them. The wheelchair stopped at the furthest door and Ellis was untied and unceremoniously dumped onto the floor inside the solitary confinement cell. The door slammed shut, locking behind him. He was left in total darkness.

Odors of damp and rot were prevalent in the box and the chill factor was much worse here than in the general population area. Ellis got to his feet and felt around in the dark until he found what felt like a steel bunk without a mattress. He closed his eyes and waited for the burning to subside, and for whatever they had planned for him next.

CHAPTER 6

In the neighborhood of Elmvale Acres in Ottawa, frost was forming on the lush lawns and glistened like tiny stars in the reflection of the streetlamps. Victor Redpath was strolling down Corry Street, three blocks away from his mother's house on Weston Road. Rusty, the Australian Terrier that had kept Sheila Redpath company for the last seven years following her husband's death, was sniffing every dark corner of the abandoned street searching for the next target upon which a hind leg could be lifted. The canine was only too happy to be out, despite the freezing weather. Sheila was pushing eighty with a troublesome hip and as a result Rusty's walks had become fewer and further between.

Victor's mind had been overwhelmed by a cacophony of scenarios since arriving in Ottawa just over a week ago. He'd been trying to find Ellis without raising any red flags to whoever may be watching or listening. The first thing he did was pick up a burner phone after dumping his iPhone in the McKay Lake. He also installed an untraceable browser onto his laptop computer. From there he corresponded with John Barton, his Private Investigator. Barton's specialty was finding people who didn't want to be found and given enough incentive he'd deliver you the archaeologist's El Dorado, ahead of schedule. The P.I. had called Redpath an hour ago. He had left no stone unturned, as per usual, yet came up short in his effort to locate Ellis Neill.

"It's like he vanished into thin air. Poof! Gone!" Barton had said in his native Boston accent. "I don't know who you're taking on here, Victor, but they've either got deep pockets or really sharp knives. Even my go-to guys in the prison system don't know shit. I've *never* been stonewalled like this before."

After the phone call, Redpath had felt increasingly agitated with the lack of answers. He'd decided he needed some air and volunteered to take the dog for a walk.

This suburb of the city went quiet after 9 p.m. and Victor appreciated the silence. It helped him think. He racked his brain to get to any plausible solution as to where Ellis was and even considered that he might be dead. Why not? Clearly whoever had ransacked his office and threatened his mother were not people who played by the rules. On several occasions he had considered walking away from this, but he couldn't just leave Cynthia and Rose to their own devices. Redpath knew that Ellis had to be found and that there was nobody else to help. He was the only one who could do anything for them and so he had accepted the inherent dangers of continuing on this path. Now that he was here, Sheila would be okay and he could finally solve this puzzle, but how? Something in the far reaches of his memory provided a possible answer.

Rita Bowman was an old girlfriend who worked at the Royal Canadian Mounted Police as an investigator, last he had heard. It wouldn't hurt getting her on board and she would definitely be able to track his client down. Besides, she owed him one after he helped her dad with a legal dispute when she was in college. He had just begun to practice law. Their relationship had ended back then on a bit of a sour note, but she was the kind of person who was willing to put her pride aside and help when it was really needed. He remembered that clearly of her, along with her flowing auburn locks and mile-long legs. Their relationship had been fiery and passionate, and Redpath considered it the best six months of his life. But as the saying goes: Life is what happens when you're making other plans. Rita got an offer to do a one-year stint with the FBI in Dallas as a part of her training to be an investigator and she couldn't pass it up. He had selfishly asked her to stay and that had been the catalyst which prompted the breakdown of their bond. He didn't regret what he said but he did regret the ensuing result.

The attorney's mind was in such a faraway place, one that was wrapped in silk sheets, champagne and memories of the warmth of Rita's body, that he didn't notice a pale blue van turning the corner and approaching him from behind, or the outline of the dark figure that was seated behind the steering wheel. The vehicle's headlights went out and it was moving at a crawling pace, barely making any sound as it steadily rolled forward.

Rusty let out a light growl at the sight of the van looming closer. The sound from the pup's throat hurled Redpath back into reality and he glanced over his shoulder. He spotted the van, now clearly driving at the exact pace he was walking at. It seemed to be floating in pursuit. His heart skipped a beat then gradually quickened its rhythm in conjunction with his increased walking speed. The moonlit night cast a long, ragged shadow behind the vehicle, making it appear much longer and thinner than it actually was, like a large black serpent crawling along the smooth road. The lawyer fumbled for the burner phone in his pockets then promptly realized he had left it at the house. A mental image of the device resting atop the refrigerator in the kitchen floated before his eyes. Remembering that there was a busy gas station a block away, he decided that he and his four-legged companion would have to make a run for it.

He bent over, picked the dog up and initiated his sprint across the road. Half a second later the van's headlights flooded the street and the unmistakable roar of a V8-engine echoed through the air, smoke billowing from its rear tires as it bore down on Redpath and the dog. The attorney's legs stretched to capacity as he mounted the sidewalk. The toe of his left shoe caught the edge and stayed behind. He dove through the air and landed on the uncompromising concrete sidewalk. Rusty slipped from his arms and soared off to the left. The van was right behind Redpath. It mounted the sidewalk closely behind him. He jumped to his feet and headed for a brick wall bordering a house fifty meters away from the gas station which was lit up like a hospital surgery ward. The engine roared to life once more. As he was about to scale the wall, the vehicle leapt forward and sandwiched the attorney between its front grid and the coarse, rocky surface. The wall gave way and Redpath's body made a crunching sound as he fell backwards onto the front of the vehicle. A large section of the wall broke off and bounced off the attorney's chest and onto the road. He rolled over, gasping. Blood streamed from his mouth and over his chin. He tried to get to his feet but his legs weren't responding to the signals from his brain. The pain in his abdomen and chest came in waves and contorted his face into a grimace.

The driver side door of the van opened and the figure, now wearing a red ski mask, climbed out and stood beside Redpath, who was propped up on one elbow. The bloodied attorney turned his head upwards, still gasping for breath that wouldn't come. His vision began to darken from the corners of his eyes as he coughed and spluttered. The last image he saw was the perfectly circular opening at the end of a silenced handgun. Three muffled gunshots later, it all went dark.

In the distance, the small dog stood across the road stared at the van for a few moments longer. It whimpered then turned and made its way home, the blue leash devoid of a guiding hand dragging on the ground behind it.

*****

"Fuck!" Warden Blakeway yelled and threw his mug against the wall behind his desk, its contents spraying over the wooden paneling. "Who was it?!"

"Jimmy Pritchard, one of Elroy's men. We found him in a pool of his own blood and shit in the showers," Dick Evans, the prison supervisor, said in a meek tone. His perfectly manicured moustache twitched as he tried his best to avoid eye contact with the enraged warden. This was something he had learnt from previous experience. When Blakeway was angry you treated him the same as you would handle a bear in the woods – avoid eye-contact and back away slowly.

"Those assholes better not be starting a gang war again!" Blakeway bellowed as the veins on his temples bulged outward beneath his leathery, red skin. "What the hell happened to their so-called ceasefire?!" He slammed his fists on the desk hard enough to make everything on the table jump almost a foot high.

"I've got half the wing in solitary," Evans lied proudly, knowing that it was probably closer to twenty percent. The prison didn't have enough basement cells to host half of Gen Pop but he guessed that the warden didn't know that or didn't remember. "If there's something going on, we'll know soon enough."

"Will you now?!" the warden scoffed. "There *is* something going on, you moron! Moves are being made and we don't know shit about it!" Blakeway dropped into the oversized, leather chair behind his desk and leaned forward with his elbows on the table. "I want Leonard *and* the Purgs' leader, whoever the fuck that happens to be this month, in solitary together so I don't have to repeat what I have to say. Got it?!"

"Yes, sir," Evans replied and vacated the office, ecstatic to have the opportunity to do so and get away from this raging, semi-intoxicated bull.

Twenty minutes later, the warden of Stone Hill Prison was seated inside a windowless basement cell which temporarily housed Elroy Leonard, leader of the Aces and Roberto Bonitas, unofficial front man of The Purgs. The multi-ethnic gang *did* in fact have an official leader but they kept his identity hidden for security purposes. Prior to meetings they would nominate a spokesperson who would represent their interests and report back to the faceless king upon his return to the block. Today, it was Bonitas' turn.

Both men were chained to opposite ends of the room. Neither was overly impressed by being forced into each other's company and they were exchanging glares to convey their dissatisfaction.

"You two want to tell me what happened in the showers this morning?" Blakeway asked as he stood up and put his arms to his sides in a feeble attempt to stamp his non-existent authority.

Bonitas spoke first. "You tell me, boss. I just work here." In his speech, there was a marked tone in the last word of every phrase and a reduced accentuation of some vowels. Blakeway hadn't met him before and guessed that he was a native of somewhere in South America. He continued, "I don't have no beef with anyone. Not today anyway."

Bonitas was a short, well-groomed man with thick, black rimmed glasses who looked more at home behind an accountant's desk than fronting for a violent gang in a SuperMax prison. Blakeway looked over to Elroy, who shrugged.

"Okay," Blakeway said. "We'll play it your way." He nodded over to the guard standing in the corner and pointed to Bonitas. "Get him out of here." The guard obliged and a moment later it was just Blakeway and Leonard in the cell. The warden turned to face Leonard and continued, "What the hell happened?"

"A plan that went sideways. That's it," Elroy said, stone-faced.

"*Your* plan?" After ten years in the "Ice Box" Elroy wasn't easily intimidated, not by anyone. Blakeway gave him a stare anyway.

"Our mutual friend's plan," Elroy replied with a hint of apprehension in his voice. He could see the warden's face go from bright red to pink and then to a pale off-white.

"Well, that changes things. I hadn't realized that it was on yet." Blakeway rubbed his palms together then rested them on his knees. Elroy picked up on the faint tremble in the warden's hands and he wasn't sure if it was caused by the alcoholic shakes or out of good old-fashioned, shit-your-pants fear. "How did Pritchard fuck that one up?" the warden continued after a pause.

"I don't know. All I know is that the new guy from Toronto was supposed to go down," Elroy said and lit a cigarette from the flower-tin in his pocket. "Obviously, he got one over on Pritchard somehow and now we're all in the shitter."

"Have you … told him?" Blakeway's eyes were wide, like that of a toddler awaiting a scolding.

"*He* called *me*. Wants to send his own guy in to do it right, as he puts it." Elroy scoffed and drew on his cigarette. "Like we're a bunch of fucking amateurs."

"What? I'll never get him in without someone noticing." Blakeway fidgeted with his tie.

"That's *your* problem, boss." Elroy grinned. "Not my dog anymore."

"What's the guy's name?" Blakeway asked.

"Ellis Neill. He's in a cell with Bobby Drake, up on the second floor."

"Is he connected?" Blakeway said while wiping sweat from his brow even though the room was a frosty ten degrees Celsius.

"Don't think so. Doesn't look like the type," Elroy said, the cigarette now gripped between his teeth.

"They never do," Blakeway said, got up and knocked twice on the door.

"Am I going back to Gen Pop? You know I can't sleep down here. This place has rats the size of Labradors."

"Tomorrow morning. If I let you out on the same day the others will get to talking," Blakeway said as the guard opened the door to let him out.

"Warden," Elroy began and Blakeway turned in the doorway to look at him. "I'd make our friend's request work if I were you. We're *all* replaceable."

The warden left without saying anything, but deep down he knew there was only one way forward.

*****

The Neill residence on St Andrews Road in Bendale, Toronto was a modest, three-bedroom house with ample outdoor space that surrounded the tan colored walls. The fact that it bordered the West Highland Creek had been an instant draw card for Ellis, Cynthia and Rose the second they laid eyes upon it just over six months ago. They were all keen nature lovers and to be this close to downtown *and* have an abundance of beautiful scenery at their doorstep had been an opportunity not to be missed.

Lazy summer Sundays were spent sprawled out on the lawn underneath a Balsam Poplar while enjoying a picnic which was always dutifully catered by Rose. Her cooking skills had appeared out of nowhere one afternoon, as all this child's revelations did. To her parents' amazement she had woven together a mouth-watering chicken parmesan dish complete with steamed broccoli and a French salad all on her own *sans* cookbook as a guide. Ellis and Cynthia were so taken aback at the discovery of yet another talent Rose possessed they decided on the spot that this was to be celebrated by enjoying the meal outdoors, and since then it had become one of their many traditions. Ellis hadn't been too big on these kinds of family gatherings in the past but had come to see it as a way for him to reconnect with both of the women in his life. These occasions were a stark reminder of what he had missed out on when he was preoccupied with work – moments of joy and laughter, Rose's smile that could melt the coldest of hearts and the expert way that Cynthia had taken to motherhood and had established herself as the cement that held their unit together and kept them all happy and healthy. Their lifestyle had taken a hit as far as luxury went, but they wouldn't have changed a thing, even for a six-figure paycheck. As he inched his way closer to Rose and became able to connect with her like they had done when she was just out of diapers, Cynthia's heart filled up more and more with a peace and tranquility that could only be described as complete contentment.

Tonight she was on the living room sofa with half a glass of Pinot Noir in her hand and Rose dozing away next to her. The television was on and a man in a suit with long, dark hair avenging the death of his beloved dog was doing his best to make as much noise as possible, even with the volume turned low. Cynthia grabbed the remote and pressed the mute button. The abrupt silence revealed the calls of frogs, birds and other fauna just beyond the edge of their property. She was deep in thought; her mind looping from the time this horrible nightmare began until right now, where she sat with not a clue about what her next move would be. It had all come upon them like a tidal wave and everyone involved was still reeling from the shock of it all, not to mention the fact that they now had absolutely no contact with Ellis and no idea where their husband and father might be. Redpath couldn't be her only option in tracking her husband down, she thought. There had to be another door that could lead to his discovery. She just had to keep digging and expand her horizons. That was easier said than done, though. On the odd occasion, her mind would push her towards losing control and prompt her to crawl under a blanket to hide from this world of pain, fear and uncertainty. But she knew that she had to keep resisting it. Rose deserved her best efforts, now more than ever, and Ellis had been her rock for twelve years. She owed him everything.

His strength shone through to her ever since the day they met at Debbie's wedding. Cynthia's older sister had invited a work colleague to the event and Ellis walked in as her "plus-one". As soon as he and Cynthia laid eyes on each other the connection was palpable, so much so that others in the room were able to pick up on it as well, like the shockwave that followed an earth tremor. At first, she was reluctant to speak to him, but it became clear as the night went on that Ellis and the woman he had arrived with were merely good friends. Cynthia had been relieved and elated all at once and Ellis reciprocated. A year after the wedding, she moved in with him at his one-bedroom apartment in downtown Edmonton and they were married during an intimate ceremony on the island of Bali six months later.

Not too long thereafter, little Rose came into their lives. She cemented their bond and extended their happy home, turning it into a life that she could only have dreamed of. The couple had fought their way through countless obstacles – Rose's birth and early life complications, the sudden loss of Cynthia's father whom she had been inseparable from since childhood, and the nightmares that had plagued Ellis following his return from Iraq. Many a night she had woken up to find his side of the bed vacant. She would search the house, room by room, and usually found him applying CPR to an unsuspecting sofa cushion during one of his numerous sleepwalking sessions. Tears would flow down his face like rivers in flood as he subconsciously recounted, once more, the events that took place on the night of August 31st, 2007, three weeks before his unit had been ordered to return to home.

Ellis had been dispatched as a Military Vehicle Engineer alongside the 150 troops who were on exchange with US and British forces in proximity to combat. His duties included maintaining the efficiency of all combat and transport vehicles in their unit which consisted of one personnel truck, three armored light utility vehicles and one M1-Abrams battle tank brought in by the US Army. They were stationed just outside of Karbala following the conflict in the city which lasted from the 27th until the 29th of August. Their main purpose was to direct citizens fleeing the city towards safe zones and to keep an eye out for hostiles who might be tracking the deserters. In reality, the mission turned out to be more of a waiting game than anything else, as they saw no other souls cross their path aside from a young boy and his small herd of goats that frequented the area. He would often bring a football along and coax the soldiers into a game with the lad providing on-the-spot commentary. Through broken communication, Ellis eventually discovered that he had learned this skill through watching hours of online football videos.

The sixteen men in the unit spent their days trying to avoid the feverish heat of the desert sun and their nights drinking rum smuggled in by one of the soldiers, unbeknownst to their commanding officer who rarely left his air-conditioned tent. On the fourth day of inertia a few of the men had begun to fray at the edges, acting erratically. Fistfights broke out every so often. Two nights later the rum ran out and almost everyone was at the end of their tether. A small group of six, Ellis included, were sitting around a campfire admiring the sunset. During evenings like these the sweltering desert would transform into a wind-chilled whirlwind of sand and debris that hit their skin with the texture of sandpaper.

Chris Maxwell was also seated by the fire, directly across from Ellis. He had been a mild-mannered young recruit who was easy to get along with. His bright red hair had been the subject of many a joke cracked by the other men but he took it on the chin as this had been something he had experienced all his life. The last two days, however, he had retracted within himself, separated from the group and became aggressive at the drop of a hat. Some of the others had reported seeing him walking off into the desert at night without a shred of clothing on him, muttering and gesturing to no one except for the grains of sand and the unseen creatures that lurked beneath it. The medical officer had given him a once-over and proclaimed dehydration along with heatstroke as the main culprits and instructed him to stay out of the sun. The majority of the group put it down to different people dealing with things in their own way. Others weren't convinced and kept a close eye on him. One of them was Ellis. From across the flames that licked skyward that night, he caught Maxwell staring at the fire with a glassy expression for a long time. Then, as if awoken from a dream, he shifted his eyes to the rest of the men around the fire. His voice was soft and broken when he spoke.

"We're all going to die here."

"What?" Ellis said, his ears now perked.

"All of this. It's nothing. *We* are nothing. Just meat and bones."

"I thought the rum was finished," Roy Baxter, seated to Ellis' left, said which caused a chuckle. Maxwell's eyes grew focused and he stared at them. It appeared as if he were looking at someone who had done him great harm, his expression filled with rage. Then, like a switch being flicked, his eyes turned soft, and he returned his gaze to the fire once more.

"Dad said I have to go home now," Maxwell continued in a dreary tone. "He said if I stay out too late again, my mom will get the pipe ready for me. I don't want that." He began to sob lightly, and tears began to fill his lower eyelids. "Please Daddy, tell Mommy to put it down. I'll be a good boy. I promise."

Ellis and his companions around the fire sat motionless, their mouths agape. None of them were too sure about what to do next.

"Quit fucking around, Maxwell!" Roy barked, but the young man's demeanor was unflinching. Slowly, as if the reel that the movie of life had been playing on was set to a lower speed, the trench coat that Maxwell had on to shield him from the sand slid off his knees and onto the floor, revealing a C7A2 Automatic rifle. The barrel of the weapon rose slowly and everyone's eyes followed it in disbelief, as if it was the ghost of Elvis or Kurt Cobain manifesting before them.

"I'm sorry, Mommy!" Maxwell let out in a sobbing wail, his voice echoing into the starry skies. "I'm so sorry!"

Muzzle flashes erupted from the gun and a rain of bullets tore through Roy Baxter's chest. Drops of blood splashed onto Ellis' face. The gun kept firing and two of the men around the fire rolled off their chairs and crawled at the speed of light towards the undercarriage of the personnel truck to their left. Ellis was one of them. From beneath the vehicle's chassis, he could see Maxwell, still sitting in the same position he had been before the shooting began.

Suddenly, their commanding officer burst from his tent and demanded to know what the unauthorized gunfire was about. Maxwell slowly got to his feet and mowed him down in a hail of bullets. Tufts of uniform fabric and chunks of flesh exploded from his body as the projectiles pierced his frame. Then, Maxwell turned and headed over to the soldiers' tents and continued to fire. Ellis got out from under the personnel truck, opened the driver's side door and retrieved a pistol from a mounted holster under the steering wheel. He crept toward the front end of the truck and took aim at the redhead who was now walking around aimlessly, waving his weapon around like a beach towel covered in sand.

"Drop the gun, Maxwell!" Ellis yelled and was met with the

clanking sounds of bullet fragments ricocheting off the hood of the truck, mere centimeters from his face. His heart was pounding and his head ached. The young soldier was now striding towards him with intent. He had switched the weapon to semi-automatic and single shots were being fired in Ellis' direction. He ducked behind the truck. "I don't want to shoot you!"

"Liar! You're a filthy, fucking liar!" Maxwell screamed as tears ran down his cheeks. In contrast to his crying, there was a snarling grin on his face that seemed to protrude his jaw. He was only four meters away now and still firing. Ellis dropped onto his stomach, took aim at the boy from under the truck's engine compartment and squeezed the trigger of the Browning side-arm three times, hitting the machine-gun-wielding soldier in the chest.

Chris Maxwell fell to his knees and landed on his back. He looked up at the sky filled with stars that seemed to disappear then return behind rolling clouds and drew his final breath. His legs twitched as he exhaled, then went still.

Ellis faced court martial upon his return to home soil and was found not guilty of manslaughter, by reason of self-defense. Even though the situation had worked out fairly well for him, all things considered, the military saw the entire incident as a black mark on his record, as well as theirs. They put him behind a desk for the next six years. In early 2013 he was transferred to the mechanical training department in Edmonton and in April 2016 he was discharged, the top brass stating that he had been made redundant.

In the following months and years up until their move to Toronto, Ellis had picked up work through private contractors who provided VIP protection. The paychecks were hefty but this meant that he had to travel to dangerous locations all over the world. During one month alone, he'd spent a week in Mogadishu, six days in Khartoum during a civil war and eight days babysitting the Prince of a Middle Eastern nation who was vacationing in Russia. Ellis had, on average, less than one week at home each thirty-day cycle and to Cynthia this had rapidly become unacceptable, not to mention the effects that it had on Ellis.

He was distant and on edge when he was with them, and she could see that Rose had become withdrawn from him. Add to that the obvious risk to his life that were involved and an ultimatum was soon laid down. Cynthia made it clear that she didn't care what career path he followed, as long as it wasn't this. Ellis had fully understood and had been receptive. He cut all contact with that world, said goodbye to savage work environments and began a new chapter as a civilian. A change of scenery was agreed upon by all three members of the Neill family and Rose had picked Toronto. Clear skies and smooth sailing seemed to be ahead for all involved.

But as Cynthia now sat on her sofa with the rustling of leaves outside and the chill of early winter creeping into her bones, she couldn't help but think that, even though the move had been well-intentioned, it had all been a grave mistake.

CHAPTER 7

In the living room of an apartment on the seventh floor of an old building, a dark figure sat in a sable leather armchair. It was poorly lit in this room, except for a faint green glow creeping in through a window adjacent to a large billboard for custom made shoes that catered towards those in their later years of life. The figure in the chair found it quite ironic that he looked out at an advertisement which referenced something that his purpose in life prevented others from achieving– old age. He figured that, if there were signs in the world that directed you towards a path in life as some people proclaimed to see, surely that one was not meant for him.

He had never believed in signs. As a young boy, his mother had instilled in him the belief that those who followed the paths most traveled were weak and did not honor their talents and true purpose. She hadn't always been kind to him. In fact, there were times when he despised her, but in his teenage years he had come to understand that she had only wanted the best for him – to not be afraid of the judgments and standards promoted by society, regardless of the actions and pleasures that called to his soul.

His long, slender fingers moved effortlessly over the pistol, first unscrewing the silencer, then gracefully taking the weapon apart, placing every component in symmetrical fashion on an impeccably clean polishing cloth. With his brushes at the ready, he peered through the barrel, then carefully inserted the tip of the bristles and gently twisted the handle back and forth. There was an odor of animal hide and wood in the house as most of its contents were constructed from these materials: from the pinewood floors to the leather sofa and armchairs, as well as the custom-made cover of his king size bed. The figure loved the feel of the hide against his bare skin. It was as if he were embracing the animal that had made the ultimate sacrifice. At times he could even hear its cries as its blood was spilled and could feel its panic as the blade sliced through its neck, the experience somehow imprinted on its skin. It made him feel electrified, as if all his senses had been reborn and were absorbing every last drop of the juice of life. This was the force that drove him. There was only ever one other time when he felt this way. When he was working.

He could hardly call it work, though. How did that quote go? *Do what you love and you'll never work a day in your life.* It released an unadulterated joy in him, thinking of that, and he smiled with great delight. He viewed every task handed to him as a gift, an opportunity to create his own form of art, constructed from the tears, blood, flesh and bone of those who were called to the end of life. Of course, this was a philosophy that not many others shared or would agree with. Yes, there were those who would have him in chains but they had not done so yet. He would rather die by his own hand than bow to the vermin that made the rules that were aimed to stifle his natural talents.

A sound echoed from the bedroom and the figure got up from his chair to see that he had received a message on his laptop. He typed a password into the slot and an email popped up.

Dear Friend,

I thank you for your last performance. It was exquisitely done. I trust you have received payment.

We do have another opportunity for you. Make your way to Stone Hill Prison just outside Fort Resolution, NWT. The coordinates are below.

61.1721° N, 113.6738° W

I have attached a photograph hereto in assistance. Your contact will meet you there.

The compensation is double the amount of the previous order. Please ensure that it goes smoothly as per usual.

VL

The dark figure opened the attached document, a JPEG file which displayed the headshot of a man in his mid to late thirties with dark hair, blue eyes and a jawline shadowed by three-day old stubble. At the bottom of the picture printed in bold, black letters was the name *ELLIS NEILL*.

He stared at the picture for a long time, mentally caressing every feature of the man's face. He imagined what the man smelled like, how his flesh felt and what ecstasy his blood would release in the figure's ever-yearning soul. Every single one of his victims gave him a gift upon the dimming of their lights and the figure knew he would gain immeasurable strength from this one. His excitement was so overwhelming that he expanded in his underwear, and soon felt his fingers reaching downward.

*****

As daylight rose outside amid the snow-white skies, Ellis awoke to a darkened world. The first sensation he encountered was cold. An agonizing and relentless sense of numb extremities and a chill that ran marrow deep. He lifted his head from the frigid steel surface that he had spent the night upon and slowly stretched from the fetal position beneath a single, woolen blanket that was seemingly made for a child and had the texture of a dish rag. His head was splitting and a ringing filled his ears as if he had spent the night in a barroom chugging Tequila shots. As dire as they were, Ellis was certain that he would give all the money in the world to trade the position he was in right now for a simple hangover.

He got to his feet and stretched his arms and back. The resounding cracking noise brought much needed relief to his stiff joints. As he stepped closer to the door he could hear footsteps approaching, then stop. The lock of his cell turned and the door swung open. Bright fluorescent light spilled into the room and Ellis was temporarily blinded. His left hand covered his eyes instinctively. Through the gaps between his fingers, he could see two guards with handcuffs at the ready.

"C'mon, tough guy," one of them said and stepped forward to fit the cuffs. "You're late for work."

On the quarter mile walk from the basement level of the facility, which housed the solitary confinement units up to the upholstery repair shop where Ellis had been stationed for work detail, he gathered information about the previous night's events from the guards' conversation. All of the inmates had been placed in lockdown, some in their cells and others in the basement or "shoe" as a precaution following the discovery of the body in the shower unit. The two hundred centimeter long, 140 kilogram body of a James Pritchard, or "Meatsack" as he was known to Ellis, had been found by the guard who was currently holding Ellis' left elbow as they mounted the steel steps toward the second floor which contained cells to the north, and woodworking shops and the upholstery repair workshop to the south.

"Heavy as a damn ox, that guy," the young guard had said to the other. "Took seven of us to get him down to the fridge, and he was dry as a bucket of sand. All his blood was on the floor next to him. It was savage!"

Savage, Ellis thought. Maybe it was. All he could remember was the suffocating weight of the man on his neck, crushing his throat and the increasing darkness that followed as the circulation was being cut off from his brain. And then the grinding feeling from the knife in his hand. The knife that was handed to him by Alfonso's partner. Ellis still couldn't figure out why the man had saved his life. Maybe there was no specific reason. Maybe he was just a decent human being who had made a judgment call in the spur of the moment. Ellis couldn't be sure of anything, aside from the fact that he would be forever grateful for the man's actions and would do what he could to repay him if they ever crossed paths again.

The two guards unlocked the door that led to the workshop

and led Ellis through to where his two colleagues were already seated at the sewing table. He was uncuffed and the older guard shoved a small, folded piece of paper into Ellis' breast pocket and walked off, his keys making a jingling sound in the silent room. After handshakes and a quick catch up with his two colleagues, Ellis took a seat at his regular table, pulled his workload closer and settled in. When he was sure that nobody had eyes on him, he reached for the note in his pocket and unfolded it.

See you soon, brother.

Elroy.

A chill reverberated down Ellis' spine. He suspected that Elroy knew he had killed Pritchard, but he didn't know the gang boss had received solid information. Or maybe he hadn't. Perhaps he was bluffing to see how Ellis would react. Fishing, looking for signs of guilt to ease his vengeful mind. Unless Alfonso's buddy talked, but why would he? They were sworn enemies and rival gang members. Elroy tried to have his partner killed, for God's sake. No, it couldn't be that.

Ellis just had to maintain his composure and think of a story. A believable one. If the gang leader didn't buy it Ellis knew his days were surely numbered. He gripped the mailbag he was working on tighter as he forced the thick needle through it, the veins in his hands and forearms bulging out. The constant feeling of unease that had inhabited his body and mind since he arrived at Stone Hill climbed from the pit of his stomach into his throat and stayed there, like the thermostat switch on an oven that was adjusted to increase the heat on whatever was unlucky enough to end up within its hellish bowels. Deep down, contrary to all the rationalizations that his mind could come up with, Ellis knew he was going to die if he remained inside these walls, and soon too. There was only one solution – he *had* to get out of here. But how? He had no attorney to speak to, no contact with the outside world and no viable options. He was trapped like a rat in a cage, waiting to be discovered and disposed of. And this time, they would make sure of it. It wouldn't just be one man. It would probably be half the gang going to town on him for a while, and then Elroy would step in with a rusty blade and that stupid grin on his face to finish him off, leaving Rose fatherless and Cynthia a widow. It could *never* happen, not like that. He had too much to do still, too much to experience with his family.

He felt a sharp tinge in his left index finger and looked down to see that he had impaled it while stitching. Droplets of dark red blood were forming around the edge of the needle. For a moment he just stared at it, seemingly lost about what to do next. His eyes focused on the appendage, then refocused on the blue mailbag beneath it where a small red trickle had ran onto the glossy surface. The bags themselves were huge, roughly two meters in length by one-and-a-half meters in width, with a large industrial grade zipper at the top that could be secured with a padlock. Ellis looked around to see where the guard was standing, as if he feared that his thoughts could be heard by anyone standing close enough. He wondered if a man could fit into one of these bags. Easily, even with the zipper closed. He would need some sort of aid to supply oxygen but that could be done. Yes … yes it could. Then it would just be a case of making sure that the bag was loaded onto the pallet of repaired bags that were scheduled to be forklifted to the barn outside the prison perimeter where they would be picked up the following morning. By then, he would be long gone.

He needed more information from a reliable source, somebody who knew the area and would be able to point him in the right direction. But who? And could that person be trusted? The answer suddenly came to him and he spoke it aloud, making the other two men in the room cease what they were doing and stare at him, puzzled.

*****

"You are out of your goddamn mind!" Bobby said and Ellis hushed him. When the old man spoke again, it was in a barely audible whisper. "Do you know what happens to guys who escape? They get their asses shot off without warning. That's what. And it's *legal* for them to do that. Not to mention the freezing fucking weather. How long do you think you're going to last out there? Huh? It's below zero at night. You'll be a popsicle even before the guards catch up with you, which they will. You are one crazy son of a bitch, I'll tell you that for free." Bobby wiped his brow and swallowed hard. "There is nothing out there, my friend. Nothing but snow, ice and a whole lot of animals who want to eat you for miles in every direction. Even if you made it to the ..." Bobby stopped as if he were a cassette that had abruptly reached its end in the middle of a song.

"What?" Ellis leaned over the edge of his bunk to look Bobby in the eyes. "The what? Tell me, Bobby."

"There's a train." Bobby sighed, then continued, "It runs non-stop between Yellowknife and Winnipeg. It loops around all the time carrying supplies to people in the Yukon and up here."

"What kinds of supplies? I thought folks around here are self-sufficient." Ellis rolled back onto his bunk.

"This isn't your run-of-the-mill supply train. It carries weird shit that definitely can't be found around here. Gourmet foods, rare wines and cigars, the kind of stuff that rich people like."

"Where does it stop?"

"Ellis, don't even think about …"

"Where, Bobby?"

"Ten kilometers from here," Bobby said after a pause and Ellis could hear the hesitation in his voice. "The train runs itself, like one of them self-driving cars. It passes by every three days, and it only stops if orders have been placed. If not, it just blasts on by. The fucker is fast too – runs at a steady one-twenty kilometers per hour."

"How do you know all of this?"

"Where do you think a lot of my shit comes from, genius?"

"So, if you place an order, it's guaranteed to stop?" Ellis asked, making mental notes as he went along.

"Yessir. One of the guards, the young skinny guy, loads it up from the station's platform where an automatic lifter drops it off. There's never more than about four or five people there to get their stuff at once. At least that's what I'm told." Bobby got up from his bunk and sat down at the wall-mounted table and single chair. He turned in his seat to look at Ellis. "There's something you need to understand. Only three men have ever tried to roll out of here early and they're all dead now. Think about that. It's not full-on winter yet, but it's cold enough out there already.

You don't know the area and these bastards have snowmobiles and horses to track you down with. What do you have besides your two feet? It's suicide."

"What other choice do I have, Bobby?" Ellis felt powerless and it was written all over his face. "Elroy and his goons are coming for me and if I stay here I'm dead anyway. God knows what's happening to my family. Are they even alive? I have no fucking clue! I *can't* stay here."

"Look, I get that." Bobby rubbed his head with the heel of his hand. "But that doesn't mean I think it's a good idea. You're going to need help. A lot of it." He turned his head and looked out of their doorway where several inmates could be seen sitting in the distance. "When are you pulling the trigger on this?"

"As soon as humanly possible."

*****

Later that night, as Ellis and Bobby continued their conversation in their cell, a nervous Warden Blakeway crossed the prison parking lot through a blanket of snowfall towards his car. He opened the driver side door and a tall man got out wearing a Stone Hill prison jumpsuit and a red ski mask. Avoiding the lighted areas, they made their way toward the rear entrance to the main prison facility. Blakeway handed the man a set of keys then returned to his car. The figure with the ski mask entered the building unnoticed.

The next morning Ellis went to work on the two men that

he was sharing a workspace with. He laid the entire story out, explaining that his life was in imminent danger and was surprised to find them more than receptive. They agreed to help straight off the bat and between the three of them they formulated a plan to keep the guards distracted until the device in question was ready.

In the woodworking shop, Bobby had called in a favor from an inmate that owed him money. They agreed that, instead of repaying the debt financially, he would manufacture a three-foot-long wooden tube. The kind that could be used as a snorkel if someone were to get caught underwater, or perhaps if a man were to be sealed inside a mail-delivery bag for an extended period of time.

CHAPTER 8

The corners of the window next to Rose's desk were caked with light brown snow following last night's blizzard. From inside the heated classroom she peered through the glass. A white blanket covered almost everything outside except for the five cars in the parking area, the juvenile White Spruce and Hackberry trees lined up on either side of the concrete walkway that ran through the school's front lawn, and the red brick columns that supported the roof of the assembly hall to the left of the open grass area that glowed green in summer. To Rose, it looked like a winter wonderland. She loved the scenes that the snowstorms left in their wake. Except this year, all of it appeared slightly duller, almost fake, and it didn't conjure the same exorbitant joy as it had during previous winters.

Her mind was always on her dad. Around this time of the year he would take them out to the lakes for the last bit of fishing before the waters would ice over. He always said that the fish would be more likely to bite then because they were fattening up and he had been right every time. They would return home at the end of the day with a couple of Lake Trout, Whitefish or Northern Pike which would then be prepared in the forms of fish pies, curries and stews for days to come. Even with their family fairly new to Toronto, her dad had already scouted the best spots around Lake Ontario with the plan of continuing their annual angling trips. But it wasn't to be this year and even a small memory of what had been taken away from them would get Rose into a heightened emotional state. She was good at keeping it at bay and not succumbing to despair. Mostly. Her life so far had been a happy one and she felt fortunate to have the kind of parents that taught her how to deal with the stresses of life and to see the bright side to every situation. But it had become increasingly difficult lately. She could deal with anything, but not the reality that she had no idea what had happened to her father. Was he okay? Was he … alive? These were the questions that weighed on her, making her feel numb to everything else in the world. She was not without her own resources, though. She had made hundreds of phone calls of her own to prisons across the country and had sent numerous emails to government officials pleading for help to find her dad. Most of them went unanswered and those who had sent replies were all automated "confirmations of messages received". The phone calls were met with promises of returns which never materialized. Nevertheless, hope was something that she never loosened her grip on. She knew deep down that, even though bad things sometimes happened to good people, her dad was too good of a person for this to be the path that would lead to his end. They had a strained relationship but that motivated her even more to see him again – so that they could continue to heal and get back to where they once had been.

She was snapped back from her thoughts when the pen she had been lightly chewing on fell from her grip and landed on the desk. Her English teacher, Mrs. Britz, was reading a chapter from Robert Hill's "Child in Darkness" when something Rose saw outside triggered a red flag in her young and overly alert mind. A large black sedan was parked alongside the principal's minivan. It hadn't been there five minutes ago and she'd never seen it at the school before. Somehow it looked out of place among the other teachers' vehicles. The windows were darkened but through the windshield she could identify the outlines of two men in the front seats. They weren't moving at all, just sitting there. Rose thought that maybe it was one of the other kids' parents here to pick them up but swiftly dismissed the thought. It couldn't be that, especially when they were only halfway through the day. She raised her hand.

"Yes, Rose?" Mrs. Britz raised her eyebrows to look over the rim of her glasses.

"There's a strange car outside," Rose said and pointed at it. The rest of the students needed no invitation to jump up from their seats and fight for a spot along the window to catch a glimpse of it for themselves. The teacher walked over to Rose's desk, looked out through the glass and squinted. She returned to her own desk, picked up the phone and dialed.

A few moments later, the campus security vehicle rolled into sight from behind the assembly hall. It came to a stop ten meters from the black car. The officer exited and approached the unknown vehicle cautiously. Like a sprinter out of the starting blocks, the black sedan quickly reversed out of the parking bay, spun around and bolted towards the main gate. Clouds of white mist erupted from its exhaust and snow spewed from beneath its tires and followed in its wake. The officer ran back to his car, bounded in and sped off in pursuit, much to the gleeful cheers and excitement of the entire class.

But Rose was not cheering. She sat silently in her chair and a faint quiver ran through her frame.

Later that day she traversed the pathway toward the same parking area, but she was smiling this time. She spotted her mother's face through the open driver's side window of her green station wagon situated among the other parents' cars. Her smile faltered slightly when she recognized how tired her mom looked. Sometimes late at night she could hear movement in the kitchen followed by crying, and when she went downstairs she found her mom sitting in the dark, tears running down her face. Sometimes she would try to console her and other times she would leave her be. Rose knew that she was also afraid. Neither of them was used to not having her dad around. They'd *never* get used to it.

"Hey, honey!" Cynthia said with an animated cheer as Rose shifted into the seat beside her. "How was school?"

"Same old, same old." Rose looked up at her mother. "Any news about Dad?"

"No, doll. Not yet." She stroked the hair from Rose's face and brushed snow from the collar of her jacket.

"Do we have a plan? Or are we going to just sit and wait?"

"No plan, darling," Cynthia lied. There most certainly was a plan but she didn't want to involve her daughter in it for fear of the risks it carried. "The only plan is for you to focus on school. Let ol' mom take care of the rest."

"Okay, that means you *do* have a plan, you just don't want

to tell me." Rose scoffed and shoved the seat belt clip into the buckle a few times before it stuck. Cynthia didn't respond right away. She waited for Rose to take a breath while putting the car into drive and pulled out of the school's driveway. Two blocks further, they came to a stop at a red traffic light and Rose broke her silence.

"I'm sorry, Mom. I didn't mean to snap at you."

"I know. I also know how you feel because I feel the same way. To answer your question: yes, there's someone I need to go and see who might be able to help us. But I have to go alone." The light turned green and they continued down the street.

"Why?" Rose protested and her voice cracked.

"Because, Miss Neill, believe it or not, you are still a child and where I'm going is no place for kids, that's why." Cynthia immediately regretted the harsh tone she had used and proceeded with a lighter one, but was careful not to sound patronizing. "It'll be an hour tops. You're having dinner at Nelly's house. I already spoke to her mom."

"Mom—"

"No more arguing, please, Rose," Cynthia cut her off.

"No ... not that." Rose said as she looked in the rear-view mirror mounted on the outside of the passenger door. She was as white as a sheet. "That car. I saw it at school today."

"Which one?" Cynthia checked the center console mirror and saw several cars behind them. Traffic was light which made it easier to distinguish between the array of vehicles on the road.

"The long black one. It was in the parking area." Rose's

voice rose in pitch and Cynthia recognized it as her I'm-scared-as-hell tone.

"Okay, I see it," Cynthia said and gripped the steering wheel tighter, her knuckles going white. She had also seen that car before. On a few occasions it had been sitting across the road from their house. She didn't think too much of it at the time. Some of their neighbors rented their homes out on Airbnb sometimes. But now that Rose had seen it as well, it had become a different ball game altogether. "Listen to me very carefully. When we stop at the house you walk in like nothing's wrong, okay?"

"Mom, I'm scared."

"I know, honey, but it'll be alright. Just do what I say and we'll be fine. I promise." Cynthia grabbed her daughter's hand and squeezed it, not sure if she just lied to her only child's face or not.

At the next freeway exit they got off and made the turn into their street. Cynthia continued to speed up until they reached the house, and she parked the car curbside, not in the driveway in front of the garage like she usually did. She could see the black car making the turn onto their street. It was about a hundred meters back. Rose got her school bag and did the best nonchalant walk towards the house that she could muster with her mother following closely behind. They entered and through the open doorway Cynthia saw the black vehicle park directly across the road as it had done before. As soon as the large, wooden front door was closed and locked, she turned to Rose.

"Go upstairs, pack only what you *need* and come downstairs.

You have one minute. Go!" Rose heeded the instruction and charged to her bedroom. Cynthia dropped her handbag and went straight for the kitchen, stopping in front of a small cupboard above the refrigerator. She opened it and got rid of the spice containers with one sweep of her arm. They crashed to the floor sending the sound of breaking glass echoing through the house.

"Mom?!" Rose, from upstairs.

"I'm fine! Keep packing!" Cynthia barked. With the heel of her hand, she punched the back wall on the inside of the cupboard and the paneling popped out, revealing a Colt 1911 Classic .45 Caliber handgun. She retrieved it and checked the magazine. It was fully loaded.

"Rose! Downstairs! Now!" Cynthia strode towards the front door. Her pulse was throbbing in her neck and temples, and she could hear the blood coursing through her veins. Rose arrived in the living room.

"Stay put!" Cynthia ordered.

She swung the front door open and crossed the lawn next to the driveway. With a straight arm she raised the gun and aimed it at the black car. She saw it had two male occupants in the front seats. One of the men turned to face her through the passenger window and she pulled the trigger four times, unloading the weapon in the direction of the car.

The vehicle's back window exploded and the bullets made golf ball sized holes in the rear panels and doors as Cynthia kept unloading the weapon relentlessly. The sedan's ignition was sparked and the engine roared to life. The driver of the vehicle slammed on the accelerator, clipping a white BMW parked in front of it. Red and white glass scattered onto the tarmac as headlight met taillight with force. The black car's tires screamed as it swung out and careened down the road. Cynthia managed to get four more shots off before the black sedan made a hasty turn at the intersection and disappeared out of sight.

For a few seconds she just stood there, in the middle of the road, breathing heavily, then lowered the weapon to her side. She glanced over to the house and saw Rose standing in the doorway, gripping her backpack tightly to her chest and staring in disbelief at her mother, the warrior woman.

"Mom?" was all that Rose could utter.

"Let's go, Rosey. In Daddy's truck." Cynthia felt spent from the adrenaline coursing through her but had enough left in the tank to help her daughter load their bags into the Dodge Ram and drive off, headed for a destination unknown to everyone but her.

*****

There was a foul stench invading the dark figure's nostrils as he stood, biding his time in the lower basement-floor of Stone Hill Prison. To his left was one of three giant water heaters encased in copper sheeting with pipes running to and from it in a symmetrically webbed network. To his right was a sewage processing tank which vibrated as the gears driving the giant stirring paddles rotated in an endless cycle. The room was dimly lighted and the rank air was thick. It was unpleasant but bearable. He was much warmer here than he had been curled up in the back of the warden's car outside.

As he began to make his way through the tunnels that led to the cell blocks, he checked his watch. It read 10:48 p.m. in amber colored digital segments. According to the warden, the guards changed their shifts at 10 p.m. and he had to wait at least another thirty to forty minutes until the day shift had left before moving; they were not privy to his arrival and would surely sound the alarm if they saw a strange prisoner walking the halls by himself after evening count and lockdown. After ten-thirty the place would be his playground.

He ascended the first set of stairs and he could feel an electrifying excitement fill his chest. It made him feel like he was floating on the surface of the moon, gently bobbing around among the stars. That feeling of temporary weightlessness filled him and made him grin under the ski mask. This is what he was made for, his purpose and his calling. He never felt more alive than when the anticipation of his gruesome tasks would take hold and drive him forward.

He passed the upper basement floor where all the solitary confinement cells were neatly stacked in rows and stepped onto the ground floor landing. A large door was looming in front of him. He tapped a code into the keypad that was mounted to the left of the handle, opened it and walked through into the main prison complex. From the guard tower in the middle of the common area a flashlight was ignited and shone onto his masked face. The light lingered for a few seconds while the figure stared back and then it went out. There was a silence here that the figure reveled in which was only broken occasionally by the light snores and coughs of the inmates resting in their cells.

He stood quietly for a moment and breathed the air deeply, as if he was inhaling the essences of the 144 souls that graced the rooms of Cell Block A. With the light tread of a cat, he mounted the stairs onto the walkway that serviced the cells to the right. He stopped at each barred door, peered in and listened. This also gave him great joy – knowing how close he was to these warm-blooded bodies. He could reach in and snatch one and they would never know.

The figure continued on the steel walkway until he reached a cell marked 7B. He produced a set of keys from his pants pocket and slid it slowly into the lock, being careful not to graze the springs on the inside. He noticed that the man on the bottom bunk was snoring intermittently and waited until he did so again before lightly turning the key to mask the sound of his entrance. He nudged the gate open just wide enough for his body to fit through and stepped inside.

The figure walked over the bunks and saw the man from the picture he was sent two days ago, laying on his back in the top bed. His eyes were closed and the rhythmic expansion and contraction of his chest as he slept was almost hypnotic. The masked figure took a syringe from his trouser pocket, popped the cap off and slipped the edge of the needle into the sleeping man's arm. He knew he wouldn't have much time so he depressed the plunger on the syringe down hard and the dark yellow fluid entered its target within mere seconds. The sleeping man stirred and the figure removed the needle, dropped to his stomach and rolled in underneath the bottom bunk. He heard the target get off his bunk and his feet appeared within his line of sight. The owner of the feet walked to the basin, had a drink of water then hopped back onto his mattress. Ten minutes later, when he was sure that the drug had begun to do its duty, he rolled out from under his hiding place and got to his feet. He held two fingers above the target's nose and felt warm air. He shoved the sleeping man's arm hard and when there was no response he grabbed him by the chest and yanked his body from the bed. Once on the floor, the figure tied the man's hands and feet together using a zip tie and dragged him out of the cell, back towards the lower basement where he had come from.

*****

Dusk had fallen and the final remnants of sunshine fell through wide cracks in a blanket of cloud cover, giving the sky a pink and golden tint. The ravaging wind had eased off and the snowfall had also subsided, now gently caressing the ground as if it were a pair of kind hands caring for a loved one. It was peaceful and silent, aside from the occasional call of a Great Horned owl atop its perch, lazily stalking a group of Eastern Bluebirds that were looking for a safe spot to retire for the night.

Cynthia's breath made a small circle of fog on the window as she continued to survey her surroundings, splitting the pale brown curtain narrowly in order to avoid drawing attention from anyone who might be passing by. Since they had arrived a few hours ago, only a cream colored Winnebago had graced the single-lane road and there was only one other car in the parking area – that of the motel manager who, when they had checked in, had kept trying to look down her top while eagerly offering his twenty-four-hour assistance with whatever she needed. She had booked in under the name *Bess Marvin,* a character from the teen-sleuth novels she had read during high school. It was the first name that came to mind when "Creepshow" had asked her for one and she was convinced that there was no way in hell he would be able to figure out her pseudonym. Upon hearing it he smiled a near-toothless grin, brushed his greasy locks back and said, "That's a real purdy name." Maybe he hadn't said "pretty" in that way, but she thought that he should have.

Her mind was tired and had been racing frantically during the two-and-a-half-hour drive north to the town of Huntsville as she was continually on the lookout for the car that she had emptied the eight-round magazine into earlier. Halfway through the trip, she had realized that the drivers would probably have exchanged vehicles by now, as a car with a smashed out back window and several massive bullet holes in it would surely attract the wrong kind of attention.

"Mom, do you want some?" Rose said, holding out her cup of instant noodles. She was wrapped in a towel with her wet hair hanging down to her shoulders, sitting cross-legged on the bed while watching a local news bulletin on a television that had apparently been sent here from the 1980's. The room itself was equally old yet cozy and the heating was surprisingly much better than Cynthia had expected. For thirty dollars a night it would do the job until the time came when she could decide where they would move on to next.

"Don't mind if I do," Cynthia said, plonked down next to her daughter and took a huge bite from the soupy concoction. Its aroma was full of promise, but it didn't really deliver on flavor.

"Hey!" Rose shrieked and pulled the cup away, laughing. "Get your own, then." She hugged her mom tight and spoke softly. "Mom, are we ever going to see Dad again?"

"Of course, Rosey. We just need to figure some things out first," Cynthia said.

"Did you call Grandma?"

"Yup. They're on a plane to Cape Town as we speak. They'll be just fine. Your grandma is a tough lady." Cynthia hoped once more that what she was saying was true.

"I hope so." Rose smiled and then something caught her eye on the television set. She shoved the half-eaten instant meal into Cynthia's hand, hopped off the bed and turned the volume up.

On the grainy image there was a photograph displayed beside the news anchor's face. It was a mugshot of a man she instantly recognized as her father. In a monotone, unassuming voice the reporter stated that a prisoner by the name of Ellis Neill, an inmate at Stone Hill Prison just outside of Fort Resolution, Northwestern Territories, had died from a massive coronary thrombosis earlier today. The prison was yet to release a formal statement.

CHAPTER 9

Ellis tried to open his eyes. He managed to get the left one open slightly but the image before him appeared foggy and muddled. In the distance he saw a shape moving around. It was oval in form and moved from left to right, stopped then moved again in intervals. He tried to lift his head to get a better look, but he couldn't do it. Something was preventing his head from moving. Attempts to bring his hand toward his face in an effort to solve the puzzle of the mysterious force that bound his cranium were also unsuccessful. He realized that his arms were restrained as well, and an instant sense of panic gripped him.

His breath quickened. Ellis gritted his teeth and summoned all available strength against the unknown force. The sound of leather stretching provided additional information on his situation. This was followed by the rattling of a chain around his feet, and it dawned on him that his entire body was bound.

Once more he tried to open his right eye, blinking furiously. The eyelid was heavy, but he managed to unfurl it. His vision was still blurry and nonsensical. The images that came to him were of a white fog through which motionless shadows were rendered. Footsteps approached. Heavy ones, with long stretches in between. To Ellis' trained ear it indicated the imminent arrival of either a tall person or a very slow one. He turned his head to the left as far as the restraints would allow and could see the distorted shape of a dark figure standing next to him, leaning over his upper body. He had calculated that he was in a horizontal position tied to some sort of platform which, by the feel of his fingertips, was made from wood. He strained his body against the ties again and heard a creaking sound from the table. The figure ran the edge of a knife over Ellis' face and the beard stubble under the blade made it sound like coarse sandpaper slowly grating over rugged timber.

"Who are you?!" Ellis shouted as his vision began to clear. In response to Ellis' question, the figure let out a high-pitched giggle, like that of a young girl. Ellis shuddered and the hair on the back of his neck stood on end. The disturbing laughter echoed in the room as if it were emanating from several different corners. The face of his captor came into focus, then receded again. It seemed to be covered by a red circle with two dark holes that hid the eyes behind narrow slits.

The figure raised the knifed hand and slammed the blade down hard. It missed his captive's left hand by centimeters. The force behind it made the weapon peg into the wood and stand upright. Ellis jolted. He heard footsteps again but this time they were moving away. A door opened, then slammed shut, and silence enveloped the room. He used this opportunity to have a look around, albeit in a limited capacity.

By his first impressions, he appeared to be in some sort of basement. A massive, copper water tank stood a few meters away to his left and next to the door to his right, a stack of boxes were withering away under the damp that hung in the air like a dense cloud. He looked straight down and saw that his ankles were shackled to the table. His eyes ran upwards along his legs, and he noticed that his wrists were tied down with leather strappings, just as he had suspected. The ties were old and withered but they still held tight. He surveyed the room further and it seemed as if the figure that had nearly stabbed his hand had left his hostage by himself. No other souls were present. None that could be seen anyway.

Frantically, Ellis began pawing at the knife pegged into the table. It was just within reach of his index and middle fingers. At the first grab he misjudged it and the blade nicked his skin. It wasn't deep but it bled, making him rethink his strategy. Curling his fingers around to the opposite side of the knife, he managed to make contact with the spine of the blade, where there was a much lower risk of being cut. He pushed at it with the fingers that could reach but the knife didn't budge. He tried to recruit his ring finger to improve the leverage on the weapon, but it wouldn't reach. "C'mon, fucker," he whispered to himself through clenched teeth as sweat started to bead on his forehead. Something told him that he wouldn't have much time.

He shuffled his hips closer to the knife then lifted and launched his waist at the blade, trying to dislodge the blade from the wooden surface. He hit it once. No dice. The second hit dislodged it from its perch. The knife fell and came to rest close to the edge of the table. He pushed his arm through the leather braces as far as he could and got his fingertips to the butt of the weapon, a foot-long hunting knife with an ivory handle.

Clawing at the white edge like a cat with a toy, he inched the handle closer to the palm of his hand until he got a secure grip on it. From the room next door Ellis could hear a ferocious thrashing kick off as if someone was rummaging around in what sounded like a steel toolbox. The sound made him jump a bit and he almost dropped the knife to the floor. In his mind's eye he pictured the figure searching for a form of medieval torture device with which to inflict pain upon his prisoner. Maybe the knife had been too conventional for the masked madman.

This mental image initiated a renewed impetus within Ellis, and he used the knife to carve at his restraints in a controlled manner. The angle made it difficult, but not impossible. His main worry was that the knife would slip and he'd accidentally stab himself in the side. *Wouldn't that be a hoot,* he thought. *Do the maniac's work for him and bleed out on the table. Just great.* With this in mind he proceeded more cautiously and a few seconds later, the leather strap popped off its mounting. Ellis' hand flew up towards his neck, praying that whatever was limiting his movements was not made from steel. He breathed a sigh of relief as his fingers brushed the same texture of that which was around his wrists – rough leather.

Slipping the blade in between his neck and the band, sharp edge outwards, he severed the tie with one forceful tug. His hands began to shake as he heard a door slam and footsteps approaching the entrance of his would-be torture chamber. He needed to act quickly. The knife did a similar job to the leather that clamped his right hand and he sat up, studying his ankle cuffs. They were of the standard prison issue variety – two steel restraints tethered by a fifty-centimeter long chain. The links of the chain were threaded through a thick, steel ring that was screwed into the wooden platform. Ellis pulled at it, but it didn't move. He noticed that the ring was quite badly rusted, then retracted his right leg as far as he could and gave it a kick. The entire table shook. He kicked it again and again. Three frantic kicks later the ring broke off at the base of the screw and he was free. From the table, at least.

He rolled off the flat surface and onto his feet. The footsteps outside were now just beyond the door. The knob turned and Ellis stood frozen, watching it rotate as if in slow motion. It felt like his feet were welded to the floor. The door started to swing open when finally, his legs thawed and he bolted towards the water tank in the corner of the room, taking quick and nimble strides to compensate for the limited length of the chain. When he reached the tank, he squeezed his body through the narrow gap that separated the copper structure from the wall. He was still feeling the effects of whatever drug the figure had given him, but his memory began to return. The last event it threw at him was the conversation he'd had with Bobby in their cell before lights-out. Anything after that was still a mystery, aside from waking up in a dungeon.

With his face almost hugging the warm barrel of water that he was hidden behind, his only focus was on the opening he had just come through. He heard the figure giggle that same eerie laugh. Then, as if someone, or something, had flicked a switch, it evolved into whistling. The heavy boots he was wearing made it relatively easy for Ellis to pinpoint the figure's location beyond the water tank. The overhead lights began to flicker, making the objects in the room disappear and throwing everything into temporary darkness. Ellis breathed slowly and listened carefully, the hunting knife gripped tightly in his fingers. The figure moved closer to the water tank and Ellis recognized the whistled tune as Elvis Presley's "Suspicious Minds". *Interesting choice for an agent of torture,* Ellis thought to himself.

As the attacker approached the gap in the wall Ellis stepped closer and raised the knife above his shoulder. His body was poised like that of a predator seconds prior to leaping at its prey. His eyes widened as an arm with a pistol shot through the gap and began firing in all directions. The suppressed sound coming from the silencer on the tip of the firearm resembled heavy raindrops impacting on a corrugated steel roof. Ellis ducked and skidded as small plumes of dust filled the space from bullets hitting the wall behind him. He knew it was only a matter of time before the figure would get lucky and one of the projectiles would pierce his flesh. That would be all she wrote. Lunging forward he stabbed at the arm and made contact. The gun-wielding limb recoiled back through the gap and drops of scarlet tainted the floor. A subdued moan came from the figure behind the tank. Ellis heard the unmistakable sound of a gun landing on the floor and seized his opportunity.

He dove headfirst through the space that separated the wall and the boiler. As he landed on the other side and scrambled to his feet, he could see the ski-masked man clasping the wound on his arm with the gun on the ground between them. He leapt at it, but the figure closed the space with lightning speed and tackled him backwards, dislodging the knife from his hand and sending it arching across the room to where it landed underneath the table of torment. The figure drew his knees up and mounted

Ellis' abdomen, wrapping his legs around to gain stability, and began to throw punches at his head. Ellis blocked as best he could with his elbows and forearms. One or two of the punches penetrated and hit him on the sides of his head, stinging as they landed. The figure drew back to land a knockout punch and Ellis reached up, wrapped the assailant's head in both arms and pulled him downward until his neck was right on top of Ellis face. He sunk his teeth into the figure's neck meat, biting down as hard as he could. The figure cried out and tried to push him away but to no avail. Ellis tightened his grip around the masked head as blood gushed down his chin and neck. He rolled them over and squatted on top of the figure, unclenched his jaw, and began to land blow after blow into the red mask. He heard a cracking sound, then another and felt the figure's body go limp and all manner of resistance dropped away. Ellis landed two more punches for good measure and heaved himself onto his feet, trying to catch his breath. His arms felt like they were made of lead and his head throbbed. He knelt down and placed his index and middle finger to the figure's wrist, feeling for a pulse.

Nothing.

Ellis dropped his gaze and ran his hand over his face. As grateful as he was to be alive, he certainly hadn't meant to kill anyone. Not *again*. His mind ran over the alternatives, and he soon came to the conclusion that the man in the mask had certainly intended to kill him. What other reason could there have been for dragging him out of his cell and strapping him to a table with a knife and firearm in his possession? It would always come down to either one of them not walking out of this room, one way or another.

He thought of Cynthia and Rose. A wave of intense relief came over him and tears ran down his face. Yes, this man was dead but because of it he still had the opportunity to be with his family again. They needed him and he needed them. He had to get out of here and find them. His wife and child were his life's purpose. They had always been that to him and he couldn't bear to be away from them for one second longer. He didn't even know if they were safe or if they were facing the same onslaught that he was. This whole affair seemed to have been conjured up to ensure the demise of him and his family - to erase all trace of them. Ellis slammed his fist into the ground, stood up and gathered the gun. He checked the magazine – empty. He gripped the ankles of the man on the floor and dragged him towards the water tank with the defunct firearm returned to one of its owner's trouser pockets. Once he reached the gap where he had found cover earlier, he picked the figure up and pushed him through the opening. At first, he wouldn't fit but after removing the thick coat from the body it slid through effortlessly and landed out of sight. Ellis picked the jacket up and was about to toss it in along with the dead man when he felt a small, hard object wrapped inside the garment. He hurriedly felt all the pockets and pulled a set of keys from the inner sleeve.

"You've got to be kidding," Ellis murmured as he stared at the contents of his hand. He wondered if this guy was from the outside. Must have been. That's how he got the weapons he was carrying inside these walls. And who sent him? As these thoughts ran through his mind, Ellis knew that he couldn't wait any longer.

He had no choice but to leave tonight.

*****

Atop the stairs to the second floor Ellis paused and glanced over his shoulder towards the guard tower. The officer on duty was in the same position as he could usually be found – feet up on the control panel and fast asleep. There used to be a small television in there to keep the night shift guards entertained in between their rounds but both resident gang-leaders had complained about the noise, which left the warden no choice but to get rid of it. Ellis turned back and proceeded towards his cell. He arrived at the door to find Bobby still out for the count. There were several keys on the set and the third one Ellis tried released the lock on the door. He crouched down beside the lower bunk and gently nudged his cellmate's shoulder. Bobby stirred then opened his eyes, blinking a few times to bring his world into focus. The room was dark except for a thin beam of moonlight that entered through the small window and spilled over the threshold of their enclosure.

"What's going on? What are you wearing? And what the fuck happened to your face?" Bobby asked in a well-practiced hushed tone as his eyes studied Ellis' mug and newly acquired garment.

"It's a long story. I'm leaving. Right now," Ellis whispered. "You coming?"

Across the abyss that separated the two rows of cells, another inmate got out of bed and stood with fingers wrapped around the bars of his cell door. He stared directly at them. Ellis wasn't sure if the man could see them or what they were doing. A few moments passed and he appeared to lose interest and returned to his bunk.

"You're out of your fucking mind, you know that?" Bobby scoffed through a grin. "Maybe twenty years ago, yeah. But I'm too old to be pulling a stunt like that now. Besides, everything's locked down."

"Perhaps," Ellis said and held the set of keys up to Bobby's face. "But not for us."

He folded Ellis' hand closed around the keys. In Bobby's eyes there was a look that Ellis had only seen a few times before – one that showed when he was deeply conflicted about something. He appeared to sift through a wide range of emotions before he spoke again. "Go. Go now. Run and don't look back. Go find your family."

"What about you?" Ellis asked.

"I've had my time, son. Anyway, what would I be running to? I've got nothing out there. My whole life *is* the system."

"You can still start over, Bobby. It's never too late."

"I've been in the trash heap too long, Ellis. Now stop giving me that inspirational quote bullshit and get the hell out of here," Bobby said, letting out a stifled laugh.

"Thank you, Bobby. For everything." Ellis shook Bobby's hand, exited the cell, and locked the door behind him. Before moving out from under the shadow cast by the walkway above he checked on the sleeping guard once more who was still snoring peacefully. Another glance across the expanse toward the nosy neighbor's cell revealed nothing but silent darkness.

He crossed the open floor downstairs and exited through the door that he had entered through. Two flights down, passing the floor containing the solitary confinement units, he arrived back at the lowest level of the facility. There was a sewage processing unit and a water heater located inside a room similar to the one he had been kept in by the masked man and he passed through a door that led to an adjoining passage.

Once inside, his eyes scanned the area. Several low light fittings were mounted on the walls, giving the place an atmosphere as that of the tunnels in a coal mine. There was moisture in the air and on the floor, water dripping from the automatic sprinkler system's pipes and several rodents could be seen skirting the puddles, looking for their next meal. Ellis broke into a light jog as he advanced through the subway which, by his own estimation, was about three hundred meters long and ran underneath the yard to well beyond both of the facility's walls and fences. At the other end of the passage were several steps that led up to a steel door. Ellis ascended them and tried the door. Locked. He retrieved the keys from his coat pocket and found one that fit.

As he pushed the door open with caution a gust of freezing wind took his breath away momentarily. A blanket of white contrasted by a deep, black sky greeted him as he stepped over the threshold. Foot-deep snow crunched under his boots as he stood there, breathing outside air for the first time in weeks. He buttoned the coat all the way and folded the collar up, partially covering his neck and ears.

The area was deserted except for two cars parked in front of the building – a Jeep Cherokee and another SUV branded with the Stone Hill prison logo on either side of the front doors. Several free-standing spotlights flooded sections of the area up to where the tree line began but for the most part it was covered in darkness. Ellis stood in one of the darkened corners and contemplated his immediate future. He knew which direction to go in and how far it would be – approximately fifteen kilometers according to Bobby's briefing the night before, but he hadn't spent too much time considering provisions for the trip. By his calculations he would reach the train station in ten hours, give or take, and he had only grabbed a liter of water and five slices of bread for the trip after he'd said goodbye to Bobby. It wasn't easy smuggling food from the prison mess hall to his cell and that was all he could manage the day before. So far, Ellis considered this fact the only downside to his expedited escape plan.

Urgency reprised itself within his mind and he set off toward the tree line, giving the floodlit areas a wide berth. The snow on the ground was dense and every step he took submerged his feet completely beneath the white powder. Reaching the first of the pine trees that beckoned him deeper into the forest he then turned back to have a last look. He hadn't been inside the prison walls for long, but to Ellis it felt as if ten years or more had passed since his arrival here. The facility seemed much smaller from the outside, as if it somehow expanded once you passed through the doors and they were locked behind you. So much happened in such a limited time, Ellis thought, and there were so many things that he had been forced to do in the short time he had been there. None of it was worth reminiscing about. He hoped that Bobby would be okay. His friend had been the single shining beacon during his passage through the proverbial hell that was Stone Hill.

Ellis waved a final goodbye to his friend, deep in the belly of the beast, then turned away and took the next step forward as the shadows of the forest swallowed him whole.

*****

Cynthia awoke on the motel room floor with Rose cradled in her arms. Her face felt flushed and swollen from the copious amount of tears that she had shed the night before. Long strands of hair were sticking to Rose's cheeks. Her expression, even in slumber, appeared to be shrouded in morbidity. The young girl had been inconsolable following the news report that announced the death of her father. The cocktail of emotions served up as her response to the bulletin had ranged from shock to sorrow, followed by anger, fear and defeat. It took everything Cynthia had not to fall apart herself, which would have driven her daughter over the edge.

She had been in a state of disbelief at first. A heart attack seemed implausible, especially considering Ellis' age and the hours he spent cantering the roads of their neighborhood every day. He had never once had a high cholesterol reading or any form of vascular complication. Once the initial shock had worn off and she gave herself time to think about it, she realized that it just didn't add up, and in her heart she felt the same way. She was convinced that it must be a mistake, a false identification or the result of some incompetent moron who didn't give a shit about his job or the inmates they were charged to look after.

Cynthia tried to convey this message to Rose last night, but she feared it went in one ear and out the other without striking even a semblance of a chord. She had to find out what the truth was. One way or another, she swore that she would see it for herself.

Rose stirred and rolled backwards from her mother's embrace, yawning and stretching. She sat up and Cynthia could see the fleeting serenity vanish from her face as the memories of yesterday reignited within her. She slowly lay back down.

"Hi, honey," Cynthia said softly while caressing the sweat-soaked hair that had gone rigid overnight from Rose's face.

"Hey, Mom," Rose said and forced a crooked smile. Her pale complexion enunciated the newly-formed dark patches underneath her eyes.

"I think we should get some breakfast."

"I'm not hungry." Rose sighed and laid a forearm over her eyes, identical to the way Cynthia had seen Ellis do many times in the past.

"Well, we have to eat," Cynthia said. "Not much choice in the matter. Why don't you hop in the shower, and I'll start packing?"

"We're leaving?" Rose peeked out from under her arm.

"Yes. I think we should keep moving."

"Alright," Rose said after a few seconds of contemplation and drudgingly made her way into the bathroom.

Forty-five minutes later they were seated across from each other in an old school diner. The red and white checkered tablecloth blended in seamlessly with the chrome and neon decor and the nineteen fifties style outfit the female server was wearing while topping Cynthia's coffee up. Rose was picking at her toast without interest. She had made easy work of the bacon, fried eggs and beans though, which satisfied her mother's watchful eye.

"We need to go back to Toronto." Cynthia broke the silence and Rose abruptly stopped fiddling with the bread.

"What? Why?"

"We need help, Rosey. I haven't heard from Dad's lawyer in a long time, and we can't keep going in circles like this."

"But Mom, what about the people who were following us? They won't be happy to see us after you pulled a *Dirty Harry* on them."

"I know." Cynthia sipped her coffee. "But we can't find Dad on our own."

"Dad's dead—" Rose said, grimacing.

"No, he's not!" Cynthia snapped and Rose jolted back in her seat. "I'm sorry. Okay? I just … I need to get to that prison to see it for myself and I can't do it alone," she continued, the corners of her mouth turning downward slightly.

"You're not alone, Mom." Rose folded her fingers around her mother's hand. Her palm was still warm from holding the coffee cup. "Who's going to help us?"

"There might be someone, but it won't be easy to convince him," Cynthia said while staring through the window at the bare trees. Their branches reached toward the sky like the arms of a giant scarecrow buried under the white, frozen landscape.

*****

Steam exited through Ellis' lips as warm breath escaped his lungs and rose into the frigid air. The sun had begun to rise, and he figured it was somewhere around 9 a.m. He had been making good progress during the dark hours, much better than he had expected. He was feeling strong as the faint daylight grew around him, exposing winter in all its deadly beauty. Ellis knew that he had only four to five hours of daylight and he planned on utilizing it to its fullest extent. He had been traveling for around three hours already and was about a third of the way toward his destination, according to the law of averages.

Beyond the clearing he was now crossing, the Slave River loomed large. Bobby had told him that the sizable body of water was, on average, five hundred meters across and he had assured Ellis that by this time of year it would almost certainly be frozen over. His cellmate had also shared that there were some sections that remained as open water during winter, but Ellis should be able to find a safe crossing easily at random points along the riverbank. The "escape gods" had also been kind to him insofar as they had graciously steered him clear of any dangerous wildlife. Shortly after leaving the prison's surroundings, he heard a few wolf howls in the distance, but the sounds soon dissipated as he trudged ahead; the canines had seemingly continued in the opposite direction.

He slowed down from a brisk walk as he approached the river. His legs were grateful for the decrease in intensity. Stopping at the riverbank he surveyed the scene. As he studied the texture of the ice, he wondered how long the prison guards had been looking for him and what progress they had made. Morning count was at six forty-five sharp, and surely Bobby would be grilled for answers. Hopefully he had somehow thrown them off and, in doing so, helped buy him some more time. The first leg of the trip had gone down without a hitch, but he still had more than ten kilometers to go and the terrain on the other side of the river appeared much more treacherous. Underfoot it had been mostly flat earth dusted with hard snow up until this point but looking at the picture ahead of him, Ellis spotted several mountainous areas where the going would be much tougher; snow tends to pack more loosely at angles, which would make the journey increasingly perilous. This would undoubtedly add minutes or perhaps even hours to his trek across the frigid tundra.

Ellis placed both hands on his jury-rigged safety pole – a relatively straight branch, about three meters in length with the girth similar to that of a soda can – which would hopefully stop him from going under if he fell through a thin patch of ice and took his first step onto the frozen surface. He stood still for a few seconds, kept his ears perked for any cracking noises, then took three more careful strides. The ice was as quiet as the rest of the environment, but he was still on high alert as he walked on. As his bootheels strode across the river a noise that was unmistakably familiar made him stop and listen. It was faint but growing louder. His mind scrambled, trying to identify a match for the sound within his memory. Then it hit him like a knee to the groin.

"That's a helicopter," he said aloud. He needed cover, and soon. His pulse quickened. Looking back over his shoulder he saw that the tree line he had emerged from before was about two kilometers away. Too far. Looking ahead, there was a small cluster of trees on the far side of the riverbank. Much closer. He would have to run across this untested veneer which could give way at any point. The sound of the helicopter drew nearer which made Ellis' decision for him. He hoisted the pole onto his shoulder and darted off like a sprinter unleashed from his starting blocks, praying to all manner of god and deity with every impact that his feet made on the river ice. The sun was now gleaming high in the sky and Ellis knew his dark clothing would be easily spotted from above. He may as well have been wearing neon green against a canvas of purest white.

Ellis glanced over his shoulder to see where the helicopter was, mid-stride, and as his right foot landed on the ice, he heard a loud crack like a shot from a small caliber firearm. Before he could look to see what had happened, he felt a sharp pain in his legs. The sensation rose rapidly to his waist and chest, then the freezing water covered his head. He was completely submerged and as he glanced upwards, he saw that the hole he had fallen through was floating away from him as if it were performing an escape of its own. He lunged toward the opening, but the weight of his clothing acted like anchors, dragging him down to his doom. He wrestled out of the thick jacket and broke out in long strokes, his booted feet kicking furiously against the current. For a long moment he seemed to be stationary in the water, but then noticed that he was in fact making slow progress back towards the hole that was his only lifeline. His chest was burning and his eyes felt like they were transforming into ice cubes in their sockets. Fatigue overcame his arms, and his legs went into overdrive, propelling him forward. With a final push he reached up, felt something coarse in his hand and latched onto it. It was the safety pole that had somehow gotten lodged in the ice beside the hole. Half of it was underwater and the other half stuck out above the ice like a spear wedged into a carcass.

Ellis' head breached the surface and he drew a long breath followed by a coughing fit, expelling freezing liquid from his lungs. As soon the water cleared from inside his ears he noticed the sound of helicopter blades. The aircraft was headed in his direction but was still quite high up. He wasn't sure if they would be able to spot him if he exited now and began to run on the ice, but he wasn't going to take any chances. As mercilessly cold as it was in here, he would have to stay put for now. His eyes scanned the sky above as the helicopter descended and got much closer. Ellis took a deep breath and went under, using the submerged half of the pole to stop himself from being swept away by the current. A large wedge of ice that had broken off as he fell through was lying beside the hole. He reached for it and slid it into the opening as if it were a manhole cover. It closed most of the opening and the water darkened to an ominous shade of deep blue, almost black.

Ellis could feel vibrations in the water as the helicopter crossing the river several times. He knew that, even if they had spotted him, which he hoped they hadn't, there was no way they would be able to land on it. His chest tightened as his body began to scream for oxygen and his grip on the pole loosened slightly while fighting the current of the river. His face was stinging and a numbness was taking hold of his legs. After several sixty-second counts, he couldn't hold it any longer and breached the surface once more, expecting the barrels of several guns to greet him as he climbed out and rolled over onto the frozen surface.

He looked around and saw nothing that resembled the scenario he had predicted. The scenery sat undisturbed and the sound of the helicopter was now fading into the distance.

Ellis breathed hard as his lungs fought to replenish themselves of air and his heartbeat began to rectify itself. His hands shook and the sensation spread through his whole body. Every muscle was vibrating in an attempt to get warm. He knew he was in serious trouble. Hypothermia had not been a part of his plan. Heat was required and a *lot* of it.

The drenched and freezing fugitive struggled to his feet and every fiber of his legs cried out against the forced movement. He gave the wedged safety pole a shove and it slid down into the dark waters below. Ellis checked the skies again and found it clear of any disturbance, the echoes of the helicopter now also a thing of the past. As he ploughed ahead, he couldn't be sure if the search chopper had spotted him or the hole in the ice. He figured if they had, the aircraft would now be standing in the clearing just beside the riverbank and several armed officers would be storming him with guns drawn. If it was even a search party that he had encountered. Ellis didn't have too much information on the capabilities of the authorities in this region of the country, but his best guess was that a prison break would be something that they would want to wrap up as soon and as effectively as possible, so a search from the skies couldn't be ruled out.

He reached the edge of the riverbank after a strenuous effort and his whole body began to go numb from the extremities inwards. Crossing the threshold of the clustered pine trees something deeper within the miniature forest caught his eye. Through the mesh of pine needles, he spotted a structure that resembled a vehicle of sorts. Ellis instinctively ducked down and crept closer, being careful not to step on any pinecones or dried branches protruding through the snow-covered ground. As he got closer, he could see that the vehicle was an old campervan, possibly a 1970's or 1980's model. It was modest in size and as Ellis approached it, he saw that the van had been parked in this spot for quite some time. A thick bank of snow was resting on top of the roof and the side panels were stained brown with rust. Three of the four tires were flat and one of the headlights was broken. Ellis sat on his haunches, holding onto a nearby tree for balance. His body was now trembling like that of an octogenarian attempting a solo trip to the bathroom. Creeping as silently as he could, Ellis approached the door and tried the handle. It was locked but the elements had worn its structural integrity and it felt loose under his hands. Summoning all the strength his body had left, he gave the handle a solid pull and the door flew open. He clambered up the double steps, his shivering legs making the simple task near impossible.

Once inside he checked the bathroom and the bedroom for occupants. There were none and by the condition of the interior it appeared as if this particular motorhome hadn't seen people in a long time. Ellis stood in front of the gas stove. He checked underneath the burners for a gas bottle and found one. The hose had been disconnected but as he nudged the bottle, he could feel that it wasn't empty. With fingers turning blue from the cold, he painstakingly reattached the pipe and opened the cylinder valve. Getting back to the burners he held down the ignition and cranked it. Several clicking sounds later a bright flame ignited from the front burner and Ellis managed a twitchy smile. He held his palms down over it and after a few minutes, he could feel life returning to his hands. He took his prison-issued clothes off, wringed them in the basin beside the stove and hung them over the edge of the countertop to dry out. Leaving the flames going he walked over to the bed, wrapped himself in the duvet, which was dusty but clean, and lay down on the mattress. It wasn't the best bed he had ever been on but compared to the beds in Stone Hill this one felt like it belonged inside a room at the Ritz-Carlton.

His mind was clear of all the troubles he had dealt with and all the worries still to come as he closed his eyes and drifted into sleep.

CHAPTER 10

Detective William Black sat at his desk, bludgeoning his way through the mountain of paperwork before him, as was customary on Monday mornings. He didn't mind the workload but often wished that there was a faster and more effective way of getting through it. Some of his colleagues were quite fond of this side of detective-work, treating it more like "down time" than anything else. In William's opinion, a cop who was sitting in an office and didn't have his ass in the streets where the real work was done was no good to anyone.

The Homicide Division office was on the fourth floor of the Metropolitan Toronto Police Headquarters building and consisted of three desks positioned in an L-shape layout. There were two cops stationed at each desk, bringing the total number of detectives at this station to five souls. Black had a desk to himself – there was a vacancy in the squad after the retirement of his long-time partner a few months ago. Over a joint venture that spanned fifteen years they had weathered gunshot wounds, perps high on meth and the bureaucracy of the police force together, and this had forged a friendship that was still strong as ever.

On this particular kick off to the week, he was catching up on two open and active cases at the top of the heap. The first was of an elderly woman, Dolores Jones, found murdered in her apartment a week ago. This usually would have been an unusual crime in this part of the city, however, the neighborhood of Stonegate had experienced a slew of break-ins during winter seasons since 2018. A male suspect had been entering the homes of elderly women in the early mornings, sexually assaulting them and cleaning them out of any cash and jewelry they might have. This group of cases was covered by the Robbery and Sex Crimes units and all the evidence pointed towards a serial perpetrator. This time, however, the suspect had gone way past his usual *modus operandi* and the case was passed to Homicide.

The second folder on Black's desk was of a victim found inside a dumpster in downtown Old Toronto yesterday known as Theodore Rifle, a twenty-eight-year-old male prostitute who frequented the area. Rifle was reported missing several days ago by his two roommates, Steve Murray and Rodney Furlong. According to the report, Rifle would often stay overnight at a client's abode upon request, but the two friends became suspicious when he hadn't returned after three days away. In addition to this, Murray had received a strange text message from Rifle's phone after day two, stating that he would be leaving town for a few weeks. This spurred the friends on to get the police involved. The coroner's report indicated blunt force trauma as the cause of death and markings on Rifle's head and torso indicated that a weapon had been used, possibly a tire iron or a hammer. There was no mention of witnesses and the CSI unit found nothing worth noting at the crime scene aside from a crumpled piece of paper with a phone number on it in the victim's back pocket. When dialed it came back as disconnected and after handing it to the tech-unit the number itself was connected to a burner phone. There wasn't much to go on which led the detective to re-examine accounts taken from friends and acquaintances in an effort to spot a lead that could have been overlooked.

Black removed the stack of statements from the folder and was about to commence reading through them for the umpteenth time when his desk phone rang.

"Homicide," he answered.

"Detective Black?" A woman's voice was on the other end.

"Speaking."

"My name is Cynthia Neill," the voice said and Black's memory banks flared up. He unwillingly chose silence as a reply. "I'm sure you remember my husband," she continued.

"Yes, Mrs. Neill, I do. I have to say, this is not a call I ever would've expected."

Black remembered her from the trial. The dejected wife who tried not to show any emotion but failed miserably, especially during sentencing. Black had actually felt sorry for her at the time, regardless of the way she had habitually glared at him.

"Believe me, Detective, this isn't a call I ever thought I'd make either so please bear with me," Cynthia said.

"Of course. What can I do for you?" Black said while running the possible motives for this call through his mind and came up empty.

"I'm sure you've heard by now that my husband seems to

have passed away in jail."

Her tone and inflection made Black wonder if this was a statement, or if he had been asked a question. The detective in him needed to figure out the reason behind this conversation. "Yes, I have. I'm sorry for your loss, Mrs. Neill. Are you having trouble getting the body released? I know the guys up north can drag their asses with it sometimes."

"No, Detective, I have not." Her voice rose in Black's ear. "No contact with the prison, the police or my lawyer for that matter. I think at this stage I have a better chance of getting a phone call from the Dalai Lama."

"Mrs. Neill—"

"I'm sorry," she interjected. "It's just been a really rough time and I'm not getting any answers."

"I wish I could tell you more, Mrs. Neill. I really do. But this is something that you have to discuss with your attorney." As Black uttered these words, something in the back of his mind started to squirm, like a worm at the end of a fishhook about to be submerged into murky waters. He couldn't put his finger on what it was, though. Not yet.

"Detective," she said with a faint break in her voice that grabbed his attention. "I need your help. I have no one else to turn to. Please."

There was a long pause before Black spoke again. "Alright, sure," he said. "Can you meet me at the Chelsea Hotel Bar downtown at six o'clock? We can talk there."

"Yes. Thank you, Detective. I'll see you there."

*****

Cynthia handed the driver a twenty, stepped out of the cab and walked through the wrought iron arch that led to the entrance of the Monarch pub, which served the customers of the Chelsea Hotel as well as those who dropped in for a drink from the business district nearby. The outdoor area was busy for six o'clock on a Thursday during winter. A group of suit-clad men accompanying women in office attire were talking and laughing in animated fashion under crimson colored patio umbrellas with *GREAT BEER LIVES HERE* printed in gold letters on the side flaps. The frigid weather hadn't affected the spirits of these revelers even a little bit, however, Cynthia thought that most of them looked like they had been more than a few drinks deep which probably influenced their perception of the dropping temperature. To her, downtown always felt just slightly colder than any other part of this city. Perhaps that was because she found the inhabitants of the area to be sharper in personality compared to what she and Ellis had been used to.

Crossing the threshold inside, she was greeted with instant warmth from the indoor heating system, supplemented by the gentle sounds of an old jukebox that played a smooth cover version of Jimi Hendrix's "The Wind Cries Mary". The bartender smiled as she walked toward him and pointed to where William Black was sitting on the far side of the room. She thanked him and her heels sank into the lush, layered carpet as she made her way towards the detective.

When she reached him, he got up and held his hand out. She shook it briefly and sat down on the leather armchair opposite him. Black was in jeans and a charcoal blazer, and she noticed the gray streaks among the dark hair around his temples, which had increased in number since the last time she saw him.

Mounted on the wall behind them were several pieces of memorabilia from artists that had performed at the venue over the years. The one that stood out to Cynthia was an autographed acoustic guitar encased in a glass box. The copper plaque on the inside stated that the item had been a gift from the Montage Grille in Rochester, New York and sported, among others, the signatures of Jorma Kaukonen of Jefferson Airplane and Dave Alvin from The Blasters. Cynthia thought – no, *knew* – that Ellis would've appreciated this shrine to classic rock music.

"Did you find the place okay?" Black asked and sipped his beer.

"Yes, I took a cab," Cynthia said and ordered a Shirley Temple from a waitress who looked like she had been working there for a few years too many.

"How's your daughter? I'm sorry, I don't recall her name."

"Rose. She's fine, thank you. Obviously, she has her days."

"Of course. Losing a family member is never easy," Black said, and Cynthia detected a stifled quiver in his voice. She decided she wasn't going to ask him about it, but the words came out anyway.

"Have you lost someone close to you, Detective?" she asked, realizing this question may have been too forward.

"Yes," Black said while staring at his almost empty beer bottle. "My son was killed during an armed robbery."

"I'm sorry to hear that," Cynthia said, and she was. She was also taken aback at his willingness to talk about it. "How old was he?"

"Seventeen."

"I'm sorry. Did they catch the guy who did it?" she asked. She knew she needed an opening to get this man to trust her and this might just be it. That didn't mean that she wasn't harboring any feelings of guilt about it.

"No, I ... *They* didn't. It was a street gang, so everyone was too afraid to talk." Black looked up at her. He had a defeated look to him.

"That's something nobody will ever get used to, that loss. I know that Rose won't either. I can't even answer her questions because I don't know anything. I only found out where Ellis was after they said he had died." Cynthia bit her lip as if she were scolding herself for saying that word aloud.

"What does your attorney say about all of this?" Black asked, his calm and collected manner having returned.

"Not much. I haven't heard from him in over two weeks. I'm fearing the worst. He received a threat from someone and then he left town. That's the last time I spoke to him."

"What kind of threat?" The red flag that was raised in Black's mind during the phone call resurfaced with a vengeance.

"A video," Cynthia said. "There was a man with a gun in his mother's house. He didn't shoot her or anything, but the guy definitely wanted Victor to know he was there. Looked like they wanted to spook him."

"Did he call the police?" Black said and took the final sip of his beer. The jukebox had moved on from Hendrix to Steely Dan's "Do It Again".

"Mr. Black, let me share something with you that I've realized lately. Not everyone who wears a badge is a good guy, regardless of your personal opinions. You can't possibly be that naïve. This whole case against my husband was cooked up and whoever is responsible had help from the boys in blue. Victor knew that. So no, he didn't call the police. I didn't call the police either when I realized that my daughter and I were being watched and followed wherever we went. I took care of it myself."

"I heard about that. The shooting in your neighborhood," Black said.

"Exactly!" Cynthia could feel herself getting worked up. "And what did you do? Nothing!" She picked up her handbag and began to get up off the chair. "You know what, this was a mistake. Thank you for your time, officer."

"Mrs. Neill, please." Black stood up as well and held a palm up. "Please sit down. I *can* help you."

She looked at him for a moment then responded, "How can I trust you?"

"I have some information to share with you about your husband. Please. If you still think I'm full of shit afterwards, feel free to leave."

Cynthia hesitated a few times then sat back down, her eyes never leaving him. "I'm listening."

"A few days ago, one of the forensics guys at my office

showed me a report of a double murder that was committed back in October 2007. At first, I didn't think much of it but there were definite similarities to the one your husband was convicted of. Same M.O. and the same kind of weapon was used. For all intents and purposes, I'd go as far as to say it was the same guy."

"Okay," Cynthia said. A flutter ran through her stomach like someone had released butterflies inside it. "What does that mean?"

"Your husband was in Afghanistan during that time so either he's a copycat killer or he's innocent. This made me wonder about the whole thing, so I began to dig a bit. I'll admit that at the time I was hot and heavy for Ellis to take the fall for this and I hadn't noticed how perfectly stacked the evidence against him was. I studied the case file again and it just didn't add up. That and the fact that the judge dismissed his alibi outright and the prosecution never established a motive." Black paused as the waitress returned and he ordered another beer. Cynthia declined, her Shirley Temple still half-full. The office-dwelling patrons outside were now singing along to Neil Diamond's "Sweet Caroline", much to the amusement of three elderly men sitting at the bar.

"Even Victor, with his thirty years in courtrooms, was left blown away by those decisions." Cynthia shuddered at reliving the moment.

"The thing is, the more I tried to work this, the more doors got slammed in my face and that's never happened before. Judge Reiner doesn't return my calls and the prosecutor refuses to see me. These are people that I'm closely involved with almost every day. I got a bad feeling about it all and I've gone out of my way to make it look like I've dropped it."

"So, we're both out of options, is that it? I'm considering driving up to that prison and banging on the door myself," Cynthia said, sipped her drink and suddenly wished she had gotten something stronger.

"Don't even think about it," Black said without hesitation. "You'll be playing right into their hands, whoever *they* are."

"What, then? I can't do nothing any longer, Detective."

"*I'll* go. There's a better chance of getting information when you're flashing a badge. The only thing you need to do for now is keep laying low. In the meantime, I'll see if I can track your attorney down." Black pulled a small notepad and pen from his jacket pocket. "What's his name again?"

"Victor Redpath. You can try his number but it goes straight to the answering service," Cynthia said and produced her cell phone from her handbag.

"No need. I'll find him," Black replied, jotting the details down as he asked, "How can I contact you safely?"

"My old phone is on the side of the road somewhere between here and Edmonton, but I have this." She held the small phone up and recited the number to Black.

"Is it linked to your name?"

"No."

"Good," the detective said and pocketed his notebook. "We should get out of here. I'll take you home."

"No." Cynthia shook her head. "I know we're supposed to be

on the same team here but I'm sure you'll understand if I don't entirely trust you yet."

"Of course," Black said, thinking twice about protesting. "Make sure you take the scenic way back and ask the driver to check if you're being followed. Just slip him an extra fifty and he'll be happy to do it. They get stranger requests than that, believe me."

"Alright. Thank you, Detective."

"Please, call me William," he said and smiled.

"Okay … William," Cynthia said and half-smiled back. He had a strange familiarity to him that made her feel like she wasn't alone for the first time since this ordeal began. She also felt the first flicker of hope spark up inside her and she let out a breath that felt like it had been stuck in her chest forever.

They parted ways and after a forty-five-minute cab ride that was supposed to take only twenty minutes, Rose was sitting in the backseat beside her after spending the evening at Nelly's house. She was covered in make-up. The girls had been following tutorials from the hottest new cosmetics influencers on the web, much to Rose's disgust. Cynthia looked her over and thought that, though some of it looked quite good, there were other areas that needed much more practice. The job done with the eyeliner made her look like Uncle Fester from the Addams Family.

"So?" Rose's face gleamed. "What happened?"

"I'll tell you later," Cynthia said and nodded towards the driver who most likely couldn't have cared less about their conversation, but she decided not to chance it. Thirty minutes later they arrived at their hotel and Cynthia spent the ensuing hour recounting every detail of her conversation with William Black to Rose. The girl kept asking for double confirmation on everything and Cynthia wondered if Rose was trying to catch her in a lie or if she wanted to hear the news more than once in an attempt to savor the morsel of good news they had received. Later that night as they were getting ready for bed, Cynthia received a text message.

Thank you for reaching out.

Let me know if you spot any raccoons in your yard.

W.

Cynthia saved the number in her contacts, checked the windows and doors again, then curled up next to Rose, who was already sound asleep.

CHAPTER 11

Vito Lombardi nodded with accentuated approval as his *capos* shook their leader's hand, one by one. He had been having a remarkable time lately and it showed on his face. Three months ago, he had assumed the throne as the new boss of the *Camorra* clan's Toronto wing, receiving with it all the power and prestige that he had worked for his entire life. Business had also picked up and the cash flow from the slot machines, massage parlors and private protection set ups had been pouring in. The proverbial cup had runneth over.

But today was one of the highlights of his life, something that he had been anticipating ever since the day he became a father. It would top all the achievements he had or would ever amass, legal or illegal. Today his beloved daughter was getting married and the fairytale day he had promised her was teetering on its precipice and about to slide into its all-encompassing glory. Every detail was immaculate. The backdrop to the ceremony was Mother Nature herself. Pure white snow and skies pristinely decorated with lightly dusted pine trees dotted the canvas as if it were professionally crafted for the occasion. The podium was set up a few feet inside the venue, which was a gigantic, renovated barn with the back wall removed to allow the scenery to stand out. Guests were seated in rows separated by an aisle, the walkway strewn with rose petals and various other flora. Behind the back row of guests, a symphony orchestra was setting the mood with elegant notes and impeccably groomed servers were floating gracefully among the crowd, handing out flutes of Dom Perignon and bite size portions of Beluga caviar and a selection of the finest Swiss cheeses.

Vito and his wife Christa took their seats in the front row of the bride's allocated seating area. His eye caught the bullish frame of Nick Castello, one of his father's former bodyguards who now headed up the horizontal refreshment department of their organization, standing in a corner and he nodded in greeting. Castello raised his glass and plastered a grin on his face which had all the sincerity of a crocodile smile.

"Look at that prick," Vito whispered to his wife. "What the fuck is he even doing here?"

"He was invited, darling," Christa said and laid a manicured hand on her husband's forearm. "You can't expect him not to turn up. It would be disrespectful." She smiled and winked at Castello, who didn't respond.

"I'd like to shove that glass down his fucking throat," Vito seethed under his breath.

"I know, but now is not the time." She tightened her grip ever so slightly on his arm and kissed his cheek. "Soon he will realize that badmouthing the boss comes with repercussions."

"They think I'm my father, him and his little following. I can see it. The disdain drips from them like bile."

"Hey, look at me," Christa said and turned his face towards hers with a featherlight touch. "You are nothing like that rat bastard. You hear me? I won't have it. Now let's enjoy our daughter's wedding, please."

Vito heeded his wife's advice and remained engaged during the entire wedding ceremony. Violet, his daughter, appeared much more mature than her twenty-two years of life had previously shown on her. She had somehow been transformed overnight from the teenage girl that used to ride bikes and play rugby with her brothers into a distinguished, confident, and well-poised woman who accepted any challenge with gusto. Vito knew deep down that she was the only one of his three children who would have the stomach to take over the reins of the family business successfully. Her choice of husband, however, had not pleased him one bit.

Burt Sylvester Foreman was *not* Italian, *not* a man of strong frame or character *nor* was he a potential supplier of high income to Violet. He made a living as a used car salesman and would speak of it in a similar manner to an award-winning cardiothoracic surgeon explaining the intricacies of his procedures in the operating room. The man's overinflation of himself and lack of drive infuriated Vito, but his daughter made it quite clear that she loved the guy, so her father could do nothing except to accept him or run the risk of driving the apple of his eye into voluntary exile. She was bull headed enough to make that decision and follow through on it. He had conceded and given her his blessing. At least this way he could keep an eye on her and rein Burt in under the guise of a supportive father figure if – no, *when* – he needed to.

As the evening progressed the guests mingled, and after dances were done and speeches were made the boss and his *capos* retired to the card room. Brandies were poured and cigars were lit among leather armchairs surrounded by velvet carpeting, all shrouded in dim lighting supplied by green desk lamps. Vito was congratulated once more, then discussions promptly turned to business.

The main topics included the initiation of an aggressive campaign to collect all outstanding debts from beneficiaries of the protection program as well as placing a tail on the leader of their Irish counterparts. Rumors had been spreading about a shift of power in their ranks and Vito had learnt that it was always a good idea to know what your rivals are doing, even if it appears not to involve you. Discussions were had, plans were set in motion and the meeting was closed.

Ray Vettori, Vito's right-hand man, was the only one to linger after the others had left. He was a rotund man with thinning, gray hair and deep-set eyes that made his face look like it was a fleshy mask.

"Any news from our guy?" Vito said as he reignited his cigar.

"No," Ray said, holding his glass up to the light. "Heard from the warden, though. He said the mechanic is probably dead by now. Turned into a popsicle or eaten by a bear, take your pick."

"I don't know how I feel about the word 'probably' added in there." Vito scoffed. "What about the wife and kid?"

"Still M.I.A." Ray shook his head. "There's no movement at the house either."

"Okay, let's keep eyes on it. And tell Blakeway I want that

mechanic's body or head or whatever the fuck he wants to show me as proof, and I want it yesterday."

"Sure, boss. One more thing." Ray took a swig from his glass. "There's a city cop asking questions."

"So? Just give him an early Christmas bonus." Vito smiled through cigar smoke rolling from his lips.

"Squeaky clean, this *ragazzo*. Sees himself as a bit of a lone wolf of justice-type."

"Fucking idealists." Vito shook his head. "Alright. Put a tail on him but outsource to one of the street gangs. I want this shit wrapped up."

*****

On the drive home, after the festivities had concluded and everyone had waved the newlyweds off to their honeymoon, Vito's mind was running like the wheels turning on his luxury sedan. He didn't like loose ends, especially the kinds that hid under the illusion of probability or likelihood. Under his father's tenure *he* had been the one to clean up any messes but now he was forced to trust in others to get the job done. Vito liked to think that he surrounded himself with the right people. Ray had been a trusted soldier and a good friend since their formative years and proved loyal beyond a shadow of a doubt. This could not be said for his entire crew, unfortunately. Vincenzo Lombardi, Vito's father and the previous boss of the outfit, had left a bitter taste in some of the *made men*'s mouths when he had departed.

At sixty-four years of age, the law had caught up with him following a substantial surveillance program. He was charged with murder, racketeering and conspiracy to commit murder, to name a few. The old man chose to run and hid in Salerno for ten years. All went well. He stayed out of reach and out of trouble until he decided, on a whim, to take a trip to the US and in his relaxed state had packed the incorrect travel documents. He was flagged upon departure and cuffed as soon as his feet touched American soil.

After his extradition to Canada, he was facing life with no chance of leaving the institution alive, considering his age. The thought of this filled him with a deep-seeded dread and he promptly cut a deal, turning state's informant. The fallout was intense with several underbosses baying for blood. Not only his blood, but that of his entire family for committing what was considered the ultimate betrayal. Vito rose to the occasion, openly declared war on his father and put out a contract on him. Two million to the man or woman who brings him the head of Vincenzo Lombardi. This put Vito back in good stead with the crew but as these things go, a small faction within the organization was not convinced. To them, being a rat is in your blood and they argued that Vito could end up burning everything they had worked for to the ground. They wanted him out and the whispers began, spawning the birth of a cancer among the Toronto mob that seemed to spread quicker than he could stamp it out. But a week ago, Vito had a breakthrough. The ringleader of the mutinous group had been identified and grabbed straight after the wedding, and that's exactly where he was on his way to now.

"Do you want me to drop you off first?" Vito asked Christa who was staring out through the window, seemingly deep in thought.

"I wouldn't miss this for the world, darling." She flashed him a devious smile, the one he usually got just before they made love.

Gliding over the blacktop at a fast pace, it wasn't too long until they reached their destination in the industrial section beside downtown. The snow had turned to rain and the tires of Vito's car disrupted the reflections of the streetlights in the pools of water that lined the entrance of the meatpacking warehouse when they made the turn. They crossed the parking area and a garage door slid open as they approached, let them enter then abruptly rolled shut.

Inside the structure there were two other cars parked with their high beams on. In full view of the flood of illumination sat a man bound to a chair. Vito parked and they walked over to where the man was tied up. He was being guarded by two large suits with menacing demeanors about them. Not far away, a collection of animal carcasses hung from meathooks giving off the smell of fresh meat mixed with blood.

"Did you enjoy the wedding, Nick?" Vito asked Nick Castello, the man in the chair who was responsible for the split in his organization and had been sipping champagne with them a few hours earlier.

"Vito? Is that you? Jesus, Vito, get me out of here! What the fuck is going on?" Castello's eyes were swollen shut from the beating he had received from the two bodyguards upon his abduction.

"What, you can't see me? Let me help you out." Vito pulled a small knife from his belt, grabbed Castello's head and slashed at the puffy, bruised bags above his eyes. Blood and pus oozed from the wounds and Castello yelped like a dog that's tail had been stepped on.

"Jesus!" Castello blew spit from between his clenched teeth. "You'll fucking burn for this, Vito!"

"Excuse me?! You try to turn my guys against me, and *I'll* burn?! Fuck off!" Veins bulged on Vito's forehead as he yelled. He turned to one of the guards and snapped his fingers. The guard pulled a pair of garden shears from his pocket and handed it to Vito. "There's something I want you to see," Vito said and retrieved his cell phone from his jacket pocket. He unlocked it and held the screen up to Castello, who was now able to see after the swelling on his eyes had been drained.

"What?" Castello huffed like he got a gut kick. Then his face grimaced as he stared at an image on a live video call of a man holding a gun to his wife and son's heads. "Where are they?"

"You don't need me to tell you what happens next, do you, Nick?" Vito said and cut the rope that bound Castello's hands behind the chair he was seated on. He slumped forward and looked up at Vito, who handed him the shears. Tears were now mixed in with the red and yellow mixture flowing from his face. He bent down and removed his left shoe, pausing to stare at Christa this time with nothing but remorse and pleading on his face. She stared back and drew on her cigarette with no change in her expression.

"Please!" Castello said, securing the sharp edges of the shears over his now exposed big toe.

"Go on, Nicky." Vito said and held the phone closer to his face. Nick looked away from his foot and squeezed the handles on the shears. He let out a sound somewhere between screaming and gargling. The toe slid over the floor as it detached from the foot and from the gruesome stub came a single squirt of blood which subsided to a steady flow.

"That's my boy!" Vito yelled and slapped Nick on the back, almost sending him rolling off the chair. "Whoa, big fella. We're not done yet! Next one!"

"Vito, please!" Castello was sobbing heavily, trying to clutch at the wound.

"Nickeeee!" Vito screamed with an unnatural shrill to his voice. "I'll filet that beautiful wife of yours, bow to stern." He paused to let his words sink in. "Do it."

Castello picked the bloody shears up off the floor and cut off the toe next to where his larger one used to be, wailing and blubbering as he did so. As the fleshy appendage popped off Castello's brain decided it had seen enough and shut his lights off. The man's body rolled off the chair and landed in the pool of blood on the floor.

"Goddammit!" Vito yelled. "It's no fun if they're not awake!" He walked over to the bodyguard closest to him, yanked a gun from his belt and put three bullets in Castello's head. The gunshots echoed in the wide-open space and smoke from the muzzle hung in the air as if suspended by small wires. Vito looked over to the man whose gun was in his hand and tossed him the phone. "Kill them both."

A series of blood curdling screams could be heard from the phone's compact speaker followed by a hail of gunfire.

CHAPTER 12

With darkness in place for the next eighteen hours, the forested tundra that surrounded the small camper van seemed lost in the vast blackness of the night. A faint glimmer of moonlight paved a slim streak over the frozen terrain, providing visibility that was marginally better than the nothingness that descended over this landscape once the sun clocked its card for the day.

Ellis was peering out from the back window of the darkened interior of his refuge. In his almost thirty-eight years he had never quite experienced the level of desolation that he was seeing through the Plexiglass. It reminded him of a painting that hung in his father's office called *The Sea of Ice* by Caspar David Friedrich. The image was of a shipwreck among a multitude of jagged icebergs and Ellis made the connection between his immediate surroundings and the message that the artwork had conveyed to him, as if it had been a premonition of his present and near future – that nature was sublimely beautiful yet could be equally and brutally indifferent to human will.

He had managed to sleep for a couple of hours with the gas stove providing sufficient warmth. When he awoke, he had found two tins of corned beef and baked beans in one of the cupboards in the kitchenette, which had replenished his energy levels far beyond what he had expected they would. In addition to that glorious discovery, he had rummaged through the closet next to the bed and found a pair of fishing pants, complete with fur lining on the inside, a pair of hiking boots that were one size too big but would certainly do the job and a long-sleeved fleece shirt with a snow cap. Everything fit to a degree and once he slipped on the jacket he had taken off his would-be killer, he felt very well insulated.

A quick look under the bed had revealed an antique-era double barreled shotgun and three shells, wrapped in a wool blanket. The gun was rusted and worn from years or possibly decades of use, and the shells looked older than he was, but Ellis figured it would certainly come in handy. He fashioned a strap for the weapon by tearing his prison-issued pants into strips, twisting them into a braid (a trick he learned early on which came with having a girl-child) and slung the gun over his shoulder. Two of the shells were in the barrels and the third was pocketed. Whether or not the bullets still fired was a question that he might eventually get the answer to. He hoped he wouldn't have to find out.

He said goodbye to the warm cabin, stepped outside and closed the door firmly behind him. The air was still, the night silent and the cold seemed less aggressive than when he had arrived here. Perhaps that was because he had been close to being frozen solid after his dip in the water earlier. Ellis liked to think it was his newfound attire that was providing him with much needed shelter on the go and he realized that he was subconsciously giving his clothes a pep talk. *New armor don't fail me now. There's a long, cold road ahead,* he thought to himself.

As he crossed through the edge of the tree line and onto yet another clearing, his mind traveled into the past then got stuck on a single point – Cynthia and Rose. Someone was out to get him, of that there could be no doubt, but had they involved his family? He didn't even want to consider all the possibilities. It filled him with dread and fear. If his family had been made mortal victims of this collusion or set up or whatever it was, he would be lost to the world forever, an inanimate object that would eventually just wither away and die under the weight of the years and the elements. Ellis shook his head in an attempt to somehow discard the thoughts from his mind but then promptly stopped himself. He ascertained that, as his family had been his driving force in everyday life, they had now become his motivation to keep going. Solving this puzzle and all attempts at proving his innocence would be secondary endeavors because without *them* he would have no desire or drive to perform the latter.

A fresh spark was building up inside him and he knew that, up against these nameless and faceless people, he would have to pull out all the stops to get the job done, regardless of how wrong it would seem or how much his morals and values kicked against it. He was desperate and the means, however grim a journey it would turn out to be, would definitely be justified to save his two girls. He knew he was able to be merciless although it was a part of him that he had tucked away and didn't enjoy tapping back into. It seemed that this conundrum that his life had been turned into was hellbent on unleashing this side of his personality. He had been forced to kill two men and although he felt no remorse for the deeds, he knew that someday it would come back to him. Was he still an innocent man? Had the very establishment he had been sent to, that was meant to rehabilitate and reform, turned him into the thing that they had accused him of being?

As these trepidations were mulled over, Ellis looked up at the clear night sky and checked his bearing. He was headed south and the stars he used to navigate his route were exactly in the position that they needed to be. Adjusting his course slightly westward he picked his pace up to a light jog.

*****

"We should never have sent the horses back!" Blakeway yelled into the pale moonlight as his legs battled through the three-foot-thick snow. His chest heaved with every arduous step, and he wished he had brought more liquor. His hip flask was approaching a drought of epic proportions and the constant strain on his body made his usually permanent buzz go flying off into the night, along with any shred of patience that he had. He could feel every bit of cold and pain and for an alcoholic of his variety, that was a horrific nightmare.

"Over here!" A voice came from the front of the makeshift posse. Blakeway was the last man in a row of six and the leader, tasked with tracking the fugitive, was Herbert Lancaster. Herbert was of middle-age, lean and muscular with shoulder length blonde hair and a full, dark beard that engulfed nearly his entire face. His connection to Blakeway and Stone Hill was made a year ago when the last men who were brave enough to spring themselves from the institution needed to be tracked down. Herbert Lancaster was known as the best tracker of all things wild and domesticated south of the Great Slave Lake and Blakeway wasted no time in enlisting him on a part-time basis, if and when required. "I've got something!" the tracker shouted again.

"What is it?!" Blakeway barked as he elbowed his way past the others towards the front, coming close to losing his footing a few times.

"There." Herbert pointed a gloved finger towards the ground. "If that ain't the imprint of a prison issue boot then I'm the Pope," he declared with glee while puffing on a withered tobacco pipe that was clenched between crooked and stained teeth.

"Which way, Inspector Morse?" Blakeway asked, making no attempt to hide his insolence as he studied the footprint.

"That way." Herbert pointed to where a small cluster of trees stood out among the vastness of snow, which appeared as a dark shade of gray in the low lighting. "Over yonder, in them trees."

Blakeway led the way and the four prison guards, all armed with shotguns and flashlights, followed with Herbert making his way back to the nose of the party. Every few steps the warden would kick at the snow in frustration. He had never before in his entire career in Correctional Services been made to trudge out to find an escaped convict. He clenched his jaw as he thought of the injustice of it all. It was beneath him, a job made for foot soldiers and dogs, yet here he was doing the bidding of his master who sat a million miles away in his comfortable chair with his hot wife, probably knuckle deep her pussy right now. Blakeway scoffed and retrieved the flask from his pocket, emptying the final drops down his throat. It burned all the way to the bottom of his stomach, and he savored it as best he could.

The guards racked their shotguns almost in unison as an old camper van appeared among the trees. Blakeway froze in his tracks. He had no intention of going one more step forward without having a few meat shields in front of him. Luckily for him Herbert pulled a .44 Magnum from beneath his bearskin coat and crept towards the door. He signaled for one of the guards to back him up and the other two surrounded the vehicle.

"Inmate!" Herbert yelled after rapping the butt of his gun on the door. "Get your ass out here, now!"

Nothing.

Blakeway nodded at the guard next to Herbert and he rushed towards the door. One swift kick and it flew off its hinges, folding inward like a sheet of paper. Herbert clambered in and after five seconds he gave the "all clear" signal.

"Fuck," the warden hissed. He stepped inside and surveyed the surroundings. Nothing seemed out of place, but then again, he supposed he wouldn't know if it was. Two of the guards checked all the cupboards and closets and came back shaking their heads. Herbert opened the small bar fridge under the cooktop, studied it then pulled a single can of beer from inside. The appliance had long since ceased to work but the drink was still cold. He opened it but before he could take a swig Blakeway snatched it from his hand.

"Who's in charge here?" the warden growled.

"You are," Herbert said and turned his gaze to the ground as Blakeway chugged the beer, spilling some of it over his chin.

"It doesn't look like anyone's been in this dump for a while," Herbert finally said after letting a few seconds pass. He was glaring at the warden from the corner of his eye.

"I think that's the first smart thing I've ever heard coming out of your mouth, bushwhacker man," Blakeway said and belched. "Let's get the hell out of here."

Herbert and the guard emerged from the trailer and joined the guards, leaving the warden inside. Blakeway put the empty beer can down on the stove, turned to leave then stopped dead in his tracks. He turned back and his hand hovered over the gas burners. "Still warm," he whispered to himself and grinned. "You can't be *too* far away then."

*****

Ellis gripped the branches of the pine tree and hauled himself up, careful not to cause any scrapes or tears into his clothing that would let any heat out. He was almost at the top and the tree trunk was quickly losing girth as it reached toward the sky. Three more hauls upward, he stopped and surveyed the area from on high.

The train station lay about four hundred meters to the east, barely visible through the tree line between him and his destination. Even though it blocked his vision he knew the foliage would provide excellent cover for when he made his final approach. Ellis thought that it was an odd structure, this station. With its concrete exterior and platform plainly jutting out of the earth, it looked more like an old bomb shelter. Perhaps that's what it had been in its previous life. A remnant from wars gone by, now being repurposed as a gateway to luxurious goods for the wealthier plot owners of Yellowknife, Fort Resolution and all the land in between. He supposed they would arrive on snowmobiles, snowcats, all-terrain trucks and all other manner of vehicles, wading across the sleet to pick up their goods and rush back to the warmth of their cabins. Hopefully they wouldn't linger.

Ellis knew he'd have to move fast when the time came, making his move only when the opportune moment presented itself. There would be no time to waste. If he missed this train, it would be a long three-day wait until the next one. By then the hunting party would've certainly tracked him down and strung him back to Stone Hill. That was *not* an option. If he missed the train, he'd have to switch to Plan B.

He ran over the alternative scenario again and even though it wasn't all that bad, it would cost him another few kilometers of trekking across the tundra to Fort Resolution, where he would commandeer a vehicle of some sort and hit the highway. That, however, seemed a lot riskier. It was a three-day drive to Toronto and the RCMP would most likely have roadblocks up all over the area. With that in place it would be a matter of mere hours before he was apprehended. So, in fact then, his only *safe* option was this train. Nobody knew that this solitary spot was where he was headed, which would give him the element of stealth, if only for a short while. What he absolutely couldn't do was underestimate their efforts at retrieving him. Whoever had orchestrated his demise into the hole that was Stone Hill went through a lot of pain and effort to get it done, and they probably won't be happy to hear that he had fled the coup. Their resources would in all likelihood be pooled to stop him from reaching his destination.

Ellis adjusted his grip on the branches and began to make his way back down to solid ground. The last thing he wanted was to add a fall from a twenty-five-foot tree to his list of misfortunes, so he took his time testing every branch carefully before placing any weight on it. The bark was coarse under his gloved hands and provided excellent friction for gripping purposes.

About halfway down, he stopped. There was rustling in the snow below. He peered down over his shoulder but saw nothing out of the ordinary. The same result came from glancing over the other shoulder. The thicket below him was partially blocking his view.

He listened.

There was breathing, no – *panting* – coming from the base of the tree. He straightened his legs and looked down through the gap between his thighs and drew in a short breath. A lone wolf, black as night with luminous blue eyes, was staring straight up at him through a mesh of pine leaves. Ellis stared back, his heart rate gradually increasing as he heard the sound of a suppressed growl coming from underneath him. *It could just be passing through,* he thought. He'd give the animal a few moments to see if it lost interest, then continue his descent. But its response was *not* what he had hoped for. The wolf began to circle the tree, never shifting its eyes off the man above while feverishly hopping around and yapping. A short howl escaped its snout. Two more followed in quick succession and Ellis realized that it was calling for backup. The rest of the pack must be close by.

"Are you fucking kidding me?" he whispered to himself. Ellis thought that it had probably been tracking him for a while and he hadn't noticed. Remembering the shotgun on his back gave him some comfort, but not much. Yes, he had a weapon, but he still had no idea if it would work and even if it proved effective, every set of ears in a ten-mile radius would hear it. He may as well fire a flare up into the sky, have a seat and wait for the cavalry to arrive.

The wolf yelped again, then let out a long, deep howl. Ellis looked down and saw the animal put its front legs up on the side of the tree, snarling at him. It was huge and had a few scars on its face from squabbles with other wolves or perhaps from hunting bears before the dead of winter descended upon it. This time of year, most of the bears were in hibernation and the elk became few and far between. Ellis grasped the fact that food was now scarce for the predators out here. Not good news if you're stuck up a tree, pursued by an enormous wolf that most likely had his pack en route to join in on the feast.

"But they're not here yet," Ellis said to himself and began to shimmy down the tree until he was about three meters above the beast. It leapt repeatedly, snapping its jaws but falling well short of the targeted bootheels. Ellis unslung the rifle and held it by the muzzle. He dipped it down, butt of the gun at the bottom in an effort to entice the wolf into leaping higher, which it did. Ellis lunged at it and missed. The angle was awkward, and the wolf was quick but he had to try something before the rest of the pack arrived. He feigned ascending back up the tree which seemed to piss the animal off even more. It hurled itself up again, higher than before and Ellis seized his chance.

He gripped the tree and doubled down, sending the butt of the rifle crashing into the top of the animal's head, right above its glaring eyes. It wailed, landed on its back, and scampered away a few meters. Ellis was surprised that he had made actual contact and in a lapse of concentration the rifle slipped from his grip, hit a branch on the way down and pegged muzzle-first into the snow. The wolf jerked then went at the gun, biting the barrel a few times and shaking it around by the improvised sling. The animal let go of the weapon and it flew off in between two shrubs a few feet away. Then, reminded of the quarry in the tree, it returned to the base of the trunk and looked back up at Ellis again, its eyes boring down into his soul. The message that he was truly fucked was seemingly projected into his mind from the mind of the ravenous creature below.

A cracking sound echoed in the distance.

Ellis and the wolf were still locked in a stare down when, suddenly, the left side of the beast's head exploded, sending blood, brain matter and teeth splashing onto the tree. The bark was stained a deep crimson dotted with pink chunks. A shockwave ran through Ellis and a few drops of the animal's blood landed on his cheek. He blinked, wiped his face with the back of his glove and looked out through the branches. He spotted two men carrying rifles approaching at a canter. Without thinking, he clambered back up the tree, all the way to the top section that he had used as a lookout. That seemed like an eternity ago. He was careful not to disturb the branches too much as he ascended. Without a doubt, hunter with that good of an eye would notice something in the tree if he shook it even a centimeter. As he settled in his crow's nest, the two men arrived at the wolf's dead body. They were clad in camouflage hunting gear and one of them was wearing a high-visibility vest.

"Got you, fucker!" High-vis man tooted and kicked the semi-headless corpse in the ribs. "That's what you get for eating my fucking dog!" he shouted and laid his boot into the animal again.

"Good job, son," his partner, an older man with long silver hair and a gray beard, said and patted the younger man on the back. "That's a shot if ever I've seen one."

Ellis drew his breath in as silently as he could while he listened to the duo pat each other on the back with a collection of various affirmations as they discussed how they had probably saved a few lives today. Ellis had to admit that his was at least one that he knew of, but if they saw him that might change. As long as they didn't find the rifle in the shrub or decide to look up for any given reason, he should be just fine.

"Let's get this sack of shit back to the truck," High-vis man said as he grabbed a wolf hind leg and the older man followed suit. They began to drag the carcass off and luckily for them – and Ellis – the direction they were headed was down a steep slope, so the two hunters made easy work of moving the enormous predator. When they were four or five hundred meters away Ellis made his way down, stopping periodically to check if the two hadn't found a reason to turn back. They had not and by the time he reached terra-almost-firma they were two specks in the distance, like a couple of minuscule black dots on a pristinely white sheet.

He looked down and saw that he had been standing in the middle of a half-moon of blood that the slain creature had left behind, and for a fleeting moment he felt sorry for it. During his wartime days, Ellis came to realize that perspective was always the greatest negotiator. This animal did nothing except try to provide for its pack and ensure their survival – whether that broke the laws of man or not, it didn't matter. Once it crossed paths with another species, especially one that saw itself as superior and as the ruler of this place, it would only ever end one way – from the crosshairs to the history books. Ellis couldn't help but scoff at the similarities between the animal's predicament and his own. The ways of the world do often seem more unfair than just, regardless of the intentions.

He gathered the shotgun from behind the bushes and crossed into the forested area that bordered the train station. It was dense and well-covered, and Ellis felt like he had been transported into a different environment altogether. A light fog hung just beneath the canopy of the trees and all manner of insects were sounding off. The ice underfoot was replaced by fallen leaves, soaked by melting snow from above. The darkness that enveloped him gave welcome relief to his eyes after the glare of pure white that he had endured for the last nine hours. The sun would set soon and Ellis was grateful for that too. Every bit of cover would help in his quest to board the train without being noticed. He found a patch of thicket that was dry, just inside the tree line, and it was well concealed. Placing the rifle on the ground next to him, he lay down with his gaze firmly set on the platform and commenced the intermission until the arrival of his train.

*****

It was early evening when Detective William Black arrived at the gates of Stone Hill Prison following his flight from Toronto Pearson Airport to the small airstrip in Fort Resolution. After disembarking, he had rented a Chevy Blazer which was about thirty years old from an office in a wooden hut with a sign that read *Henry's Car Rental* in bright yellow cursive writing. The elderly woman behind the counter had stared at him intently over her reading glasses as he filled in an actual paper form, which in itself was an experience. She gave him the usual "you city folk" look when he asked how old the vehicle was, and he felt scolded when she questioned his doubts about the reliability of her cars with a sour tone. Black also wanted to inquire about half-day rates as he wouldn't need the motor overnight but thought better of it. Best not to make the natives too restless, and he also wanted to be done and leave as soon as he could. The place reeked of cat urine and looked like it had recently been mothballed.

The guard that manned the wrought-iron gate had a cheerful demeanor and let him through after his identity was verified by the flash of his badge which preceded a call up to the main building to confirm his appointment. Black had tried to fish for an opinion about prisoner deaths from the man in the box, but the gatekeeper had been tight-lipped. The detective had the official statistics on hand but sometimes it was better to receive some input from the horse's mouth, so to speak.

As he made the slow drive up to the administration building, he couldn't help but feel a sense of unease creeping up in his stomach, like the inexplicable shivers that run down your back when you walk into a house or room. His mother used to get that. He remembered as a young boy accompanying his parents to look at new houses each time they were about to move. They would arrive at a certain location and on the odd occasion, she would summarily exit the building after being inside for only a few minutes. No reason would be given for the abrupt departure. She would simply walk out and go sit in the car until the viewing had concluded. He never understood it back then, but as he got older, she had tried to explain it to him. On her deathbed a few years ago she had insisted that a long-lost relative was sitting on the bed with her. It had been so convincing that Black had decided right then that he was a believer. Not in religion but in the probable existence of spirits and lingering imprints of those who had left this plain of existence in an unsavory manner. His mother had described it as fragments of their souls, scattered about like tiny shards of glass that could still be found on a floor months or years after an ornament or picture frame had been broken.

The detective parked in front of the building and made his way up to the entrance. He pushed a button marked *BELL* on top of the keypad and the door buzzed open. Black didn't know what to expect as he walked in but what he was presented with came as a surprise. A starkly lit, bare room with a single wooden desk was stationed against the right-hand side wall and a dull-gray concrete staircase was on the left. The rest of the room was the same uninspiring color with nothing on the walls. To Black, it looked like this reception area had been put together in mere minutes. A portly woman of middle age with curly hair sat behind the desk and looked up at him with a forced smile.

"Good evening, Detective," Thelma Radcliffe, according to the plaque on her desk, said and rose to her feet. "Please, have a seat." She gestured to the chair at the opposite end of her desk.

"Thank you," Black replied and sat down.

"Did you find us okay?" Thelma asked. Her smile was now partnered with an eager sparkle in her eye that suggested that there weren't many visitors to this establishment.

"I did. The car rental people were very helpful." Black adjusted in his chair which wasn't very comfortable.

"Hmm. Really?" Thelma uttered, looking unsure. "Grace can be a bit strange with out-of-towners. I hope the old girl wasn't too rough on you." She grinned.

"Not at all. Is Mr. Blakeway on his way?" Black didn't want to sound rude but he also didn't want to spend too much time here. He had court the next morning and the last flight back left in an hour.

"Ah." Thelma's expression changed to one of dismay. "Yes … Warden Blakeway is unavailable, unfortunately. But he did leave a message that our on-site physician, Dr Rafferty, will take care of you." She grinned again but a bit less convincingly this time, Black thought.

"That's too bad—" Black said but got cut off.

"Detective Black?" a voice with a distinct London accent said from the stairs. Black got up from his chair and saw a tall man in his thirties with cropped blonde hair descending the last few steps of the staircase. He held a hand out. "I'm Doctor Rafferty. I'm sorry to keep you waiting. Do follow me, please."

They went up two floors and entered the warden's office, where Rafferty took a seat behind the desk and Black sat down opposite him. The light in the room was dim and came from behind the doctor which shrouded his features slightly.

"You'll have to excuse me," Rafferty continued. "Warden Blakeway didn't fill me in on the reason for your visit. How may I help?"

"No trouble at all," Black said and flashed him a polite smile. "Just dotting some i's and crossing some t's on an old case. Ellis Neill. I believe he was an inmate here?" Black took his notebook from his pocket and flipped it open.

"Yes, that's right. A rather unfortunate business. He was quite young."

"Mm-hmm." Black nodded. "How exactly did he die?"

"Surely you've seen the news?" Rafferty seemed taken aback by the question.

"Yes, of course. But if you wouldn't mind just giving me a quick play-by-play? It'll really help." Black tried to sound as unofficial as possible. Rafferty's previous answer suggested that this might not be as easy as he had expected it to be.

"Well." Rafferty glanced at the clock on the desk and continued. "Mr. Neill was fine at final headcount the night of his death, according to the guard on duty. His cellmate reported him being unresponsive in the morning and alerted the warden and myself."

"Right, right." Black jotted in his notepad. "And this was around 7 a.m.?"

"Correct," Rafferty said and fiddled with his tie.

"And when did you contact the next of kin?"

"Well, there was no next of kin listed so we sent a notice to the Toronto Police." Rafferty spoke in a monotone now and Black thought it sounded rehearsed.

"Really? Do the inmates complete the forms themselves when they go through intake?" Black squinted as he asked this. "Because Mr. Neill has a wife and a daughter."

"*Had.* And yes, they do." Rafferty shifted in his chair. "I can't be expected to know the motives prisoners have for omitting information on their forms, can I?"

"Of course not," Black came back and picked up a hint of annoyance in the doctor's voice. "Don't you think that's odd, though?"

"I guess so," Rafferty said with a smile that wasn't reflected by the expression in his eyes. "Some of these men have bitten their own tongues off in protest to the canteen food. That's odd too."

"I'm sure you've seen all manner of strange things in your time here, Doctor."

"You wouldn't believe some of it," Rafferty stated almost proudly. "Even if it happened right in front of your face."

"I can only imagine." Black decided to step things up a gear and asked, "Is the body still here?"

"Yes," Rafferty said after a slight hesitation. "Nobody has claimed him."

"Could I see him? If it's not too much trouble."

"I'm afraid I couldn't allow that. Especially with the warden being out," Rafferty said, looking uncomfortable *and* disgusted at the same time.

"Oh c'mon." Black put his best buddy-buddy voice on. "Just a quick peek to verify the identity and I'll be out of your hair forever."

"That's already been verified," Rafferty snapped back.

"By whom? You said that there was no next of kin. So, legally he has not been identified yet," Black lied, not knowing how far his bluff would go.

"Legally," the doctor continued as he sat back in the warden's oversized chair, "I don't have to show you anything."

The doctor's shift in tone was palpable and Black felt himself getting annoyed.

"I could come back with a warrant. Then it won't be just for the body. It'll be for your files, hard drives and personal documents …" Black trailed off, sure that his implications were received.

"Detective Black, was it?" Rafferty made no attempt to conceal his sudden patronizing tone. "Do you think that would be a wise move?"

"I'm not sure I follow," Black replied, and Rafferty leaned forward, almost whispering.

"Let it go, Detective. He was someone you didn't even know. Why ruin your life and that of your family over it? Walk away while you can."

"You know, usually I get offers of money. But you go straight for the jugular, don't you?" Black asked after a pause. He flipped his notebook closed and slipped it back into his pocket. "Do you know what the penalty is for threatening a police officer?"

"Believe me detective, I'm not threatening you. This is a warning you'll wish you heeded if you continue down this path." Rafferty reached into a drawer and Black momentarily stiffened. His hand instinctively went for his weapon then stopped short as the doctor pulled a bottle of bourbon from below the desk, before asking, "Is there anything else?"

"No. We're done here." Black paused for a moment, wanting to say something else, then got up and walked out.

Back on the ground floor landing, he brushed past the receptionist who said something unintelligible, and he waved a hand as he exited the building and made his way to the waiting Blazer. He turned the ignition key and waited for the heat to warm the vehicle's cabin up. Staring at the facility looming large in front of him, his mind began to race. The doctor had tried to scare him off but he'd only succeeded in establishing the opposite. If there was one thing that boiled Black down to the core, it was corrupt officials. He pulled out of the driveway and headed back to the airstrip, racing along the slippery road, en route back to the airfield.

As Detective Black's SUV departed the Stone Hill parking lot there was a stir in the basement of the prison and a dark figure rose to his feet.

*****

Ellis stretched his limbs out on the grass and got up. The unmistakable sound of a train approaching made his heart leap and filled him with nervous energy. He was about to step out from among the trees when two off-road vehicles came roaring over the hill to his right and parked in front of the platform. Four men emerged from the SUV's carrying several empty crates, each clasping a large bottle of beer. Laughter and loud conversation could be heard from the group and Ellis studied them, staying well within the cover of the foliage. By the light swaying of their bodies, it was apparent that they had been drinking for a while. In between the cackling and shoulder slaps, Ellis picked up that they were from around the area, had gathered for Christmas day celebrations and were sent out by their wives to collect incoming orders.

Ellis grit his teeth when he realized what time of the year it was and the fact that instead of being with his family he was stuck out in a barren, frozen land in the middle of nowhere. Memories flooded his mind, and he could smell the aroma of Rose's holiday lunch coming from their kitchen as he and Cynthia prepared the table for family festivities. Often the location would vary between their home and Cheryl's. Rose's grandmother loved entertaining and would marvel at the culinary creations her granddaughter came up with. This would've been their first family Christmas in Toronto and Ellis had to dig deep within his resolve to keep himself together. The thought of his family had been the only factor that kept him going and he couldn't cave in now. His mind had to withstand all of the onslaughts if he were to make it back to them.

Out of the black night a single headlight emerged from the tracks and Ellis could hear the rhythmic rolling of the iron wheels in his direction. The men on the platform cheered and slammed their drinks together in celebration, beer spilling from their bottles and onto the frozen concrete floor. As the train slowed down and pulled into the station, a cloud of snow followed it and settled on top of the roof.

It was a compact train with only two cars coupled onto the engine. It had a sleek look about it, like that of a bullet train except there were no windows. Ellis recalled that Bobby had said the entire operation was automated, completely devoid of manpower except when a problem arose. The car directly behind the engine was kept at a cool minus twenty degrees Celsius to keep perishables fresh and the second cart was held at eighteen degrees Celsius for items that didn't require refrigeration. This section housed fine wines and dry goods not available to the Northwestern Territories' local population. It was also Ellis' target area. The train ride would take two days and there were more than enough supplies in the cart to tide him over for the trip.

The doors slid open and the four men entered. Several agonizing minutes later, they emerged with their quarry and began to load the vehicles. Ellis noticed a lapse in their awareness and crept closer to the edge of the train track, just to the left of the platform. The single streetlamp that illuminated the station's loading area made a circle of light that Ellis stayed well clear of. The cover was ideal and he rolled in underneath the train. Crawling over the railway sleepers and ballasts he soon made it to the second cart, then rolled out from under the train and slowly rose to his feet, fingers clenched on the side of the platform. He peeked over the edge and saw that the men still had their heads poked inside of the refrigerated car, trying to stack their empty crates in the back. Ellis hoisted himself up onto the platform and hopped into the back car through the open sliding door. It was warm inside and he found a barrel which was covered with a green tarpaulin standing in the corner of the car. He removed the sheet from the barrel, squatted down behind it and put the tarp over himself, ensuring he covered every centimeter of his body and boots. Two of the men walked back into the car and Ellis' heart froze. He heard them talking and by the sound of their voices they were right next to where he was sitting. Movement by his feet almost made him jump but he managed to stifle the instinct.

"Move your ass, Henry. You know what Rhonda is like when she has to wait." One of the men said.

"I do. She'll have a face like she's been sucking on a lemon for the rest of the night." Henry replied. "And that's *all* she'll be sucking on for a while!" Henry's statement caused raucous laughter among the entire group. When the drunken bunch had regained their composure Ellis heard them exiting the cart.

Then it went silent for a moment, which felt to Ellis like it took an age.

He heard the two vehicles start up and then a loud mechanical whirring noise signaled the train doors sliding shut. Once he was sure they were completely closed, he threw the tarpaulin aside and stood up, surveying the room. From the roof an air conditioner silently expelled warm air, adding even more heat to the now sealed enclosure and Ellis' fingers and toes tingled with gratitude. He removed his gloves and jacket while continuing to scan the supplies.

The barrel he had hidden behind contained beer from Germany. In the opposite corner there was bread and cheese stamped with a French-sounding name beside a variety of vacuum sealed cured meats and four bottles of champagne. Ellis jumped as the train slowly pulled out of the station and he walked over the buffet of food. In the only other occupied corner of the car there were several empty crates, bottles of expensive looking water and root beers from Australia.

He grabbed some bread, cheese and meat, popped open a root beer and sat down with his back against the wall. It had been about twenty-four hours since he had last eaten, and the nourishment went down well as he went over his plan once more. The rhythmic movement of the train now running at full tilt provided comfort to his aching and worn-out body.

CHAPTER 13

Rose picked at her French fries without much concern. She hadn't really intended to eat anything when they sat down at the diner, but upon her mother's insistence she ordered something called a "Venus Burger with Otherworldly Fries". The restaurant was space-themed and soon after they entered it became obvious that the strategy was to draw in children of all ages and, by extension, their paying parents. Regardless of that tactic, the place wasn't busy. There were a few families scattered around but Rose thought it was fairly quiet by themed-restaurant standards.

Right across from her, an elderly couple was entertaining a baby girl of about four months old as the parents looked on. Both the mom and dad were young and had dark circles under their eyes. The mom's hair was only partially under control, and she hadn't bothered with make-up. It was clear that they were new parents and their bundle of joy had not yet acquired the art of sleeping all the way through the night. Rose would often ask her mother about when *she* was a baby and enjoyed hearing about the antics that her younger self had gotten up to. From scaling furniture to swinging from plants and falling on her head, it sounded like she gave her mom and dad a real hard time. But to her, the most special part about recounting those events was the way her parents' eyes would light up when they spoke about her. It always made her feel grateful and loved.

She took a sip of her fruit juice and was hurled back into reality by the chime of her mother's phone alerting to a new text message.

"Who is it?" Rose perked up as her mother studied the phone screen.

"Hang on, love," Cynthia said, still reading.

"Mom?" The pleading tone in Rose's voice made Cynthia look up from the phone.

"Okay, sorry. It's the detective I told you about. He said he went to the prison but didn't see Dad. He wants to meet up tomorrow."

"I'm coming with you this time."

"Absolutely not," Cynthia replied. She had expected Rose to suggest that.

"I'm not sitting in another motel room waiting to see if you come back or not. I am *not* doing that ever again. I'm coming with you and that's final," Rose said, bracing for the backlash from her mother. When it didn't come, she was surprised and also a bit proud of herself.

"Alright." Cynthia sighed. "I suppose you'll be safer with me anyway."

"So," Rose continued with a renewed interest in her food, "does that mean they moved his body? Or ..." She trailed off. A grimace somewhere between a smile and a frown floated over her face.

"Or what?" Cynthia asked and put her fork down with half a load of the "Lunar Mac-N- Cheese" on it.

"Could he still be alive? Is it at all possible, Mom?" Rose asked and leaned forward, her eyes wide.

"I don't want you to get your hopes up my darling." Cynthia was fighting back tears now, the phone still clenched in her hand. "*I* think so. At least ... I hope I'm not rationalizing here, but it's possible."

"Yes!" Rose replied with a newfound gleam in her eye. She thought her mother had all but given up and hearing news to the contrary filled her with the closest feeling to joy that she had felt since the day her dad was arrested. "I think so too. All we have to go on is that report on TV and one could hardly call that proof."

"Okay, calm down," Cynthia said as she took Rose's hand. She read the excitement on Rose's young face and couldn't help but smile through a faint sob. "Easy, now. I don't want you to get ahead of yourself. Let's talk to the detective tomorrow and take it from there."

"He's alive, Mom. I just know it!" Rose said, her smile now filled with hope and a longing that Cynthia hadn't ever seen in her daughter.

After dinner they ordered dessert on a whim – a choc nut sundae for Cynthia and a banana split for Rose. The conversation was lighter than it had been for weeks and even though it was evident that they might be celebrating a bit prematurely, it was long overdue. For weeks pressure had been building on their relationship; now they could finally both release some of it and just have normal mother-daughter chats like they used to have without emotionally tiptoeing around each other. To Rose, it felt familiar and comforting.

Back at the motel they curled up in front of a movie after Cynthia confirmed the meeting with Black over a few message exchanges. It was set for 2 p.m. at a coffee shop in Downtown. She had told Black that Rose would be accompanying them, and the detective had said that he looked forward to meeting her very much.

In the parking lot outside, at the very edge where a Poplar tree provided cover from the flood lights, a dark SUV was parked with two occupants inside.

*****

Lightning streaked across the sky in jagged patterns as the navy-blue sedan rolled into the motel parking area and reversed into a vacant spot next to the SUV. The figure behind the wheel looked over to the two men in the other car. They nodded, started up their engine and pulled out of the bay. When they were out of sight the figure shifted his focus to the row of rooms fifty meters in front of him, but mostly on the door with the number ten on it. The adjoining window had a blue tinge of flashing images visible through the drawn curtains that told him the occupants of this particular room were most likely in front of the television. The figure adjusted in his seat and winced at the pain that ran through his side. He was hurting, but not too bad.

His self-diagnosis, which was pretty reliable after many injuries sustained in his line of work, told him that he had several cracked ribs, a broken nose and a mild concussion. Every time he felt the pain, he thought of the man he was supposed to kill at the prison. The inmate had gotten the drop on him and when he regained consciousness, he wasn't sure how long he had been behind the boiler. He guessed it had been two or three hours, perhaps longer. He also wondered why the man hadn't finished him off. In his mind this seemed ludicrous. The man had taken the time and made the effort to hide him but didn't make sure the job was done. He had heard of people who were incapable of killing and it had always struck him as weak and incomprehensible. Perhaps the man thought he *was* dead and had just been careless. Either way, he would have the chance to make the man rue his mistake, that was all but guaranteed.

Shrouded in silence he sank back in his seat, breathed deeply, and folded within his mind to the place that he frequented prior to his tasks. Before his mind's eye was an image of himself standing on a deserted beach at night. The moon was red, and it provided a faint light that glimmered off the calm ocean surface. He raised his hands slowly toward the sky and the severed heads of those he had killed before rose from the water, as if suspended by thin wires, then hovered in place. The figure flicked his fingers towards his face and the heads floated onto the beach, their eyes staring lovingly at him. Their lips moved as if to speak but no sounds emerged. They silently whispered their devotion to him and gave thanks to their savior for rescuing them from the bonds of the flesh, for ending their pain and for reuniting them with the Earth. The heads then formed a line and in turn, floated toward the figure's face and kissed him lightly on the cheek. He stroked their hair and sent them back to the darkened depths of his memories, where they would be with him forever. He opened his eyes and exhaled.

The dark figure slipped into his red ski mask and exited the vehicle, ensuring he was as quiet as possible and slid the hunting knife into his back pocket. The air was cool as he crossed the empty lot and there was only one other car visible – that of the woman and child in the room he was heading toward. His boots broke through a thin layer of snow on the tarmac and that too didn't make a sound. What could be heard were several cars passing by on the main road a block away and the monotonous hum of the enormous floodlight overhead. Scanning the area before him he saw that all the other windows were dark. Nobody home – exactly how he wanted it. If screams couldn't be heard, he wouldn't be interrupted.

Arriving at the door, he stopped and put his ear to it. Muffled conversation came from the inside and the figure guessed it was from the speaker on the television set. He listened for a moment longer, then took a step back and kicked the door open.

Charging through, he hooked the door with his leg and it slammed shut. The woman and the child bolted upright on the bed, their eyes as wide as side plates. He leapt onto the mattress, grabbed the woman by the hair and punched her square in the face. She moaned and rolled onto the carpet, her body limp. The child screamed loud enough to make the figure want to slam his hands over his ears but when she jumped off the bed he went after her. As she reached the threshold of the bathroom, he snagged her ankle and yanked her back towards him. The girl rolled over onto her back and began to frantically kick at him. Her right heel landed a blow into his injured ribs, and he coughed as the pain shot through his ribcage and down into his legs.

She kicked again, but this time he blocked it and swung at her. The back of his hand grazed the top of her head and she cried out.

He reached back, pulled the knife from his pocket and lunged at her but somehow, she managed to squirm out from underneath him and the blade met nothing but air. The figure got to his feet and turned around to see the woman standing in front of him. She held a gun that was aimed directly at his head.

She fired with a trembling hand.

The bullet missed his face and hit the full-length mirror mounted on the wall behind him, shattering it to pieces. He extended the arm that held the knife towards the woman and the blade sliced her arm open. She screamed and the gun fell onto the carpet. The woman dropped onto her knees and went to retrieve it. That's when he slammed the blade into her back hard enough to make her limbs spread out beside her. Blood gushed from the wound and she wailed.

"Rose!" she cried. "Run! Run!"

The child, upon seeing her mother wounded, ran at the figure and screamed at the top of her lungs. When she was half a meter away from him, he stepped forward and landed a blow to her cheek, sending her bounding backwards. Her eyes rolled in her head, and she fell to the floor, unconscious.

The figure turned back to the woman bleeding on the floor. He pulled the knife from her back and stabbed her again, this time between the shoulder blades. She let out a barking sound, like a dog that had been hit by a car, then tried to crawl towards the child while crying and screaming. The guttural sound of blood spewing from her mouth muddled her cries. She got a hand on the child's leg before the figure grabbed her by the hair and lifted her head up, exposing her neck. In one smooth motion, he ran the blade across her throat, from ear to ear. Deep-red liquid sprayed from her neck and onto the child's legs. She tried to speak but only a gargled groan emerged. The figure stood there, staring at her with a cocked head. She flailed for a few moments, let out a moan then dropped from all fours to her belly and remained still.

A few minutes went by. She did not move again.

CHAPTER 14

William Black checked his watch – 2:28 p.m. He took a sip of his coffee which had gone cold in the Styrofoam cup and let his eyes survey the bustling interior of the shop. No Cynthia. No Rose. He dialed her number again. Just as before, it went straight to voicemail without ringing. Black knew that he hadn't been communicating with Cynthia for very long, so there was no way to tell how responsive she was in general. But from the few messages they had exchanged so far, she had rarely let more than ten minutes pass before replying. Why would she not answer *now*? Black was no expert on mobile phone technology, but he also knew that when a call went straight to voicemail it usually meant that the recipient's phone had been switched off, or the battery had died. For a moment, he had a fleeting thought that the signs were not pointing in a good direction.

He decided not to get ahead of himself. He told his mind (which was already running through every worst-case scenarios in the background) in a calm manner that something had probably come up and she'd just forgotten to let him know. However, this wasn't your run-of-the-mill coffee date to catch up on trivialities. This meeting could potentially determine the fate of her maybe-alive, maybe-dead husband. Surely that would be at the top of any loving wife's priority list.

Black took a breath and told himself to stop being a judgmental asshole. He would go about the rest of his day and wait for her call. Besides, it wasn't like he could hop in the car and go check on them. She still hadn't disclosed their location to him which didn't leave him much in the line of options.

Ten minutes later, he decided to pack it in. He paid for the coffee and made his way out towards the car when his phone rang.

"Black."

"Afternoon, Detective." It was Lawrence, a uniformed cop. "We have a homicide at a motel in Scarborough. 3126 Kingston Road." Black hung up, darted for his car and was inside in a flash.

He sped toward the destination with the blue-and-reds flashing out towards the world through the Crown Vic's windshield. Traffic was light this time of the day and within fifteen minutes he pulled into the parking lot of the *Garden Motel*. A sign at the entrance read *Satellite TV, Coin-operated beds, No "Grammers" in the pool-area!* Several marked units were stopped in front of room number ten alongside an ambulance. He exited the vehicle and was met by the uniformed officer that made the call.

"Lay it on me," Black said as they walked toward the room that had its door propped open.

"We have one victim. Female," the uniformed cop reported. "Multiple stab wounds to the upper and lower back. The place is pretty trashed, but nothing was taken so it doesn't look like it was a robbery. Also, someone is missing from the party. There's some kid's stuff in the room. Clothes, shoes, that sort of thing, but no kid."

Black felt his heart skip a beat and increased his walking pace, leaving the officer behind. He crossed the threshold and walked over to where the body lay at the foot of the double bed. She was covered with a white sheet but that didn't hide the pear-shaped bloodstain that had spread out from underneath her and soaked into the carpet. It had gone from a deep red to a rusty brown against the cream colored fibers on the floor. Another uniformed cop walked up to Black and handed him a driver's license.

"This is the victim, sir."

The name next to the picture of the attractive brunette with the bright, emerald-green eyes and warm smile read *Cynthia Neill*. Black felt his stomach churn and his face went red-hot. He knelt down, partially because his knees felt like they had come undone and also because he couldn't believe it was her. He uncovered the top half of the corpse on the floor. There was no mistaking who it was. Black pushed the lump in his throat back, re-covered Cynthia and rose to his feet.

"Anything else?" Black asked the uniformed cop beside him.

"Not much. The janitor saw a blue sedan out in the lot last night that he thought was unusual as no other rooms were booked out. We only got a partial plate number from him," the officer said.

"Okay. Send his statement over to my email." Black clapped

his hands together loud enough for all to hear then continued. "Listen up everyone!" he said and all in the room stopped what they were doing and faced him. "There was a girl in this room. Her name is Rose Neill, ten years old. I'll forward a picture of her to all of you. Your only priority right now is to find her. Get on the lines to the other units and lean on whoever you need to for information! Everything else can wait!"

A mad scramble ensued as all the uniformed officers and other detectives left the room and got onto their two-way radios and cell phones to kickstart the search.

Black sat down on the bed, taking in the carnage that was left behind after the murder. Clothes were strewn about the floor with tiny spots of blood on them and Black prayed it was only Cynthia's. In a corner of the room an old television set was on its tube-shaped screen, apparently a collateral victim of the assault.

"I hope you're still out there," he whispered, but no one heard his words.

*****

Ellis crouched behind the tree and his limbs and lower back cracked in protest. Thirteen hours on a train and another two days of being cramped up on a bus hadn't done his physical condition any favors. A small price to pay to get back to Toronto unnoticed. He had pawned the relic of a shotgun along with several bottles of expensive whisky from the train at a questionable second-hand shop when he arrived in a town called Grand Prairie in Alberta. The elderly woman behind the counter had given him five hundred dollars for the lot, but only after he managed to haggle her up from a very ambitious two-fifty as her opening gambit and fervently tried to push it as "the best deal this side of Lake Winnipeg". Ellis was grateful for the cash, considering that he had to jump from a moving train and somehow ensured all the bottles landed safely in the snow beside him. It was certainly worth it.

The next stop for the train was Edmonton. With his food supplies low and the crowded nature of that city, he didn't want to risk disembarking from there. Too many eyes in one place. Small-town folks only really noticed drifters if they spotted them more than once and he didn't plan on hanging around. He didn't know how far the all-points bulletin for his arrest stretched and didn't want to take unnecessary chances. Lucky for him the Greyhound to Ontario passed through the town and he boarded the first available coach to his home city. It had been a long journey with few stops and after arriving at his destination downtown he had walked to his home under the cover of night, steering clear of streetlights and passing vehicles. Now, as he sat perched in a tree across the street with the dim moonlight reflecting off the living room window, he examined the building for signs of life. Thirty minutes passed without incident, and he slowly made his way back down towards terra firma, checking the surrounding houses and driveways for any potential witnesses to his arrival.

When he was sure the street was clear, he crossed it and hopped over the fence, to which his tired body exclaimed once more. Ellis made his way towards the rear of the house which was steeped in total darkness. The spare key that was supposed to be under the granite flowerpot that housed Cynthia's White Trilliums, now in a dormant state from lack of care, was ever present. He slipped it into the lock of the back door and let himself in. To his surprise, the house alarm had not been set.

He detected a musty odor as he entered the kitchen, as if the house had been closed up for an extended period of time. This in itself caused several questions to arise in Ellis' mind: Are Cynthia and Rose in Edmonton? How long have they been there? Should he have made a detour and stopped at Cheryl's house to check if his family was there? He pushed these questions aside and focused on the task at hand, which was clearing the house of any likely ambushers lying in wait.

As he crossed the living room, he noted some items of clothing strewn on the carpet. A red jacket and a pair of trainers belonging to Rose and a turquoise sweater, Cynthia's favorite lounging-around-the-house garment. He picked it up, held it close to his face and inhaled his wife's scent. Heading up the stairs he was met with more silence. He checked both bedrooms and bathrooms – no warm bodies here. When he was certain the house was empty, he went back into the master en suite and turned the shower on. Soon steam began to rise from behind the glass door and he stripped down. The clothes he had spent the last five days in peeled off him like an old wetsuit. He spent a lot of time among the flowing masses of water, half an hour or more, processing the events of the last week and filing it into the appropriate cabinets in his mind. Most of it ended up in a folder called *Shit I never thought I'd have to do or experience,* and he locked it away, only to be rehashed once he had been reunited with his family.

When the hot water ran out, he switched the heating on, changed into shorts and went downstairs to raid the fridge, looking for any food that hadn't expired. He settled on fried eggs and sausage, all prepared in the dark in case there were eyes on the place. It tasted surprisingly good for a blind cook, and he felt somewhat better when he lay down on the sofa in the living room afterwards. The silence was eerie and for a moment he could hear his thoughts as if they were spoken aloud. He tried to form a coherent plan, but the fatigue of the last few days caught up with him in a rush. He was staring at the digital clock on the wall unit which read 1:54 a.m. The green numerals drifted into the distance, and he slipped into a deep and much needed slumber.

*****

A red light blinked in the corner. It was faint and hazy, like sunshine creeping through a thick curtain. There was damp hanging in the air, and it made everything feel like it was covered in a thin layer of oil or grease.

Rose turned her head and tried to focus on the light but couldn't open her eyes all the way. She could feel something on her head. It was soft and it smelled of burnt wood. It made her eyes water and it spanned all the way around her head like a bandana. She tried to reach toward the cloth to remove it, but a stinging sensation ran through her shoulders, and she winced. Her fingers were numb and she soon realized that her hands were tied behind her back. She was lying on her stomach and the floor was moving. There was a sound that was unmistakable – a car hitting its brakes. She was in the trunk of a car. Her mind tried to piece the series of events together that led her here. There was a movie, sitting on the bed eating popcorn with her mom, and then …

A groan escaped through the gag that was tied around her face, covering her nose and mouth. She curled up and screamed but only a stifled bark could be heard. Her head felt hot, like it was about to explode, and she was sure her heart was going to burst from the pain. Flashes came of her mother reaching for a gun, then firing it at the man in the red mask, the knife slicing her mother's arm open. And then … then the worst of it – the man plunging the blade deep into her back, up to where only the white handle stuck out of her. The blood squirting from her mother's mouth, and then darkness.

The car came to an abrupt halt, and she rolled over, her back pressing against the opposite end of the mobile prison cell. A door opened and slammed shut. Rose's breathing quickened and it became harder to take in sufficient oxygen through the dense rag. The trunk opened and as she looked up only the outline of the man from the motel room was discernable against the pale moonlight. He bent down, reached in, and picked her up with one hand like he was lifting a suitcase. Through the mesh that partially blocked her vision, Rose could see that they were in a rural area. The grass was knee high and there were no lights or visible buildings. Tall trees were dotted around them, and the smell of pine needles entered her nostrils, providing temporary relief from the rank odor of the restraints.

The man brought her to a decrepit structure that looked like a small barn. At the door, he put her on the ground and produced a set of keys from his pocket. He disengaged the padlock and untangled the chain that held the doors together through two holes on either side. Grabbing her by one ankle he dragged her over a straw floor and towards a trapdoor, ten meters from the entrance. His foot flung it open like he had done it a thousand times before and he sent her down a metal slide, belly first. She reached the bottom and rolled off, landing on a concrete surface. Then, the door above her head slammed shut and she could hear a lock on the other side being secured.

For a moment, Rose sat cross-legged trying to take in her surroundings. After a few minutes of internal deliberation, she decided that the rag over her eyes would *have* to go if she were to have any idea regarding the nature of her surroundings. She got to her feet, realized they weren't tied together anymore and walked until she hit a surface. It felt like iron bars, cold to the touch but there was an edge to them that she thought might be useful. Pressing her face up to one of the individual slats she maneuvered her head down and loosened both bandana and gag, sending them slipping down her face and landing around her neck like two atrocious scarves. Her head spun back and forth a few times and she saw that she was inside a wrought-iron cage. The bars were crisscrossed, providing small squares to look through. Not that there was much to see beyond them, except for wooden walls on all sides about two meters away. The cage was also sealed overhead, and she noticed that the slide she came down on was now missing. A single, dimmed lightbulb hanging above her in the center of the room provided very limited lighting and from the faint illumination she saw a thin, single mattress in the corner of the cell with a gray blanket and faded white pillow on top of it. Aside from that, the room was bare. And quiet. So quiet she could hear her own thoughts. Not that she wanted to hear what they had to say.

From the floor above her head, she heard heavy footsteps moving around. This was followed by a screeching sound, like something weighted being dragged across the room until it came to a stop right above the trapdoor where she had been deposited through. Her common sense told her the man was no doubt making it impossible for her to lift, even it if she somehow managed to scale the wall and get there, which upon initial inspection was out of the question. Besides, her hands were still tied. It felt like tape around her wrists, and she knew that with enough wiggling and stretching over time she would eventually get free. Rose sat down on the mattress with her back against the steel bars. It was uncomfortable but the pain welling in her heart was overwhelming the mild discomfort that her body felt.

Her mother was dead. Even if the man hadn't stabbed her again, that initial wound made her contort in a way that was unnatural. And that look. The look in her eyes ... *She* knew she was dead as well, even before her light went out.

Rose tipped over onto the mattress, pulled her knees to her chest and cried as a part of her slowly died.

*****

It was early dawn when Ellis awoke on the couch in his living room. He looked around confused and had to remind himself that he wasn't on the inside of a cell anymore. He plodded his way to the kitchen, switched the coffee machine on and looked through the window. The street was quiet this early in the morning and he was glad to see that there was no SWAT team prepping for a breach in the driveway. No nosy neighbors either. It appeared that he had entered undetected and that gave him a glimmer of hope in a time where Murphy's Law had dictated the flow of his life without missing a beat.

The machine whirred as it poured out the brown liquid and Ellis' thoughts drifted to Rose and Cynthia once more. They were never far from his conscious mind and this morning he was mulling on the mystery of their current location and where exactly he would commence his search for them. He considered calling the in-laws, then decided against it. Their phones would almost certainly be tapped, and Ellis didn't know whether their absence from the house was for safety reasons or if they'd just decided that they needed a change of scenery. Either way, it struck him as odd that they hadn't returned yet.

He added sugar and milk to his coffee and made his way up the stairs. At the top he turned to go to the main bedroom, then stopped and went the other way. Leaning against the arch in the threshold of Rose's bedroom, he stared into it while sipping coffee. The place was a mess and that was very unlike his daughter. Her room was always impeccably clean and organized and he knew that if she were standing next to him right now, she would hit the roof at the state of it. That could mean one of two things – either someone else made the mess or her and Cynthia left in a real hurry.

He went inside and began to pick clothes up off the floor, folded them and placed them on the bed. He bent to grab a wayward shoe when, on the way down, something caught his eye. On the desk was an open notepad with the word "color" written at the top of the page. The rest of the paper was blank. A pencil was placed under the word in a way that made Ellis think it had been intentional. The way it was positioned, like it was perfectly underlining the word, sent a shiver down his spine and a distant memory popped into his head.

When Rose was five, she was obsessed with spy movies. To quell her thirst for knowledge of the espionage-trade, he had shown her how to send a low-tech secret message using a pencil and paper by writing words on the top page then tearing it out. All the would-be recipient had to do was color the next page on the pad and the indentations made by the sender's original writing would reveal the message in all its glory. Ellis scratched his head then grabbed the pencil and began to glide his hand over the page. A few seconds later, his impulse paid off and he could read what his daughter had written:

johnfogerty2010@gmail.com

Favorite song

With the notepad in one hand and the coffee in the other he sprinted downstairs, almost falling twice. He switched on the desktop computer on the table next to the kitchen and impatiently tapped the wooden surface with his index finger as the operating system took its time to bring the machine to life. When it had completed its system checks he launched the browser. From there he clicked on *Gmail* then typed the email address into the blue-lined box that requested *Email or Phone*. He clicked *Next* and in the password box he typed in "Green River" which was his favorite Creedence Clearwater Revival song. Both Rose and

Cynthia would mock him on Sunday mornings when he blared the tune while singing along to front man John Fogerty from the kitchen as he made coffee.

There was one message in the Inbox. Ellis' fingers trembled as he opened it.

Hey Old Man ;)

Dunno if you will ever read this, but I had to have a crack at it, just in case.

Not sure where to start so I'll just talk.

Mom and I are okay. We went to Grandma's for a while but that didn't work out. Basically because I hated it there and Mom also wanted to come home. Since then we realized that it wasn't safe at home so we're on the road. Mom shot at some bad guys, she was such a badass!! But don't worry, we're safe now. We're going to find you soon, I hope. Things aren't the same without you and I really wish that we can see you soon.

Please send me a message if you get this. You probably won't.

We love you!!

Rosey and Mom.

XXXXXXXXX

Ellis read the message twice, and then once more. He got up, paced around, and took some deep breaths then sat back down in the chair. Not knowing which emotion he felt first, he got up again and lay down on his back. Joy, fear, anger, and hope flooded his system. He put his hands over his eyes and grit his teeth. So, they were out there somewhere, running and hiding from someone and he couldn't protect or even help them.

Cynthia shot at them, at least. He had to smile at that, and he bet those fuckers didn't know what hit them. He was so proud of her and hoped that she'd hurt them, no, *killed* them. It's what they deserved for coming after his family.

Ellis jumped to his feet and got back on the chair. He clicked *Reply* and began typing:

Hey honey!

It's so good to hear that you and Mom are okay! I miss you guys so much! I'll be seeing both of you real soon.

Tell Mom to meet me at the place where we go on date nights. Two days from now at 12 p.m. I'll explain everything then, I promise!

You're such a brave girl and I can't wait to see you!

All my love!!!

Dad. XXXXXXXXXX

He shut the computer down and ran back up the stairs to the main bedroom. Opening the closet, he grabbed a backpack and began to stuff extra clothes inside while getting dressed simultaneously. Back in the kitchen he opened the cupboard above the fridge and saw that the small gun safe was open and empty. *Okay,* he thought. *Cynthia used the gun I left in the secret panel, the one the cops didn't find in their search.* He felt a bit more at ease at this discovery. He opened the door that led to the garage and saw that his truck was gone. Cynthia's car was also missing, and he knew he would have to make another plan for a set of wheels. It was probably best that he didn't travel in a vehicle that was known to the authorities.

He gathered a few more essential items including cash that he kept in an old toolbox, stuffed them in the bag and left the house. He scanned the area and saw an old Ford pick-up parked a few houses over and made a beeline for it. The truck wasn't directly in front of any of the home's windows and as Ellis tried the handle, it opened. He slid behind the wheel and popped the plastic cover around the ignition off, exposing the wiring. By the layout of the electrical system, Ellis deduced that this was an F-150 XL, mid- to late-eighties model. He inserted a flat head screwdriver from his backpack into the key slot and turned it into the "on" position which activated the fuel pump. Then he completed the circuit by connecting the live wire to the starter motor's port and the engine roared to life. This wasn't the first time he had to hotwire a car, but it still made him smile every time. The previous occasions were legal, of course, when absent-minded soldiers or officers would lose the keys to their Humvees in the middle of the desert. He rolled out of the driveway, put the truck in drive and headed for Victor Redpath's office downtown.

As Ellis turned the corner to exit his street, a Crown Victoria with a single occupant behind the wheel passed him by and turned into the road that led toward his house. Neither man noticed the other.

*****

The detective stepped out of his car and his shoes left deep imprints in the rapidly expanding blanket of snowfall that covered everything around him. *This is suburbia alright*, he thought as he regarded the area. Crossing the driveway toward the front door, he didn't notice any neighbors out and about. It was mid-morning, around 9 a.m. and he figured most of them were at work. He took a set of keys which he'd taken from the station's evidence locker from his coat pocket and unlocked the door. Fully aware that he wasn't exactly operating within the letter of the law, he quickly stepped inside and shut the door behind him. Yes, he was breaking the rules, but the situation was dire, and he needed all the help he could get. A young girl's life was on the line.

The first thing that hit him as odd when he entered the kitchen was the strong smell of freshly brewed coffee in the air. He crossed the linoleum floor and put a hand on the half-full glass jug underneath the coffee brewer. It was warm. Weapon drawn, he did a sweep of the whole house, including the garage, and when he returned to the kitchen, he was satisfied that the house was abandoned. On a small wooden table beside the fridge stood a computer screen and keyboard that he had missed before, and next to it was a mug of coffee, which was also warm to the touch. He sat down and toggled the mouse, to which the computer responded with a buzz from its internal fan, and the screen lit up. The Internet browser was open. He opened the *History* tab in the top right-hand corner, clicked on *Inbox (1) johnfogarty2010@gmail.com* and crossed his fingers that whoever used this device last had enough sense to leave its history log uncleared. The page opened and he read the solitary email that was sent to the address and the subsequent reply to it, sent only thirty minutes ago. This made Black look over both shoulders to make sure he was alone, even though he knew he was. The reply was from Ellis Neill, who was supposed to be dead, and by all accounts it looked like the detective was sitting on the same chair *he* had been on not that long ago.

If this were true, Black thought, then a lot of other things made sense now and others were even more baffling. In the case for the former, he now knew why the doctor at Stone Hill had been so reluctant to show him Ellis' body. Either they didn't have one or it was the corpse of some other poor, unfortunate soul that was stuffed in their freezer. He knew he had to make contact with Ellis – and he had to do it soon. The powers in charge of this set up – and he now wholeheartedly believed it was one – had enough influence to put up a fake news report and get the entire staff complement of a state prison to back it up. Black knew he needed to move fast.

He opened the Gmail application on his smartphone and added the username and password to the list of active accounts on his phone. This way he had access to the account wherever he went. His phone rang.

"Yes."

"We have a lead on the missing girl," the voice of a uniform came said. "I'll text you the location."

Black pocketed the phone and left the house.

CHAPTER 15

It was late that night when Ellis left the comfy confines of the F-150 to venture out into the freezing darkness. He had spent the better part of that day keeping an eye on the law offices of *Redpath and Associates* which was located within a modest strip mall building on the outskirts of downtown Toronto. Several men and women in business attire had left the office in segments starting from around 5 p.m. with the final cluster locking the doors at around seven. The city had already been cast into darkness and Ellis had decided that there was still too much activity around at that time to attempt what he was planning. But now, with the Ford's old-school clock displaying 11:23 p.m., he thought the time was right to make his move. The office had a florist next door that had closed hours earlier and on the other end, the newsagent had locked up and departed at around eight. The parking area across the road, where Ellis was stationed, contained several other vehicles that appeared to have been stowed there until the following morning.

He got out of the truck, shoved a few small tools into his jacket pocket and crossed the road. Sparse snowflakes brushed his cheeks, and the tarmac was wet underfoot as he sidled to the left of the newsagent and into a narrow alleyway that was littered with wheelie bins and scattered with discarded debris – mostly broken pallets and bales of pulp paper headed for the main recycling plant in Hamilton. He scaled the wall that led to the service area of the newsagent then hopped another fence that placed him directly in front of the law office's back door. It wasn't too heavily fortified – a steel gate was fitted in front of a standard wooden door with a single lock on it. Ellis pulled the tools from his jacket and went to work, trying to keep the decibel level as low as possible. Ten minutes later, he was standing in a small kitchenette on the other side of the door. Moonlight spilled in through the windows and Ellis was grateful that he didn't need the services of the flashlight he'd packed. He approached a door marked *Victor Redpath - Managing Partner* and was surprised to find it locked when all the other office doors stood ajar. He bypassed the lock with a TTC subway card and letter opener that he found on a desk nearby and entered the office.

The room smelled of damp and a plume of dust rose from the carpet as Ellis entered. Clearly, no one had been in here for a while. He sat down behind the desk and booted up the computer. Surprisingly, it wasn't password protected and after a while browsing through the files and finding nothing of interest, Ellis moved on to the series of standing file cabinets across the room. Under N he found his casefile, removed it and spread it open on the desk. For this exercise he *did* require the flashlight but wasn't too bothered about it being spotted from outside as Redpath's office had a single window that looked out on the abandoned alley which had been deserted all night. A flutter passed through his gut as he looked over the evidence photographs and read some of Redpath's notes from the court sessions, casting him straight back to behind the defendant's table and how optimistic he had been initially only to be knocked off his feet by the result of the procedures. It hit home in a much more profound way than he expected.

Ellis sat back and took a deep breath, letting his eyes float around the office. It was neat and tidy, almost too much so. The walls were adorned with degrees and diplomas among memories caught on camera from years gone by. One of them was of a young Redpath with a woman and a baby in front of an old Camaro, seemingly from the seventies. Beside it was another where he had a few gray streaks in his hair, standing next to an elderly woman in front of a quaint, blue house with white trimmings. His mother, most likely. Just off to the right was a more recent photograph of Redpath with another man, also in his sixties with cropped, gray hair and a moustache. To Ellis, the man had a cop's face. There was an inscription in the corner of the picture that read: *To the best P.I. in the business. Happy Birthday.*

Something about the placement of the frame looked off to him, like it was slightly further away from the wall than the others. Ellis got up, removed it to have a closer look and as he did something slid out from behind the picture and landed on the floor, making him jump. He picked the small, brown envelope up from the carpet. It was thick and bulky with something hard and rectangular shaped inside. He tore the package open and spilled the contents onto the desk. A single key, a folded note and a small cassette player tumbled onto the leather trimming which lined the inside of the mahogany table. He unfolded the note first and had to read it a few times to decipher the words embedded in the shambolic handwriting.

Victor,

This is the tape that our friend told me about. Listen to it when you're alone. Call me on the number below afterwards and I'll explain the key.

886 1353

John

Ellis picked the cassette player up and stared at it. With a slight tremble in his fingers and a queasy feeling in his stomach he pressed the *Play* button. The first few seconds were silent, then a conversation between two men began. The audio quality wasn't great and to Ellis it sounded like it was a recording of a phone call.

A: *"Mr. Lombardi, thank you for taking my call."*

B: *"Of course, anything for an old friend."*

A: *"How's the family? I hear little Tony is off to college".*

B: *"Yup. He's the man right now. Hopefully he can keep his head in the books."*

A: *"I know my Max could never have done that. Too much of a hot head."*

B: *"God rest his soul."*

A: *"Yeah, God rest his soul."*

B: *"So, what can I do for you, Bobby?"*

A: *"I've been talking to Frank the Tank and it looks like you might be looking for a fall guy soon. You know ... for a job. I hope you don't think I'm speaking out of turn here, sir."*

B: *"Not at all. It's not like you're some mook on a street corner. You've come a long way with us. Speak your mind."*

A: *"I have someone. In fact, it's the only option in my opinion and we'll be swatting two flies with one hit. If you give the green light, of course."*

B: *"Keep talking."*

A: *"You get your patsy and I get the motherfucker who killed my son."*

B: *"Sounds like mustard so far. Who is he?"*

A: *"Man by the name of Ellis Neill."*

B: *"And where do we find Mr. Neill?"*

A: *"I've been keeping tabs on him since ... He dropped off the radar for a few years but then Frank recognized his name when he applied to work for you. Frank gave me a call and here we are."*

B: *"Well, it really is a small fuckin' world, isn't it?"*

A: *"Ain't that the truth. So, what do you think, Vito? Can you help a brother out?"*

B: "Why don't I just off the guy for you? It'll be much easier."

A: "No. I want to look that asshole in the eye, so that he knows it was me. I want to get him to trust me. That way it'll be much worse for him."

B: "Alright, Mr. Drake. Judge Reiner owes us one. Actually, he owes us more than one. I'll get the wheels in motion. The hit has already been planned so Frank will call you tomorrow to keep you in the loop. Sounds good?"

A: "Yes sir! Thank you, sir. I appreciate it and my boy thanks you too."

B: "Enough with this sir shit, Bobby. We're family. I know you had to get out but you've always been there for us and we look after our own. We'll get that fucker for you, don't even worry about it."

The tape stopped by itself, and Ellis dropped the cassette player on the floor. His mind ran back to his flight to Stone Hill. Now, he could see the resemblance clearly, as if he had crossed a parallel universe and both men were standing right in front of him. Father and son. Their names were different, but the same eyes stared back at him. The way both of them curled their lips up when they smiled was identical. How did he not notice this before?

Ellis' shock soon turned to concern. He had told Bobby exactly what his plans were, down to the letter. Add to that the many conversations they had shared about Cynthia and Rose and Ellis shuddered at the thought of what the old man, who had been so convincing in his sincerity, had done with the information that was given to him.

Pocketing the contents of the envelope, he returned the photo frame to its resting place on and retraced his steps as he exited, making sure he placed everything back where it had been when he entered, erasing all and any trace of him ever being there. After locking the door and gate, he hopped back over both fences and covered the corridor to where his vehicle was parked. As he reached the mouth of the alleyway he stopped in his tracks and slinked back into the shadows. Across the road, a Police Patrol car was parked behind the F-150 and two officers were inspecting the vehicle with flashlights in hand, checking the cockpit through the windows and the bed in the back through the canopy portholes. As Ellis racked his brain for a Plan B, a late-night bus came to a standstill right in front of him, blocking the cops' view of the opposite side of the road. Ellis hesitated, then boarded the bus. He dropped the fare amount in coins into the slot next to the driver, took a seat in the front and pulled the hood of his jacket over his head. As the bus rolled off, he glanced back to where the police were now opening the doors of the truck he had used earlier, and he felt fortunate to not be standing there right now.

*****

Rose stirred, then rolled over on the mattress. For a moment, she thought she was in her bedroom but when the smell of food entered her nostrils and she opened her eyes to see the barred ceiling looming above her head, her heart sank and she let out a whimper. Composing herself, in case the man was watching, she sat up and studied the tray that had been placed at her feet while she was sleeping. It had faded yellow flowers printed on it and there was a bowl placed in the middle with an apple off to the left. The bowl had a brown mixture in it that Rose assumed was soup with a spoon sticking out of it. She gave it a suspicious look and decided that it would be risky to eat *anything* provided by the man who had so brutally and senselessly killed her mother.

She could hear movement from upstairs and wondered what the man's plan was for her. Surely, he didn't have much use for an almost teenage girl. Why hadn't he killed her as well? Her mind went to a dark option that he might be considering, then she pulled away from it, as if thinking about it could manifest the thought in the stranger's mind. Panic threatened to set in once more, but Rose thought back to what her father had taught her from a young age: It was never pertinent to panic, even though the situation might seem impossible to get out of. Grit your teeth and use your brain. Whatever else needs to be dealt with can be done once you are safe and completely out of the woods.

With that thought in mind, Rose gave the bowl of soup another look. Her stomach was aching and she began to feel weak from lack of nourishment. Also, if she was going to get out of here, she needed her strength. With a reluctant sigh she pawed at the tray and drew it closer. It smelled good. Well, maybe it didn't really smell that good, but Rose thought it did, especially after a likely forty-eight hours without a meal. She scooped some of the soup with the wooden spoon and it went down well, prompting her to have more. Before long the bowl was empty and she moved on to the apple. She wolfed it all down, core included, and settled back onto the mattress.

After a few minutes, she could feel the life force returning to her exhausted body and mind. Something stirred above her and before she could prepare herself, the trap door flew open. She backed into the corner of the cell and her head hit the steel bars, but she barely noticed. A ladder slid through the hole and its feet were planted into the soil surrounding the cell. A pair of black boots, Dr Martens by Rose's guess, emerged through the opening and the man that had taken her captive made his way down the steps. His movements were slow and methodical, almost like he was some sort of mechanical contraption. Finally, he stood before the cell. Rose could see the red ski mask peeking out at her from beneath a black hood which descended down the length of his body and morphed into an ankle length trench coat. He just stood there, staring.

"Hey!" Rose shouted and she was ashamed that it came out a lot shriller than she had intended. The dark stranger didn't respond. "What do you want?! Huh?!"

Rose grabbed the soup bowl, hurled it at him but it ricocheted off the bars and landed back inside the cell.

"I'm not afraid of you! You hear me!" she screamed so violently that she had pause to catch her breath. The figure pulled a piece of paper from his pocket, rolled it into a ball and tossed it at her. Rose hesitated for a second then scrambled forward and grabbed the paper, all the while keeping her eyes firmly locked on the man in front of her. She dove back to the mattress and unfurled the page.

It was a screenshot of an email. It was a reply that her dad had sent to her Gmail address. Rose's eyes welled up with tears and she glared at the figure.

"He's alive! He's alive!" she said, wiping her drenched face with her sleeve. "He'll come for me, you know." Her voice was now low, resigned to all emotion. "He'll come for me, and you'll wish you were dead!"

In response, the figure rolled the hood of his coat back and slowly pulled the ski mask off his face, revealing features that seemed both fantastical and grotesque at the same time. He had no lips, just two thin folds of skin that constituted his mouth. He smiled and it revealed brown, crooked teeth that looked rotten to the core. The nose that protruded from in between sunken and acne-scarred cheeks was misshapen. It looked like it had been chewed away by some sort of animal and left to heal on its own. But the worst were the eyes – two bright yellow irises appeared to glow from deep inside their sockets, surrounded by skin so pale it seemed gray.

"I know," the figure said. His voice was raspy and thin. "That's exactly what I'm waiting for."

CHAPTER 16

T he lights and revelry passed by as the bus traveled down Yonge Street, the busiest road in downtown where bars, nightclubs and late-night stores of all kinds lured the lonely and hungry towards its offerings: from the partygoers lining up to sample the best that the "Little House of Kebabs" had to offer its ravenous clientele after a night of drinking and doing lines, to those drawn toward the fiery neon lights of "Club Zanzibar" where the sign read *OVER 70 HOT, SINFUL GIRLS!* and *VIP AND CHAMPAGNE ROOMS AVAILABLE.* Ellis' eyes glided over all of it. A tattered, middle-aged man sat in the doorway of the twenty-four-hour record store next door to the flesh parade, panhandling for change. No doubt a victim of this part of town that can swallow a person whole, given half a chance.

Ellis' gaze fell over the CN Tower in the distance ahead. It was lit up in green and red for the festive season but he hardly noticed as the rhythmic rocking of the bus jogged his mind into action. He wondered who he could trust with this evidence. The police were out of the question, no doubt about it. He could hand it to a newspaper, but that might send Bobby's co-conspirators into hiding or push them over the edge and kill Rose and Cynthia.

He couldn't risk it. Not until he had them both back with him where they were safe.

His phone vibrated from inside his pants pocket, and he pulled it out. It was an email notification. He opened the app and read the message.

Hi Ellis,

This is detective William Black. I'm sure you remember me. I have information about your family. We need to meet soon.

I know this is a surprise to you and that you have absolutely no reason to trust me, but I am here to help. Please contact me right away. Time is of the essence. Your daughter is missing and I fear she is in great danger.

I'll explain everything when we meet.

You can call me directly on this number – 555 5471

William.

Ellis' heart skipped a beat for the umpteenth time as he read the message over and over again. He didn't know what to make of it. His initial thoughts were that it was an ambush, but no police had been looking for him. He had been scanning the news websites since he left his house and found no mention of an escaped convict. On the contrary, he found a report that he had died in prison of an apparent heart attack a week ago. He wondered if that had gotten back to Cynthia and, if it had, how she'd responded to it. Or Rose, for that matter. The problem was that he had many more questions than answers at this stage, and with no way to find his family aside from an email address that Rose seemingly stopped responding to or had lost contact with, his options were limited. He could begin to scour the Earth for them but where to start? Going door-to-door seemed ludicrous, but he would do it if there was no other way. The problem with that was that it would be time consuming as hell and most likely wouldn't turn anything up.

If the cop was telling the truth, then he was Ellis' only chance of finding them. But what if he wasn't? What if he was just as deep in cahoots with the "string pullers" of this deadly pantomime as the ever-trustworthy, ever-helpful Bobby Drake? Ellis grit his teeth at the thought of how easily the wool had been pulled over his eyes. He remembered that, when they met, he had been wary of everyone, considering the company he found himself in. Perhaps he had let the old man in because he so desperately wanted someone to confide in. He'd dropped his guard just long enough for Bobby to snake his way in. Bobby seemed harmless enough at the time. He was pissed off at himself for not following his own guidelines of "keeping everyone at a distance until they proved themselves trustworthy" as he had done ever since the day he'd had to shoot one of his own and it opened up a world of backstabbing that he never knew existed. He shook his head at the irony of it all – being undone by the father of the man who had so influenced his rules for life. But the fact of the matter was that he had no choice now. He had to trust this cop, to an extent anyway.

As the wheels on the bus rolled through the night, he decided that he would sleep on it and make his decision early in the morning, when his mind was fresh and he had some more time to wait on a reply from Rose.

*****

Back in his office, Warden Blakeway was packing personal belongings into a black duffel bag. It had been two days since he and his crew were out in the snow looking for Ellis Neill and had come up short. Their only finds had been a pool of blood close to the train station, which his guide had rapidly debunked as evidence of an animal slaying and, of course, the warm stove top in the camper van. Neither of which proved anything. He certainly couldn't go back to Lombardi with this flimsy cluster as feedback to their progress. He'd be laughed out of the room, assuming the mob boss had a sense of humor, which he didn't.

Another factor was that there had been no communication from anyone in Toronto since he'd returned from bushwhacking through the ice and snow. That in itself was worrying, and it made the warden reach for the bottle more often than usual. When they went silent was when you needed to pay attention. Because that meant that you didn't know what Lombardi was thinking or what was coming next – and that was dangerous. As a result, Blakeway had decided that he wasn't prepared to hang around and find out. He needed to get the hell out of dodge, and he needed to do it as soon as humanly possible. Kicking himself that he didn't make this decision earlier was evident, but he didn't even have time for that. He also had to make sure that nobody picked up on the fact that he was doing a runner. There were eyes all over the place and if anyone got a sniff of his plans it would all end in painful, agonizing failure. No, not when he was so close to getting out. He could already see the Florida beaches and smell the suntan lotion that the young, bikini clad girls would be covered in as he stared at them while sipping on an array of umbrella drinks. *No more of this freezing, ice box bullshit*, he thought.

Bag in hand he made his way out past reception without stopping. It was 5:45 p.m., only fifteen minutes earlier than his usual departure time and he was sure nothing would be made of it. Waiting another fifteen minutes was simply out of the question. He only had to stop at home to grab his suitcase, then it was a one-hundred-and-fifty-mile drive to Fort Smith Airport where he would catch the American Airlines flight to Dallas/ Fort Worth and from there it would be on to Fort Lauderdale. Easy as pie.

Blakeway loaded the bag into the back of his car, slipped on the ice, cursed, and then slid in behind the steering wheel. It was a quick drive to his house and when he got there, he wasted no time. He stormed in, grabbed his suitcase which was already waiting for him on the sofa and blew back out of the front door, not even bothering to lock it. If robbers, vandals or homeless people found the place, it would be their lucky day.

His momentum was stopped dead in its tracks when he saw a black Cadillac Escalade parked next to his car as he came outside. The blood drained from his face when two men stepped out of the SUV and started walking toward him.

"Going somewhere, Andy?" came the voice of Max Ricatelli. He was one of Vito Lombardi's henchmen. Blakeway didn't recognize the other guy, but he was almost as wide as he was tall with a slicked back hairstyle and dark eyes.

"Hey, Max!" Blakeway's voice was squeaky, and he cleared

his throat. "What are you wiseguys doing all the way out in Bumfuck town?"

"Just came to see our favorite prison guard." Max smiled, exposing a gold tooth in place of one of his lateral incisors. "So, where are you going, Andy?"

"Oh." Blakeway looked down at the suitcase and dropped it on the snow as if to distance himself from it. "Laundry day. My washer is on the fritz. You know how it is."

"Can it wait? It's awfully cold out here. How about a nice cup of joe? If it's not too much trouble." Max flashed an obviously insincere smile.

"Sure, fellas. There's a great coffee shop in town—" Blakeway began but Max cut him off.

"Too far! Why don't we go inside? I'm happy with instant. How about you, Vince?" Max asked and the behemoth next to him nodded in silent agreement. They walked over to Blakeway who picked up his suitcase out of the snow and opened the front door for them. It was freezing cold, but he was sweating underneath his clothes.

The temperature indoors seemed colder than Blakeway remembered, as if the two men had brought winter in with them. He filled the kettle from the tap in the kitchen sink and switched it on, then moved to an eye level kitchen cabinet where he found three coffee mugs. His eyes fell on an object in between the two mugs right at the back of the cupboard. He froze and had to look twice to be sure that he wasn't hallucinating. The memory of him placing the object there failed him, but then again, most memories did, considering his habit of killing brain cells.

The warden looked over his shoulder and saw both men peering out of his living room window before Max drew the drapes shut. He knew what that meant. He'd known what they meant the second he saw them stepping out of their car. Sending a flash prayer up to a deity that he hadn't spoken to in many years, he asked for help. He promised to quit perving over younger women and most of all, he swore he would never touch another drop of the firewater for as long as he lived, if only he could be saved from his near certain fate – ending up in a hole somewhere, his body riddled with bullets. Deep down, Blakeway knew he didn't deserve any help, but his intentions were pure for the first time in his life. Reaching back into the cupboard, he took the object and slipped it into his jacket pocket.

"You guys take milk and sugar?" Blakeway asked, not caring much about the answer.

"Strong and black, Andy," Max replied, and the fat man nodded in apparent agreement. It seemed that he didn't have much of an opinion of his own about anything.

"Good," Blakeway said. "The milk's gone bad."

He handed a mug to the big guy, then turned to get Max's from the counter. When he turned back, he had the other coffee in one hand and the gun in the other. Max's eyes grew wide and his hand went for the concealed gun in his belt. Blakeway threw the coffee at him and he screamed as the hot liquid scorched his skin. The warden turned the weapon on his sidekick and fired three times. All three shots hit his target in the chest, sending the man stumbling backwards until he fell over an armchair behind him. Then, the warden turned the gun back on Max, stretched his arm out and fired two shots into the henchman's head at point blank range. His skull made a popping sound and small drops of blood hit Blakeway in the face. Max's hands went up to his neck in a seizure-like motion then dropped to his sides before he hit the carpet.

Blakeway stood still in the eerily silent room as smoke from the firearm hung in the air. He looked down at the gun in his hand and couldn't believe what had just happened. If he had to bet, he would've placed his money on the hitmen, even with the weapon they were unaware of thrown into the mix.

A phone ringing jarred him back to reality. At first he thought it was his own, but after checking the unlit screen his eyes scanned the room until they stopped at a faint blue glow coming from Max's pants pocket. No doubt a check-in from the boss to see if the job has been done, Blakeway thought. Either way, he wasn't going to let the grass grow under his feet.

He grabbed a dishcloth from the sink and wiped the blood off his face, then pocketed the revolver. He'd toss it out of the window on his drive to Fort Smith. Grabbing the suitcase, he made for the door and as he passed his liquor cabinet, a bottle of unopened bourbon standing on it made him stop. Glaring at it, he raised a hand to grab it then pulled back. He turned to look once more at the two men on the floor, exited the house then started his car and sped out of the driveway en route to the airport.

All without the aid of the bottle.

*****

Ellis stood in front of his hotel room window and stared at the sun peeking its head out over the horizon. The snowfall had subsided during the night and the sky was unusually clear this morning. From his vantage point on the tenth floor, he could see early risers running along the sidewalks and garbage trucks doing their morning rounds. It was a tranquil scene, a deep contrast to what was going on in his mind.

He read the email that Detective Black sent again, then returned his gaze to the scene outside and focused on his thoughts which at this stage was more akin to herding cats. Was the cop being honest? There was no way he could know in advance. Not contacting the detective would leave him in no man's land and if he did decide to take the trust-fall, he would have to put some countermeasures in place. Just in case the boy in blue was laying the mother of all traps for him. But what? The night that passed had given him no extra answers and there were no other bargaining chips to play. Besides, someone with the resources of the police force behind them would certainly be an asset, assuming he could keep them at arm's length.

Then, an idea came to him.

He took the phone from the bedside table and saved the phone number from the email to his contacts under *5-0*. Ellis' direct commanding officer had always referred to military police personnel by that name and it had stuck with him. Even when he strolled past cops on the street, he would think, *There goes 5-0,* and then Captain Warwick's face would appear.

Ellis typed a text message to Black that read:

Sichuan Garden Restaurant.

Spadina Ave, Chinatown.

4 p.m.

Come alone.

E.N.

He knew this restaurant and considered it home territory as far as a public meeting went. It was always crowded and there was a back exit that led to an alley where Ellis would park his car close by, in case he had to leave in a hurry. His thumb hovered over the *Send* button. He took a deep breath and pressed it. The little envelope animation floated on the screen then a message appeared that said "Delivered".

He checked his watch: 6:47 a.m. The plan was to grab breakfast downstairs, then head out to the meeting spot to do preparations and stake the place out until the time came. Ellis chugged the rest of his coffee and headed for the shower.

*****

William Black glanced at the computer screen as he slid the phone back into his pocket. He sensed movement and looked up to see a woman standing at his desk, staring at him. She appeared to be in her early thirties. Dark brown hair cascaded onto her shoulders and soft, coffee-brown eyes were studying his face. She smiled when she noticed him looking back at her and Black couldn't help but feel his insides melt a little at her perfect complexion. As she sat down on the chair opposite him the silk blouse underneath her suit blazer gaped slightly, exposing the lace of her black bra which encompassed an immaculately sculpted cleavage. His gaze shot back up to hers, hoping she didn't notice the half-second long involuntary indiscretion.

"Can I help you, ma'am?"

"Wow," she said and the dazzling smile reappeared with an added sparkle in her eyes. "I haven't been called that in years. You charmer."

Black smiled back. "Comes with the job."

"Maybe where *you* come from. The academy never taught *me* that," she said and saw confusion forming on his face.

"Wait, you're ..."

"Ramona Lee. Detective," she said and held out a hand. Instead of taking it, Black rose from his chair and marched to the captain's office. He stuck his head through the door but before he could say anything, the uniformed officer in his early sixties piped up, "I don't want to hear it, Bill. This comes from higher up. Make it work!"

The captain walked around from behind his desk and shut the door in his face. Black hovered for a second then returned to his seat and pretended to ruffle through his paperwork. Feeling Ramona Lee's eyes drilling two holes through the top of his head, he wondered how long he could keep this up, and if she'd say anything. He didn't have to wait long.

"Look, I get it," Ramona said in a voice that was almost silky enough to hide her sarcasm. "You're one of those 'I work alone' guys and I can respect that. I didn't ask to be here but as long as I am, I think we can help each other."

"Yeah? How's that?" Black was still mock-sifting through his desk's contents.

"I hear you're looking for someone." Ramona leaned forward and Black picked up a faint scent of jasmine. "I'm *really* good at finding people."

"And who might I be looking for?" Black said and felt a knot in his stomach. He looked up at her, expecting to hear the words "Ellis Neill". The reply he received wasn't what he anticipated.

"The girl, Daddy-O!" Ramona raised her palms in the air in dismay and dropped them on her thighs. "From the motel?"

"Right." Black sighed then tried to hide his relief. Unfortunately, he caught her eyes narrowing a bit as she observed his reaction. "Long day."

"Sure." Her interrogation-face began to fade. "Any leads on that? Captain said the uniforms called something in yesterday."

"Nope. Dead end. A junkie looking for a payday."

"Detective, do you ever speak in sentences longer than three words? Because if you don't then this blossoming, hot and steamy new relationship of ours isn't going to work out," she said, and Black shifted in his chair.

"Okay, you win," he said, moving the paperwork aside. "Yes, I need to find the girl. Where do you suppose we look?" Black didn't really want an answer from his new bombshell partner. He needed time to think. He had just over an hour before he had to meet Ellis and he needed to ditch her, soon. In his bones, he felt that this wouldn't be an easy task.

"Let's go for a drive then, Daddy-O," Ramona replied, then

looked down as her phone vibrated. The screen showed a text message from Vito Lombardi.

CHAPTER 17

Ellis adjusted the baseball cap lower as a few pedestrians passed by and his view of the entrance to the Sichuan Garden Restaurant from his window seat at the coffee shop across the road was once more without obstruction. He checked his watch – 3:57 p.m. The street was quiet, but inside the shop was bustling with those seeking a taste of Asia in downtown Toronto. He'd been seated here for the last two hours and hadn't spotted anything that looked out of place. No fake delivery men or mock street workers. Nobody had looped around the block and there were no cars parked in the immediate vicinity that had been there longer than he was. Same went for the customers of the coffee house. Before sitting down, he had parked a blue Prius that he thought was a much more inconspicuous choice than his previous boost behind the restaurant where he was to meet Black, close enough to the back entrance to make a hasty retreat as planned. By the lack of stares and glances he received as he drove to his destination, he felt reassured that he had made the correct vehicle choice.

His stomach muscles tensed when he saw the detective walk past the window, headed for the restaurant entrance. He looked like he had aged a few years since the last time Ellis locked eyes with him from across the courtroom. There were a few more gray hairs around his ears and he appeared to have a slightly labored walk. Ellis had a last look around the area and when he was convinced that the cop did not have a tail, he left the coffee house and crossed the road towards the meeting spot. Beyond the threshold he spotted Black right away, sitting by himself at a corner table. His heart was racing as he entered the restaurant, wound through the crowd and sat down opposite the cop. For a minute or two they just sat there, neither wanting to be the first to speak. Black was the one who broke the silence.

"Good to see you," he said. "For a while there I thought you were done for."

"Yeah, me too," Ellis said hesitantly. It felt strange to sit across from the man who had cuffed and thrown him in the back of a van. Like he was somehow betraying himself by colluding with the enemy.

"I know you don't trust me," the detective said as if he'd read Ellis' mind. "I'm here to help, regardless of what happened in the past."

"Or this is some sort of set up," Ellis snapped back. "I guess that makes me the idiot then, right?"

"I can only give you my word. The rest is up to you."

"Fair enough," Ellis said and took a sip of his green tea which was complementary for every customer as soon as they were seated. "You said you had some information. Do you know where my family is?"

"I'll tell you what I know, but I have to start at the beginning,"

Black said and took a deep breath. He recounted how the new evidence was brought to him soon after Ellis' conviction, which confirmed his prior suspicions that there were dirty cops and city officials within his department who liked to line their pockets, and that he could deny it no longer, despite his long-standing personal beliefs. He told Ellis about the phone call he'd received from Cynthia and their subsequent meeting at the bar where he had convinced her that he was trying to help. He explained how she had missed their appointment, and he watched the man across from him slump and shudder as he divulged the part about the body they found in the motel room and the ID in the purse that confirmed that it was Cynthia. When Ellis finally asked, in a husky and croaking voice, if the detective was sure that it was her and not someone carrying her wallet, he explained that he checked the body himself and that he was sure.

The dam wall that Ellis had strained to keep intact during this conversation was swept away by the words *Rose wasn't at the scene* and *She's missing, possibly taken by the killer* that flowed from Black's mouth like a hex. Ellis' head sunk into his hands, and he shook as the reality of it hit him square in the chest. He felt dizzy and there were dark circles narrowing in on his vision. He looked up and Black had him by the arm saying, "Deep breaths, buddy" and "Take it easy, now". Then, everything went dark.

*****

Vito Lombardi sat up in bed. The sheets clung to his back as he wiped sweat from his face. Breathing deeply, he tried to piece together the dream that he'd just had. He swung his legs off the edge and took three large gulps of water from a glass on his bedside table. As his feet grazed the thick carpet, it came back to him.

He had been in prison, laying down on a top bunk. Which facility exactly was a mystery. He had been in a few during his career, but the dream provided no detail to indicate his exact location. A voice came from below him that sounded like his father's, but every time he rolled over to look down, the face of the person on the bottom bunk would distort and fade away. The voice's words were muffled in the beginning then became clearer, as if several rags had been removed from its mouth in stages.

You think you're smarter than me.

Like the song goes about the apple and the tree.

I am you and you are me.

"No! I'm nothing like you! You're nothing but a fucking rat!" Vito had screamed in his dream state.

Vieni qui, figliolo. Come here my son. We are the same.

My boy.

My little one, of my flesh and blood.

They know.

They know and they will come for you.

Then, as if pushed from the bunk, Vito rolled off the bed and landed on the concrete floor. He turned to look at where the voice came from. The bottom bunk was now a luxurious, blue sofa. His father was sitting in between two police officers who were handing him notes of cash as the old mob boss smiled from ear to ear. His eyes bore deep into Vito's soul and there was a fury in him that built until he could take it no more. He looked down and there was a butcher's knife in his hand. Charging at the sofa he stabbed the two cops, then began to slash at his father. Multiple stabs to the throat and chest would only result in the old man laughing even harder and repeating the lines he had said before.

Vieni qui, figliolo. Come here my son. We are the same.

My boy.

My little one, of my flesh and blood...

You cannot kill me! I live in YOU!

One final stab and Vito jammed the blade into the top of his father's skull, the handle the only thing stopping the descent of the cold steel through the bone and down into the gray matter. Still, the old man laughed.

And that's when he awoke. Although Nick Lombardi was long dead, but he still haunted his son. The legacy his father had left behind, of a mob boss who ran – something that no self-respecting clan-boss *ever* did – then, upon his arrest, turned state witness was weighing on him. Like a shadow that bore down with a ton of weight, it followed him everywhere and so did the whispers. Since Vito took over the reins following his father's demise he had tried almost everything to prove his loyalty, and that he was the only obvious choice to lead. Acts of ruthlessness in the name of justice and vengeance for the family were rife.

Over time and with increased bloodshed of their enemies, the critical voices had become quieter, and they slowly began to forget the unforgivable actions of his father. Up until recently, that was. Shortly after the trial was over, the grumbling started up again, like ambers blowing in the wind.

The murder of Judge Thatcher and his wife had been kickback for a sentence he had handed to Rocco Ganelli, a *capo* and close personal friend to those who opposed Vito within the organization. This was to be a different direction for the young mob boss. Instead of simply wiping his adversaries out, thus dwindling the numbers of his own army, he chose to extend an olive branch. Though many of Vito's closest allies advised against it he chose to avenge the sentencing by not only approving the hit on Thatcher, but also taking care of it himself by using his own, most trusted undertaker. It had been a success of note and for a short while, it seemed as if the rift in the family was closing.

But now there were major loose ends. Word had gotten out that the fall guy was out of prison, his killer had gone rogue, and the warden had somehow popped Vito's number one enforcer and was nowhere to be found. This made the others uncomfortable. Warden Blakeway had extensive knowledge about their operations and the escaped prisoner could be making noise already. Sure, not many people would give him the time of day considering he was a convict, but he only needed one person to listen. And if it was the right one, their entire operation could be at risk. The cigarette smuggling, the hookers, and the cocaine they ran with the assistance of the Konahue-tribe in Michigan was in jeopardy. Vito knew the pressure was on. So, he had made the decision to send Ramona in. Outside of his *capo* she was the only other person he could trust unreservedly and her results as a fixer were unmatched. She was tougher than any hired gun he had ever come across and she didn't need much managing. Like a top-class "fire and forget missile" you could send her into any situation and know that the outcome would be exactly as desired. Nevertheless, he was still on edge and sleep came in short installments, if at all.

He looked over at Christa who was sleeping soundly, and he exited the room. Downstairs in the living room he grabbed the cordless phone and dialed a number he could recite in his sleep. The phone rang three times before there was an answer.

"Missing me already?" a woman's voice said.

"You never called me back," Vito said in a playful tone. "That's not like you."

"Easy, Daddy-O. This cop is jumpy as it is."

"Do you think there's anything there?" Vito asked and mentally crossed his fingers.

"Oh yeah." He could tell that she was smiling. "He's definitely sitting on something."

"Good." Vito smiled as well now. "I need you to squeeze harder."

"Does your wife know you're getting a girl all hot like that?"

"Don't you worry about that, doll. You turn that cop upside down and shake him if you have to. I want to know where this Ellis guy is, where his family is and what the fuck happened to my trigger man. Time is of the essence here."

"Sure thing, lover. Now, not to be rude but a girl needs to get her beauty rest," Ramona said and hung up.

Vito went into the kitchen, poured himself a whisky and sat down at the kitchen table. This thing was a mess, but it might work out for him yet.

CHAPTER 18

Ellis sat up, disoriented and confused, to find that he was in the back of a car traveling down a busy road. He looked ahead and saw that the driver of the vehicle was William Black. The detective glanced in the rear-view mirror and his eyes widened as he spotted Ellis stirring behind him.

"Jesus, you scared the shit out of me! Are you okay?" Black asked in a tone several notes higher than usual.

"What … what happened?" Ellis replied and rubbed the back of his head.

"You tell me. You mumbled something and then you flew backwards, and your head hit the floor like a ton of bricks. I had to get people sitting around us to help me put you in the car."

"I … need to … find Rose," Ellis said in between labored breaths. His head was killing him.

"Easy, tiger," Black said. "I'm taking you to get checked out first."

"No! No hospitals!" Ellis leaned forward to get Black's attention.

"I know. Fuck, man. I'm not a moron," Black said as his eyes shifted back towards the road ahead. "We're going to my house. A friend will come out and have a look at you there, okay? Just chill out."

They drove the rest of the way in silence and eventually ended up in a neighborhood that Ellis didn't recognize. The Crown Vic pulled into a suburban area and after a few left and right turns Black stopped the car in front of his home, a modest but neat looking two-storey that had an open garden and a path laid with wooden sleepers leading to the front door. Black opened the door for Ellis and led him down the path towards the door. Once inside, the detective guided him toward the sofa and instructed him to stay put, something Ellis had no problem doing. His headache was getting worse, and it felt like he had been hit by a freight train. Black pulled his phone from his pocket and walked into the kitchen, out of sight but within earshot. There was a quick exchange between Black and somebody named Nathan, then the talking subsided. Black returned from the kitchen with a glass of water, which he handed to Ellis.

"Try to relax," Black said. He took a seat beside Ellis on the sofa and glanced at his watch.

Ten minutes later, there was a knock at the door. A young man, probably in his late twenties, walked in with a medical bag. He was wearing a paramedic's jumpsuit and had a friendly face. He knelt down in front of Ellis.

"Hi Mr. Neill, my name is Nathan. I'm just going to have a quick look at you, okay?" he said and shone a small flashlight in Ellis' eyes, darting from one eye to the next. "Any nausea or dizziness?"

"Yes, I'm a bit dizzy," Ellis said and turned his face away from the flashlight.

"Is the light bad?" the medic asked as he switched the light off and pocketed it.

"It feels like you're shining it into my brain, if that answers your question."

"Okay, how about pain? On a scale of one to ten."

"I'd say eight," Ellis said and leaned back in the seat.

"Alright," Nathan the paramedic said and turned to Black. "He has a concussion but not too bad. Strap a bag of frozen peas to his head for an hour, feed him plenty of Paracetamol and he'll be fine in a day or two. No booze and lots of rest. You can let him sleep."

Black walked Nathan out and went back into the kitchen to get the supplies that were needed. He taped a bag of frozen carrots to Ellis' head and helped him take two pain tablets. Ellis leaned on Black as they made their way upstairs. The detective led him into a room where everything was colored in various shades of pink and toy ponies were the favored decorative items. Ellis lay down on the single bed and Black looked at him with a kind of regard that was somewhere in between concern and pity.

"Get some rest," Black said, and then left, closing the door behind him.

In the dark silence of the room Ellis lay there for a few minutes trying to mull over what Black had told him in the restaurant. Cynthia was dead and Rose was gone. He tried to fathom how things had turned so bad, so quickly. He felt as if he had lost a limb. The love of his life was gone forever, and in such a horrible way that he could feel physical pain in his gut and heart. It felt like everything had fallen apart. His whole world was different once again and as he lay in the pink bed, he couldn't help but curl up and begin to cry like he had never done before. It was unbearable, the images that conjured up in his mind of his beautiful wife fighting for her life amid a madman slashing at her with a knife. And what of Rosey? Had she gotten away as the chaos ensued? Did she witness her mother being brutally murdered? Where could she be? Ellis pictured her hunkered underneath a bridge, scared and alone and it filled him with rage and sorrow all over again. He decided that he would leave right now to go and look for his daughter, but his battered body had other plans and it sent him into a deep slumber before he could even complete his train of thought.

*****

William Black sat down on the sofa where Ellis had been seated not too long ago. Next to him was a black backpack that came along with the man who was asleep in his daughter's bed. He stared at it and wondered what was inside. The thought that immediately followed was that it definitely wouldn't assist in building trust with the escaped convict if he *did* sneak a peek and was then caught out. On the other hand, there might be something in there that he could use, or perhaps a clue as to where Rose might be, something that Ellis may have overlooked. After all, he was on the run and in Black's experience, people on the run rarely paid attention to detail as their minds were constantly occupied by looking over their shoulders. It didn't leave much room or time for logical assessment or reasoning.

Before he had actually decided to do so he grabbed the bag, turned it upside down and the contents spilled onto the cushion beside him. Most of the items were random: a flashlight, a small toolkit and a change of clothes. The object that grabbed his attention was a small tape recorder. It had a cassette inside and it took every ounce of willpower to leave the *play* button untouched. He decided that he would wait until Ellis woke up then ask him about it.

The detective then called his office to say he would be out for the rest of the day and switched the television on. A news anchor was speaking in the background, but the detective's mind was too preoccupied. The Dictaphone in the backpack was haunting him like the ghost of an old lover, prodding at him and demanding his attention as the screen before him portrayed the mayhem unfolding in Afghanistan following the withdrawal of all US troops.

Thirty minutes passed and after much deliberation, he came to the decision that he would check the tape. They were in a race against time and to Black that warranted breaking a few rules, even if it went against the very fiber of his being. As he got up from the sofa to open the bag the doorbell rang, which made him jump. Approaching the door, he stopped and looked through the peephole.

On the other side, staring right back at him, stood Ramona Lee.

*****

There was a sound of water dripping in the distance as Rose lifted her head from the pillow. She looked around and tried to pinpoint its location. This wasn't the first time she'd heard it and by her own rough estimates, she came to the conclusion that it was caused by a rainstorm outside. The dripping usually didn't last long. As an additional bonus to research she did for a school project a year ago, she also learned that in winter the rainstorms in the area didn't last long. And if there was water leaking into the structure, that told her that there was an opening somewhere – it could mean a way out, assuming she could make it out of the cage. That was something that she had also been working on in her head during the long and quiet hours. The square holes created by the crisscrossed steel bars were about twenty centimeters in diameter. Rose thought that if she could fit her head through, then the rest of her body would slide through virtually unobstructed, but that theory was still untested. A measuring tape at hand and the exact circumference of her noggin would be ideal, but she didn't have access to any of these luxuries, so she decided that a field test would be the only viable option.

Since her arrival in the cage (Rose didn't actually know how long she had been there but estimated it at around four days) she had made a point of noting the figure's routine and movements. He always wore heavy boots which made it relatively easy to determine when he was approaching the trap door to bring her food and water. Aside from that, he rarely stirred, and she also knew that he only slept for short periods at a time. One of those occasions was taking place right now. Rose hadn't heard him move for what she calculated to be approximately twenty minutes and she decided that this would be the opportune moment to launch "Operation Head Shrink".

She reached underneath her pillow and removed a ball of congealed fat that she had skimmed off the soup that she had been served for lunch and dinner, every day. The broth was sparse in the meat and vegetable department but always contained plenty of adipose tissue as if it were made from whale blubber. It was about a golf ball sized dollop. She rolled the ball between her palms and as it warmed up and turned pulpy, she began to apply it to her head in even strokes, from her crown all the way down to her neck and covering her face. It had gone putrid in the humid room and she gagged a few times as the foul grease covered her whole head and hung from her hair in clumps.

A few days ago, she had noticed that one row of the square gaps in the cell was slightly bigger than the others. It was at ground level and the point where it met the floor had about a four centimeter larger gap in height which would provide excess space to squeeze through. She moved the mattress aside and lay on her belly with her head right up against the chosen square. Taking a deep breath, she prayed that she wouldn't get stuck as the assumed result would be that the figure would just leave her there until her dad arrived – if he ever did. Letting the breath out, she pulled herself onto the bars. The fat on her hair made her head slide in seamlessly until the bars reached her temples and the glide came to an abrupt halt. It would move no further. Her legs kicked against the floor, trying to gain traction and as her head advanced through the bars a sharp pain throbbed through her temples. It was agonizing and for a second, she considered pulling back. After a final heave, her entire head flopped through the gap and she just lay there, letting the blood flow return to the sides of her head, and she smiled.

C'mon Rosie, you're not out yet, she thought to herself and continued to maneuver through the small space. Her left shoulder went through first, followed by her right and then her hips, which she was thankful had not yet begun to show the signs of looming puberty. Finally, her legs slid through and a few seconds later she was standing upright, studying the bars from the exterior of the cage.

She listened for movement upstairs – there was none.

Rose pulled the blanket through the bars. She wrapped herself in it and went to find the source of the dripping water. Her fingers ran alongside the surface of the wall on the far side and then, as if highlighted by a flashlight, she saw a crack in the top where the boarded wall of the basement met the structure wall above it. Bright moonlight was pouring in along with a miniscule stream of water. She looked around and found an old, rusted jerry can and placed it up against the wall. Carefully stepping up, she mounted it and began to pull at the top of the board. It let go easily and as she kept pulling, it disintegrated completely. Shards of wood landed around her on the floor and left a hole more than ample enough for her to clamber through. Her heart leapt from her chest as the frosty air spilled in and a smile as wide as she had ever shown graced her face. She pulled herself up by the roots of a nearby tree that had previously been covered by the basement wall paneling and lifted a leg onto the top of the gap. From ground level she could see the forest that surrounded her prison. Every pinecone and needle on the trees was lit up by the shimmering lunar glow, as if they had Christmas lights attached to them.

Then, out of nowhere, pain exploded inside her ankle. She glanced downward and saw a thick chain wrapped around the appendage, anchored by a small hook that was digging into the flesh around her foot. Her eyes followed the chain that spanned the length of the room. At the other end of it stood the figure with the chain firmly grasped within his gloved hands. He wrapped the chain around his upper arm and began to circle the cage at a gallop. The pain in Rose's leg was amplified tenfold as she was violently yanked off the jerry can and dragged around the room. She screamed for him to stop, but he kept sprinting and jerking at the iron links.

After what felt like an eternity, he stopped, and Rose could hear the chains rattle as he walked over to her. She propped herself up on her elbows and stared at him through fresh tears. He was wearing the mask today.

"Fucking coward!" Rose shouted. The veins in her neck stood out and her face was red with rage. "Have you had enough fun torturing a little girl?!"

He stood there, staring at her with his bright eyes far behind the holes of the red mask. Since the day he'd dropped the email through the bars, he hadn't said another word. He said nothing now and it infuriated her even more.

"Talk, dammit!" she yelled and her voice went hoarse. "Say something! You're nothing but a coward!"

The figure stepped closer, grabbed her by the hair and dragged her back to the basement door of the steel cage as she protested and kicked, but to no avail. Once they were both inside, he took a pair of handcuffs from his back pocket and secured her ankle to one of the steel bars. He used the uninjured one, knowing that the swelling which now engulfed the other foot would eventually go down, making it easy for her to slip out of the restraints. He exited and locked the cell door behind him.

Rose didn't get fed that night or the day after, and nothing the following day either. A single cup of water once a day was her new ration. He also removed the bucket that she used as a makeshift toilet.

*****

"I know you're in there, Black," Ramona said as she ogled the peephole from the porch. "Just open the door. Jeezus."

Black opened the door and peered out through a foot-wide gap. "Hey. What are you doing here?" he said while checking the street behind her.

"What the fuck are *you* doing here? The station said you took the rest of the day off," she barked, clearly upset. "Can I come inside? I'm freezing my balls off out here."

"Alright," Black said and stepped aside. Ramona brushed past him as if she lived there and walked inside. She sat down on the sofa and crossed her legs. Her eyes never left Black as he sat down on the armchair adjacent to her.

"So? What's your deal, Daddy-O? There's a missing girl out

there and you decided to take the day to do absolutely fuck all, by the looks of things," Ramona said as her eyes darted around the room.

"I'm not feeling all that great," Black lied and rubbed his hand over his eyes.

"Really?" Ramona looked him up and down. "I call bullshit."

"Look, this isn't something that you want to be involved in, okay? I'm trying to do you a favor," Black said, realizing that she wasn't going to let it go.

"Well!" She threw her arms up in the air. "Thank the Lord, we're getting somewhere! Now you *have* to tell me."

"I'm serious." Black shifted to the edge of the sofa. "You can do whatever the hell you want. I'll tell the chief all is good and you can stay at home or something until this thing is done."

"Okay, it's your turn to listen to *me* now." Ramona placed her hands on her knees and stared straight at Black. "You clearly feel like you can't trust me with whatever it is you're doing, and I get that. The thin blue line isn't what it used to be. But you can let me in. I worked internal affairs for two years so if it's dirty cops, crooked judges or the fucking tooth fairy that's leaking your info, I know all about that kind of shit. I can help you." Her eyes were soft and sincere and Black stared at her for a minute as his mind ran into overdrive.

"Do you want some coffee?" he said after a long pause and headed to the kitchen.

"Sure." Ramona followed him. As Black prepared the joe and they sat back down in the living room, he laid the entire story out for her. From the day of the arrest up until the events that took place just over an hour ago. She was transfixed and didn't ask one question. Black didn't even remember her blinking during his explanation of the situation. When he was done, she still stared at him, her mouth now gaping.

Then, she finally broke her stunned silence. "Wait, so he's upstairs right now?"

"Yes."

"And nobody else knows he's here?"

"No. Aside from the medic that checked him out. He won't say anything," Black said. He found the question strange but wrote it off as a bit of paranoia caused by the fact that he was now forced to work under the radar of the institution that he valued and respected so much during his entire career. The term *rat* came to mind, which was something he and his colleagues used often to describe someone who betrayed their brethren. The skin on the back of his neck broke out in gooseflesh at the thought of it.

"Well, I can't wait to meet him," Ramona said and smiled.

*****

Thirty minutes later, Ellis came down the stairs with measured movement. His head felt like it was caving in and his mouth was dry. If he didn't know any better, he'd say he was severely hungover. He reached the bottom of the stairs and turned the corner to see William Black sitting in the living room with a young woman. She gave a wide grin when she saw him, and she pointed a perfectly straight index finger in his direction.

"There he is! The man of the moment!" She laughed and Black whipped his head around and gave Ellis the smile of a toddler whose been caught decorating a wall with a permanent marker. Introductions were made and Ellis sat down while Ramona went to the bathroom.

"Are you feeling better?" Black asked and Ellis gave him a thumbs up.

"As well as can be expected. You didn't tell me you had a partner," Ellis said and motioned toward the bathroom.

"I didn't until yesterday. She checks out though, don't worry about it."

"You don't think it's odd that you got a new partner on the day that you and I met?" Ellis said in a low tone. "My brain is swollen to shit, and *I* can tell you that sounds off."

"She can help us. Besides, I'd rather talk about the tape recorder I found in your bag. What's on it?"

"It's a recording of a conversation," Ellis said and rubbed the back of his head.

"Between who?" Black looked surprised and excited.

"I'm not sure. I mean … I know who *one* of them is. He was in a cell with me," Ellis said just as Ramona returned from the bathroom. She sat down on her original spot and listened.

"Where did you get something like that? It couldn't have just arrived in your mailbox," Black continued.

"I found it in my attorney's office. The one I haven't heard from in forever. The room looked like nobody had been there in a long time either. It's like he just disappeared off the face of the Earth," Ellis continued and studied Ramona's face. She smiled at him, which he found unsettling.

"His name was Redmayne, right?" As Black asked the question, something in the back of his mind lit up.

"Redpath. Victor Redpath," Ellis said, and Black pursed his lips. "What?"

"Hang on a sec," Black said and pulled his phone from his pocket. He typed furiously then put a hand to his mouth.

"What is it?" Ramona leaned in as Black handed the phone to Ellis. He took it and read the headline on the *Ottawa Sun* news website:

ATTORNEY FOUND SLAIN

Underneath the headline it read:

Victor Redpath (58) an Ottawa native who practiced law in Toronto was found dead at around 5 a.m. yesterday morning by a commuter on his way to work. Mr. Redpath appeared to have been the victim of a hit-and-run homicide. Police reported that he had also sustained multiple gunshot wounds to the head and chest which indicated ...

Ellis handed the phone back to Black and sank into the sofa, running a hand over his face. The throbbing in his head came back with a vengeance as he spoke.

"Oh my god. That article's four weeks old. He's been dead that long and none of us knew. I thought he just gave up and ran."

"I don't know about you fellas," Ramona said. "But to me it's beginning to look like this thing runs much deeper than any of us could imagine."

Ellis looked at her and thought that she looked a bit paler than when he first saw her. That put his mind slightly more at ease about their new "teammate". His thoughts went back to the news article and a few things made sense to him now. The state of Redpath's office, the Dictaphone that was hidden behind a picture frame, the seemingly abandoned state of his office and the fact that he hadn't heard from the man in ages. It all added up now. The biggest question now, aside from Rose's location, was the identity of the man that Bobby was speaking to in the recording. He figured his best bet would be to play the tape and reveal it to his new friends in the police. Surely between the two of them they would know who this Lombardi asshole was.

"There's something else," Black said to Ramona, then looked over to Ellis who met his gaze. Ellis nodded slowly.

"What is it?" Ramona asked, trying not to sound too surprised.

"It's a tape of a phone call," Black continued. "I haven't heard it yet, but Ellis has. One of them is his old cellmate at Stone Hill. We don't know who the mystery man is yet."

"Well let's pop that fucker in the stereo, Daddy-O!" Ramona said eagerly. "Time's a wastin'."

Ellis leaned over, collected the backpack, and slid his hand inside. When it emerged, he had the cassette player from Redpath's office clenched between his index and middle finger. He handed it to Black and Ramona's eyes followed the object as if it were a donor heart being passed from one person to the next during a transplant operation.

"Here we go," Black said and pressed the play button. The room was silent as the mechanical whirring of the ancient recorder seemed to echo off the walls.

A: "Mr. Lombardi, thank you for taking my call."

B: "Of course, anything for an old friend."

A: "How's the family? I hear little Tony is off to college."

B: "Yup. He's the man right now. Hopefully he can keep his head in the books."

A: "I know my Max could never have done that. Too much of a hot head."

B: "God rest his soul."

A: "Yeah, God rest his soul."

B: "So, what can I do for you, Bobby?"

A: "I've been talking to Frank the Tank and it looks like you might be looking for a fall guy soon. You know... for a job. I hope you don't think I'm speaking out of turn here, sir."

B: "Not at all. It's not like you're some mook on a street

corner. You've come a long way with us. Speak your mind."

A: "I have someone in mind. In fact, it's the only option in my opinion and we'll be swatting two flies with one hit. If you give the green light, of course."

B: "Keep talking."

A: "You get your patsy and I get the motherfucker who killed my son."

B: "Sounds like mustard so far. Who is he?"

A: "Man by the name of Ellis Neill."

B: "And where do we find Mr. Neill?"

A: "I've been keeping tabs on him since ... He dropped off the radar for a few years but then Frank recognized his name when he applied to work at the shop. Frank gave me a call and here we are."

B: "Well, it really is a small fuckin' world, isn't it?"

A: "Ain't that the truth. So, what do you think, Mr. Lombardi? Can you help a brother out?"

B: "Why don't I just off the guy for you? It'll be much easier."

A: "No. I want to look that asshole in the eye, so that he knows it was me. I want to get him to trust me. That way it'll be much worse for him."

B: "Alright, Mr. Drake. Judge Reiner owes us one. Actually, he owes us more than one. I'll get the wheels in motion. We'll get this fucker for you. The hit has already been planned so Frank will call you tomorrow to keep you in the loop so you can get your shit in order. Sounds good?"

A: "Yes sir! Thank you, sir. I appreciate it and my boy thanks you too."

B: "Enough with this sir shit, Bobby. We're family. I know you had to get out but you've always been there for us and we look after our own. It's a goddamn tragedy what happened to your boy. We'll help to get that fucker for you, don't even worry about it."

The silence that graced the room before the tape was played continued on for what seemed to Ellis like a full five minutes when it was, in fact, only one. Both detectives were staring at each other. Black's mouth was agape, and Ramona's lips were tightly pressed together for the entire sixty seconds. This was something else that didn't make sense to Ellis. He didn't know the woman very well, but it seemed like she wasn't someone who waited to be asked to give her opinion. Finally, he couldn't stand the silence any longer.

"Well?" Ellis said, and both cops jumped in their seats. "You two look like you've seen a ghost. Do either of you know who that is?"

"That's Vito Lombardi," Black said and clenched the tape recorder tightly. "He runs the Italian mob in Toronto."

"Yup," Ramona said and turned to Ellis. "They're into

cigarette smuggling, hookers, chop shops and pretty much anything illegal you can think of. Not the most savory of characters. His daddy turned C.I. so he's got a point to prove. Likes to chop people up to send a message to other crews and his own."

"That's right," Black jumped in. "We've been watching his outfit for years, but he's managed to stay clean. Runs his operation from an underground bunker that sits underneath his motor repair shop on Trinity Road in the Don Lands, where we picked you up, Ellis."

"Say what now?" Ellis turned to Black. "He owns the garage where I worked?"

"You wouldn't ever have seen him there because that's Frank the Tank's department," Black continued. "He runs all the car dealerships, garages, and chop shops. Vito stays out of sight. That's why they're so hard to catch in the act. Well, that and they outsource a lot of their hits to the street gangs."

"Fuck! The Mob?!" Ellis cried. "I thought I was doing my family a favor by getting this job. Turns out I did exactly the opposite." He clenched his fists, and his face went red.

Black's phone rang. He answered it and got up from his chair then walked briskly toward the front door and went outside.

"It's not your fault, you know. All of this," Ramona said and put a hand on Ellis' knee.

"It isn't? Whose fault is it then? *I* was the one who put them in danger. *I* shot Bobby's kid. *I* picked that fucking ad for the job. And now my wife is dead, and Rose is missing." Ellis' voice cracked and he buried his face in his hands.

"We might have something," Black said as he strode back into through the door. "Possible sighting of the same car that was seen in the motel parking lot the night that Cynthia … Anyway, it looks like I still have some friends out there."

"Where?" Ramona asked. She picked up her coffee, realized it was cold and put it back down on the table.

"Just outside Wasaga Beach, about two hours' drive from here. Got a call from one of my old informants who lives out there. Odd thing is that he said he could've sworn the man driving the car was wearing a red mask. I hope he hasn't lost his marbles out there in the sticks," Black replied and Ellis felt a cold slab of ice slide over his heart and into his stomach. He decided to keep this revelation to himself.

"Can you trust him?" Ramona asked.

"Yeah, he's not on the department's books anymore so comms with him aren't monitored," Black said and pocketed his phone.

"Let's check it out. We have nothing to lose, right? If it *is* her, we need to get there now!" Ellis said as the color in his face began to return to normal.

"We can't just go storming the place. Ellis. There's protocol—" Black began but he was cut off by the fired-up father.

"Fuck your protocol! I'm not asking you! I'm telling you! I came to *you*, remember?!" Ellis roared and got to his feet.

"I agree," Ramona piped up, her eyes wide. "Let's go check it out. We've got no other leads and I don't feel like sitting on my cute ass all day."

Black nodded. "Alright, but if this turns out to be legit then nobody makes a move without my say so. Can we agree on that?"

Ellis and Ramona agreed. Ramona volunteered to drive and after Black gathered some additional tools – his twelve-gauge shotgun and a Glock pistol that he handed to Ellis (to which he had to crack a smile) along with a couple of flashlights – they were on the road, headed north.

CHAPTER 19

Everything is good for you

If it doesn't kill you

Everything is good for you

Good for you ...

Ellis turned the volume on the car stereo down as the Crowded House tune came to its echoing conclusion. Out of his passenger side window, the scenery rolled by in a collage of snow-covered forestry, hiding deep and dark secrets within the shadows of the dense foliage. His mind traveled to Cynthia and the pain that came with her memory was reignited within his heart. He tried to push it aside, knowing that dwelling on the thought of her, for now at least, would cloud his ability to think clearly and strategically. He couldn't afford that, as hard as it was. Not with Rose possibly in the hands of a sadistic maniac. The figure that had abducted him from his cell in the middle of the night may have made a slight miscalculation with Ellis, but that didn't mean he wasn't every bit as cunning and resourceful as any super predator. And he certainly wasn't to be underestimated.

He also thought of Bobby, who was most likely waiting inside the walls of Stone Hill for his plan to come to fruition. Had it all worked out as the old guy wanted it to so far, or had Ellis thrown the proverbial spanner in the works by giving the hitman the slip and escaping? Bobby had let him go that night when he could have easily raised the alarm and stopped the ensuing events dead in their tracks, but he chose not to. Ellis knew he had to consider every interaction he had with Bobby as a complete fabrication, an act of deception intended to instill trust. But he couldn't help considering the remote possibility that at least a shred of it had been genuine. Ellis wasn't a "people person" per se but he knew when he had made a veritable connection with someone, and this had certainly taken place during his exchanges with Bobby Drake. Whichever way this thing was to play out, Ellis had begun to understand the man's motives as a parent, especially now that his own daughter's life was hanging in the balance. He concluded that there was always something to be said for perspective, the element that is always lacking when human emotion is involved.

"Penny for your thoughts there, Daddy-O?" Ramona asked, her eyes still fixed on the patchy white road ahead. "Are you still with us?"

"Yeah. Just thinking about what we might find out there." Ellis was still staring out of the window when he felt a hand on his.

"She'll be fine. You said yourself that she's a tough one, right?" Ramona's voice was soft and comforting and Ellis gave her half a smile. He didn't trust her yet, but she was making that very difficult. She was likable and quick-witted, and he didn't have much of a choice at this stage. As far as he was concerned, the path that his life had taken over the last few months was riddled with risks and unpleasant experiences and if Miss Lee turned psycho on him it wouldn't surprise him at all. But this time he'd be ready to defend his purpose without hesitation or concern. He was going to get Rose back and whoever stood in his way better make their peace – and soon.

They passed a sign that indicated a temporary road closure with a rest stop ten kilometers ahead. The weather had suddenly turned sideways and a blizzard was rocking the car from side to side. They pulled up to an officer who manned the roadblock. Black turned to Ellis and Ramona.

"Leave the talking to me," he said.

"Sorry folks, road's closed for now," the cop sporting the wide hat and flashlight said. He had plain black lapels on his uniform's shoulder mounts.

"Afternoon, Constable," Black said and flashed his badge. "What's going on?"

"Afternoon, sir." The young officer seemed flustered. "A tree came down around the bend over there. Local loggers are working on it now. Shouldn't be too long."

"There's no way around it?" Black asked, smiling.

"Afraid not, sir. Snow is thick as shit... Sorry. It's too thick to go around, sir." The young cop blushed.

"Alright. We'll pull into the rest stop. You let me know as soon as the road opens, okay?"

"Yes sir." The officer gave a hesitant salute and Black had to smile. A real one this time.

It was late afternoon and Ellis was annoyed at the forced stoppage, but a few minutes later he realized that he couldn't remember the last time he had eaten anything. "Gertie's Roadhouse and Diner" was a quaint establishment which proudly displayed that it had been serving travelers since 1955, with the bygone era prominently celebrated through tabletops made from old vinyl LP's, antique jukeboxes in every corner and old cash registers gracing the bar counter. Ellis, Black and their new partner exited the car and were soon seated by the window-table overlooking the road. All three of them settled on the "Dish of the Day" which consisted of a double BLT, chicken wings and a side of fries topped off with Gertie's pecan pie. Conversation was few and far between and Ellis noted that his companions were just about as tense as he was. When Ramona excused herself to "powder her nose", Black shifted closer to Ellis.

"Do you think we're making a mistake, bringing her along?" Black asked in a hushed tone.

"I thought you said she was good," Ellis replied while forking his pie.

"I did, but I've had some time to think in the car and recent events are making me reconsider. I don't know, I just don't want a decision that *I* made to fuck things up for you. Not after everything you've endured, and I had a hand in that," Black said and sipped his coffee while his eyes kept darting in the direction of the restrooms.

"So far, I haven't spotted anything to make me suspicious,

but that doesn't mean I'm including her in my last will and testament." Ellis put his fork down and looked at Black. "We'll keep an eye on her and if something begins to stink, we'll take care of it. Just make sure she's never standing behind you. That's a rule I learned in the desert, and it's served me well."

"Alright." Black took another sip of his coffee. "You know, I haven't even apologized to you yet for all the shit that went down. For what it's worth, I'm sorry. I got caught up in the propaganda machine and I let it fuck with my head."

"Tell you what," Ellis said, looking Black straight in the eye. "You help me get Rose back and all is forgiven. Deal?"

Ellis held a hand out and as Black shook it, he could see a glimmer of relief flash over the detective's face. The officer that they met earlier knocked on the window and when he saw that Black had noticed him, he gave a thumbs up accompanied by a wide, boyish grin.

"You fellas ready to get going?" Ramona said as she arrived back at the table and tossed Ellis the car keys. "You're driving. I'm too full of bacon."

"No way," Black protested.

"Why not? We're already breaking the law, Daddy-O," Ramona said and pointed a perfectly manicured finger at Ellis. "This tall drink of water is an escaped convict and we're all on a road trip together. Unknot your knickers, big man."

Back in the car, the mood was turning from tense to an air of nervous excitement and Ellis recalled this feeling from his days in the desert. Except this time, he was much more vested in the situation. Retrieving his child intact was the objective here, not clearing a dilapidated building packed with hostiles for some fat cats sitting ten thousand kilometers away. His palms felt damp underneath the leather upholstery of the steering wheel and he had to keep reminding himself to slow down in order to stay within the speed limit. Yes, he had two cops with him in the car who could probably badge-flash their way out of trouble again, but he didn't want to tempt fate. Not today of all days. They passed a sign that read *Wasaga Beach – 3 kms* and *Home of the Largest Freshwater Beach in the World* in faded red print on a withered, blue backboard.

"The town that time forgot," Black said, staring out of the window.

"What was that you said?" Ramona asked.

"This place. It's the town that time has forgotten. I used to come down here on holiday with friends from the academy. Then in oh-seven, half the town's main strip burned down and shit just came to a standstill. Lots of people left for good after that. If it wasn't for the beach this place would've died completely a long time ago."

"I remember that," Ellis said and met Black's eyes in the rear-view mirror. "Two kids did it."

"And that right there is why my birth control is more important to me than my weapon," Ramona said and scoffed. "No thank you, sir."

Ten minutes later, they were driving through the quiet town and Black was directing Ellis to the location where the suspect vehicle was seen. The houses were sparsely scattered on either side of secluded roads. The run-down domiciles were endowed with expansive front and back yard areas. The roofs and terrace awnings were burdened with thick layers of packed snow and the sky seemed darker here than the stretch they covered on the main road. Ellis didn't know if it was because of the concentration of trees flanking the streets or perhaps just the mood of the town that appeared to be reflected in the sky. To him it felt wrong, being here. Like something in the air was issuing a warning that this was a place of ominous things.

They passed an area labelled by a road sign that read *Wasaga Beach Village* then turned right onto Ramblewood Drive. When they reached an area where there were two dilapidated houses on the right and dense forest to the left Black spoke up.

"Right here. Stop the car."

Ellis pulled to the side of the road and parked on the shoulder. "Which one is it?" he asked, eyeing the two houses out.

"Neither. It's in there," Black said and thumbed in the direction of the tightly clustered forest. Ellis and Ramona turned around in unison and stared into the lines of pine trees that were coated in white powder. Ellis thought it looked like they were standing guard, as if to protect what was hidden inside. Visibility was low because of the density of the trees and past the second line of pines nothing was distinguishable from the shadows cast by the canopy.

"Right," Ramona said and cocked her pistol, "what exactly are we looking for here?"

"Anything that looks like it might contain an abducted girl," Black said and Ramona rolled her eyes. The detective removed the shotgun from under the blanket next to him on the backseat and loaded it with five shells, its maximum capacity, then dumped four more into his coat pocket. The two cops and the con exited the vehicle and stood before the mammoth sized trees which loomed over them like sleeping giants.

"So, what's the plan?" Ellis asked as he checked the magazine on his firearm.

"Simple," Black said, his eyes scanning the forest. "We split up into two groups. Ellis, you're with me." He turned his gaze to Ramona. "You can range toward the right. Ellis and I will go left, and we'll meet in the middle. Happy?"

"Roger, Dodger," Ramona said and swapped her heels out for a pair of running shoes from her bag. "Just don't fucking shoot me, please."

"Alright. Stay frosty, we don't know what we're walking into here," Black wrapped up and they set off into the forest.

The floor was thick with snow and dead leaves, and it made a strange crunching noise as Ellis and Black pushed forward, trying to avoid stepping on the really dense areas to minimize their noise levels. Ramona was walking in the same direction, about fifty meters to their right, and Ellis was amazed at how little sound she was making; her dainty feet appeared to float on the snowpack. The forest was quiet except for a few distant bird calls and the creaking of the tree trunks as the tops swayed in the wind and their bases resettled in the frozen soil. As they slowly moved forward, steam rolled from their lips and Ellis noticed that his exhalations were more frequent and jittery. He calmed himself, remembering that this might be the place, yes, but it was just as likely that it would turn out to be a wild goose chase.

Suddenly, a blood-curdling scream came from his right. It was sharp and high-pitched and seemed to echo through the entire forest. Ellis turned towards the sound and saw Ramona lying flat on her back in between the leaves and snow, her head only barely visible from his vantage point.

"Oh shit!" Black screamed and rushed past Ellis towards where Ramona lay. Ellis shook the chill that gripped his neck after hearing the scream and followed the detective. What felt like a hundred footsteps later, they finally arrived at where she was sprawled on the ground. Her left foot was covered in blood and around her lower leg were the gigantic jaws of an old, rusted bear-trap. Her shin was bent where the steel teeth had snapped shut around it and Ellis instantly knew the bone was broken. She was squirming on the ground and kept trying to sit up and paw at the jaws clamping down on her leg.

"Fuck. We've got to get this off her," Black said and tried to pry the trap open, but it wouldn't budge. She was trapped.

*****

Rose was torn from sleep as heavy footsteps approached the trap door at a frenetic pace. It swung open and the figure leaped down, his feet landing hard on the concrete floor. She jumped up and backed into the corner instinctively and her knees gave way in fear and panic as he ripped the gate open.

The figure lunged at her, and she swatted his hand away. He grabbed at her again and got a hand firmly clenched around her forearm. The figure twisted it and turned her back to him then forced onto her stomach.

"No! No! Please!" Rose cried out and tears rolled over her gaunt cheeks. She felt his full weight on top of her then her wrists were gripped behind her back in one of his hands. He secured her arms together with zip ties then attached an excessive amount of duct tape over her mouth, stifling her cries. The figure rolled Rose over onto her back and stood over her, staring blankly. His eyes were cold and dead as he raised a single index finger to his mouth, then turned and left the room locking the steel gate behind him.

Fighting through her tears, Rose began to try to make sense of what had just happened. Why did he want her to keep quiet? Why did he bind her hands and gag her? Was there someone coming? Could it be her father? Her heart jumped into her chest at the thought of it and she cried even harder. *It must be him*, she thought. He was here and he had come to save her from this animal that kept her without food and a bucket to shit in. It was finally time to go home.

Then another thought entered her mind. The figure had been waiting for him to arrive all this time. Surely he would've prepared for that. She had to warn him or whoever was out there. Rose strained against the gag, mustering all her strength to shout, but only a muffled moan escaped from her lips.

*****

"Hang on, let's try together," Ellis said and looked at Ramona whose complexion had gone whiter than the snow that surrounded her. "Ramona! When I say *three* you pull that leg out as hard as you can, okay?!" Ramona gave half a nod, then leaned to her right and vomited. Ellis grabbed one half of the jaws and Black the other. "Let's go! One! Two! Three!" Both men leaned back and pulled. The jaws gave a short screech and began to open. When they could widen the gap no more, Ellis checked the width.

"Now!" he yelled and Ramona yanked her leg out. Her stockings were fused to the metal teeth as they tore from her leg. The wound wasn't bleeding too badly but the pain was enough to make her go limp, and her eyes rolled in their sockets.

A gunshot.

A branch from the tree behind them shattered, sending bark and wood splinters raining down on them. Ellis grabbed Ramona around the waist and dragged her behind another wide tree trunk. He propped her up with her back against it. The sound of the gunfire made her return from Neverland.

"What the fuck is going on?!" she shrieked and another gunshot clapped into the air. This time the bullet hit the opposite side of the tree they were leaning against. Fragments of wood and snow exploded behind them. "Fuck! My leg!" Ramona screamed and Ellis put a hand over her mouth.

"I'm sorry but you *have* to try and be quiet. We're under fire," Ellis said as calmly as he could. Shots went off right next to him and as Ellis looked left, he saw Black in a crouched position, firing his Glock in the direction of the gunman. The detective unloaded six rounds then ducked behind the tree next to Ellis and Ramona.

"I can see the muzzle flash. Fucker is about a hundred meters ahead. There's an outline of a barn as well." Black's eyes were wide, and he was breathing hard. "How's she doing?"

"I'll live. Probably won't conga ever again," Ramona said through the tears and blood that streaked her face and she managed a wry smile.

"You stay right where you are. Your job here is done," Ellis said and gripped her shoulder softly. She looked up at him and winked, then laid her head back against the tree. Her eyes rolled a few times then closed but Ellis saw that she was breathing steadily.

Two more gunshots.

Tree bark flew and snow mixed with brown leaves popped off the ground into the air between Ellis and Black.

"We can't stay here," Ellis said in a low voice just above a whisper.

"I'll draw his fire," Black said and slid the shotgun over to Ellis. "You go get your kid."

"Watch your step," Ellis said. He motioned to Ramona who was now fully unconscious. "What about her? Will she be okay?"

"She'll be fine as long as she stays quiet. I'll come back for her."

The two men nodded in agreement and Detective William Black darted out from behind his tree and dove in behind another one three meters away, which resulted in two more gunshots echoing from ahead. He leaned to the left of the tree trunk and fired his weapon three times. Ellis knew this was his cue and he bounded forward past two trees and stopped behind the third. He could see the barn now. It was covered in early evening fog and drifted in and out of sight. Ellis breathed steadily and waited. A few seconds later, he heard Black fire his weapon again and he set off, passing three trees this time, and stopped behind the fourth. With every footfall he prayed that there were no more bear traps laid. The barn was ten meters in front of him now. He could also see the shooter holding a rifle at shoulder height standing just past the far corner of the building and as he fired, a cry came from the bowels of the forest, and he knew it was Black. He'd been hit. Ellis racked the shotgun and fired in the direction of the shooter. The figure ducked then ran into the brush, disappearing in the rapidly encroaching darkness. Ellis slid around the tree, shotgun raised, and aimed in the direction that the figure had run off into. He slowly stepped closer to the barn. He turned the corner and found a door. Stepping even lighter now he approached it, counted to three then kicked it down as hard as he could. He stormed inside, checked the corners and crevices for occupants but found none.

The place was furnished scantily with a single bed, stove and small wooden table and chairs, but no Rose. His heart sank as he looked around in the empty room. Turning to exit and continue his search outside, he heard a faint clunking sound. It was rhythmic and repetitive and sounded like it was coming from outside. On his way back towards the door that was now hanging from one hinge, his boot caught on something underneath the tattered rug on the floor. He stopped, pulled the carpet off to the left and had to catch his breath as a trapdoor in the floorboards revealed itself. Ellis unlatched it and swung the creaking panel open and saw a metal slide that ran down and ended beside a steel cage. Next to the slide, on the right, was a narrow steel ladder.

He took the steps two at a time until he reached the bottom floor. Before him was a wrought-iron structure almost the same size as the dugout room and inside the cage lay his daughter, frail and quivering with a rag tied around her mouth and a set of cuffs connecting her ankle to one of the bars. Ellis fell to his knees and crawled to the side where Rose lay. When she turned and saw him her face grimaced, and a wail escaped her lips through the cloth around her mouth. She tried to crawl closer to the bars on her stomach but couldn't get there. Ellis reached in through the bars, managed to snag the sleeve on her shirt and pulled her right up to him. He embraced her tightly through the bars. The edges of the steel were digging into his shoulders, but he didn't care. Ellis could feel Rose's body shaking as she sobbed uncontrollably and kept trying to talk. He pulled back and removed the gag from her mouth.

"Daddy! Oh my god! You came!" Rose managed through the tears. "Mom ... She's ..."

"I know," he said and hugged her tightly, feeling the lump in his throat expand. "I know, darling."

As they embraced and Ellis felt Rose relax into his arms, a sudden dull pain shot through the back of his head and his vision went dark. Rose screamed. He fell over and the last thing he saw as he lost consciousness was the red mask on the man standing over him who was holding a rifle.

*****

Ellis rubbed the back of his head and he flinched as he sat up. He could hear voices in the distance, muffled like a conversation over a bad phone line. Gradually, it cleared, and he recognized one of the voices – it was Rose.

"Dad! Dad! Can you hear me?!" There was a panic in her voice that Ellis had never heard before. He looked to his right and saw that she was sitting next to him on the floor. He realized they were both inside the cage now. A pair of men's shoes stood before him and as his eyes traveled upwards, he saw the red mask. The one he saw in prison – the same one he had laid elbows and fists into. The same one he thought he had killed. The masked figure was pointing a rifle at his head.

"I'm okay, honey," Ellis said to Rose, not taking his eyes off the figure before him.

"When you kill someone," the figure's thin, reedy voice spoke from behind the crimson nylon, "you better make sure they're dead."

The figure cocked his rifle and tucked the butt firmly into his shoulder, staring straight at Ellis as he readied his shot. Rose began to scream, but her father couldn't hear her. He looked over to his daughter, smiled and said, "I love you, honey. I always will."

"I love you, Daddy," Rose said softly, her face the picture of pure hopelessness and despair as it dawned on her that she was going to have to watch her father die too.

A shot rang into the air and reverberated around the room. Then, two more shots. Tiny drops of blood landed on Rose's glistening cheeks.

Ellis opened his eyes. The figure was lying in front of him, his red mask now a deeper shade of crimson. Through a hole in between his eyes, there was gray matter and blood pouring out. Ellis looked up and behind the figure, propped up on one leg with her Glock still aimed at the body on the floor, stood Ramona Lee. Rose leapt over and wrapped her arms around her father's neck, still crying but now for a different reason. Ellis hugged her, kissed her forehead, and stroked strands of hair out of her face. For a moment they just stared into each other's eyes, both in disbelief at the living presence of the other.

"Honey," Ellis said. "This is Ramona." He turned to look at her but the spot where she was standing mere seconds ago was now vacant. Like an apparition that had the ability to dissipate into thin air, their savior had made off as quickly as she had appeared. Ellis turned back to face Rose. "Let's get out of here."

Ellis helped Rose to her feet, and they began to ascend the ladder. They exited the barn through the broken-down door and around the corner Ellis stopped as he laid eyes on William Black, sitting on the ground and clutching his left elbow. Faint trickles of blood were flowing from in between his fingers. The detective smiled as he saw Ellis and Rose approaching.

"You must be Rose," Black said and she gave him a smile back.

"Did you see Ramona?" Ellis asked.

"No. She's probably still where we left her." Black grimaced as he clutched his arm tighter. "I think we should get the fuck out of here. Someone may have heard all the gunfire.

"Agreed," Ellis said and helped Black to his feet. Together

the three navigated their way through the dark and the snow back to the car that was patiently waiting for them on the side of the road.

"We can't leave her here," Ellis said and opened the door for Rose.

"I know. But we need to go *now*," Black said.

With Ellis behind the wheel, his daughter safe and sound in the passenger seat next to him, and William Black tending to his wounds in the backseat, they drove off into the night.

CHAPTER 20

Ellis couldn't help but sit and watch Rose as she devoured the pizza – that wasn't that great – as if it were her last meal. He was surprised at the lingering ferocity of her appetite even after two days of eating very well. The results were also beginning to show. Her cheeks were once more flushed with the rosy tint they had been graced with since the day of her birth and she had regained her energy. The glistening gleam in her eye had also made a welcome return. It was quite the contrasting image to when they had arrived at the "R&R Motel" which was situated a few blocks away from the airport.

In addition to her drastic weight loss, Rose had barely been able to walk and had developed chills brought in by malnutrition during the drive from the forest where she had been kept. Black made an emergency call to Nathan, the stand-by paramedic, and upon their arrival at the motel he had administered two intravenous nourishment bags. The first was a combination of half-strength Darrow's solution with five percent dextrose, followed by a cocktail of Ringer's lactate solution – shaken, not stirred – with five percent dextrose. The next morning, Ellis breathed a sigh of relief as the girl rose with an appetite similar to young Claudia's after her turning to the dark side in *Interview with the Vampire*. Rose did not appreciate the analogy.

As she reached for the final slice of pie, Ellis' phone chimed. It was a text from William Black.

CBC News. Now.

He pressed the power button on the television remote and a bleak looking Vito Lombardi appeared on screen. He was being escorted out of his house in handcuffs and a bathrobe, accompanied by several men in suits and sunglasses. The caption at the bottom of the screen read: "MOB BOSS AND *CAPO'S* CHARGED WITH MURDER, CONSPIRACY AND TRAFFICKING". Ellis turned the volume up as a blonde female reporter standing in front of the scene gave a breakdown of events.

... A police spokesperson has informed CBC News that they received a recording of a phone call where Lomardi and another unnamed party can be heard discussing the planned murder of Judge Stephen Thatcher and his wife earlier this year. If found guilty, Lombardi and his co-conspirators will most likely face a life-term in prison. I'm Stacey Hawkins for CBC News, Toronto.

Ellis smiled and as he looked over to Rose, he could see that she was smiling too. It was a good day. The best day that the father and daughter had experienced together in a very long time.

*****

Black shifted the gear lever into park, grabbed the brown manilla envelope and newspaper from the passenger seat and exited his car. The sling that his arm had been placed in was tight and uncomfortable, but it didn't limit his range of movement much. He ascended the two flights of stairs beside the motel office and knocked on the burgundy door with *3F* in bold golden print on it. Ellis opened the door. William was surprised to see him smile as he shook his hand. He walked inside and broke out in a similar smile when he saw Rose sitting on the bed, her eyes sparkling like two polished diamonds.

"Hey, missy," Black said and pulled a chocolate from his coat pocket. He tossed it over to her and she caught it with one hand.

"Hi, Detective. How are you feeling?"

"Just fine, thank you, Rose. How about you?"

"Hungry! All the time!" She rolled her eyes and started to unwrap the chocolate bar.

"All according to plan then," Black said and sat down on one of the chairs at the modest dining table. Rose got up, as if she could tell that the grown-ups were going to discuss something private, went into the bedroom and closed the door.

"How's the shoulder?" Ellis asked when Rose was out of sight.

"It's okay. I had to write a bogus report about someone trying to rob me in my driveway just to get people to stop asking questions. That was more painful than any wound I'll ever sustain," Black said and tossed the newspaper to Ellis. "Have a look at the front page."

Ellis unfolded the paper and stared at it. On the front page were several photographs lined up in a row. The first was a fresh mugshot of Vito Lombardi. The three men next to his picture were named: Georgio Lambretti, Sal Vettori and Nick Figliomeni. All three were labeled as *Capo's* in the organization. The final picture was of an attractive woman in her early thirties and Ellis had to catch his breath as he read the caption beneath it – Ramona Lee. The words *STILL AT LARGE* were printed next to her name.

"You're fucking kidding!" Ellis said and ran a hand through his hair.

"I shit you not, my friend. She was one of them the whole time." Black shook his head as he continued, "But … she had a million chances to stop us. I don't get it."

"Beats me. Maybe she had a change of heart. It doesn't say what exactly she did for him, but it looks like she was quite important to ol' Vito's business."

"Well." Ellis sighed and folded the newspaper. "I'm just glad it's all over."

"It's *kind of* over, Ellis. Unfortunately, it'll never be completely over. That's why I got you this," Black said and handed Ellis the manilla envelope. "We can assume that the ones that remain within Vito's organization will always be on the lookout for Ellis and Rose Neill."

Ellis opened the envelope and turned it over onto the table in front of him. A few cards and two passports fell out. He looked them over. There was a California driver's license with Ellis' picture for a "Lawrence Kruger" along with US Social Security cards, one with the same name as the driver's license and the other had "Sophie Kruger" printed on it. The passports were United States of America documents with the same corresponding names on them, all with fake stamps from previous travels to ensure authenticity upon inspection.

"When did you get the time to do this?" Ellis asked.

"I made the call to my guy just before we left for the forest to look for Rose. Figured it would come in handy."

"I don't know what to say. Thank you, William."

"Think of it as my final apology for dropping you in the turd-mixer," Black said and smiled.

"What about you and your family?" Ellis asked. "It can't be completely safe here for you either."

"You're right about that. We'll wait a few weeks until the dust settles then I'll put in for a transfer or tender my resignation. We can start over anywhere. In the meantime, we'll run a tight ship."

"Yeah. Perhaps that's the best thing for everyone. A fresh start."

*****

The sun was setting low in the sky as Rose peered over the dashboard and through the windshield. Her excitement was tangible, and Ellis felt it too.

"There it is, Dad!" she shouted as the border crossing into the

US came into sight in the distance.

"Are you excited?" Ellis asked, fully knowing what the response would be, but he was enjoying seeing his daughter glow.

"Duh! What a silly question," she said and looked at him with softness in her eyes. "I think mom would have loved our new home in Colorado."

"Yes, she would. She would also be very proud of the woman you're becoming. She really would," Ellis said, and that lump returned to his throat.

"And of you, Dad. For saving me. I love you," Rose said and leaned over to hug him.

"I love you too, honey," Ellis said and hugged her back.

"Dad." Rose looked up at him. "This feeling I have inside about Mom. I don't know what it is, and I don't know what to do with it. All I know is … that it hurts. What do I do with it?"

"I know exactly what you mean, my Rosey," Ellis said and ran his hand over her hair. "I wish I could fix that for you, but I don't know how either." He saw her gaze drop to the floor. "But do you know what?"

"What, Dad?"

"We will figure it out together. As long as you know that you're not alone. Your old dad is right here with you, always."

Rose smiled and nuzzled her face into his chest.

The car rolled forward, toward their new destinations and their new life. Ellis knew there was healing to be done and the deep wound inflicted by the loss of his beloved wife would haunt him for years to come. There would be hard days ahead but also good days. He knew one thing above all else – that Cynthia would want them to make the most of their time together, to squeeze every bit of joy and happiness from the fruit of life while they could.

*****

Several months had passed when, on a crisp Rocky Mountain morning, Ellis picked up the phone and dialed the number for Stone Hill Prison. He introduced himself to the operator using his new name and social security number then waited.

"Hello, this is Bobby Maxwell."

"Hi Bobby. This is Lawrence Kruger," Ellis said and there was a pause before the reply came.

"Who? Did you punch the wrong inmate number, Mr. Kruger? I can relay you back to recep—"

"No, I didn't. I was stationed in Karbala with your son. I was there the night that he died," Ellis said. He could hear the familiar sounds of the prison playing out in the background and it gave him a momentary shudder.

"Well … um." Bobby sounded confused and apprehensive. "I thought I had met all of Chris' friends. It's been such a long time."

"We didn't know each other for very long. But we did have some conversations. About life and family," Ellis said.

"Oh yeah?" Bobby chuckled. "He probably told you about his father, the criminal and what a fuckup I was?"

"No, in fact that's not what my impression was. You're just a father who has suffered a great loss. An unimaginable loss that has filled you with anger and fear."

There was a long silence before Bobby replied.

"The man that killed my son is walking free. That will drive any father insane." Bobby had a defeated tone in his voice.

"The man that killed your son, Mr. Drake, does not go to sleep *one* night without thinking of him. He lies awake and replays that night in his mind, looking for ways that he could've stopped him without shooting him. And after fourteen years, neither he nor those close to him have come up with an alternative solution. Your son wasn't well, Bobby. Yes, we should have noticed it earlier and many of us thought it was nothing. Just the desert getting to him like it did to all of us. I know that if the man who killed him could change the events of that night, he would, in a heartbeat. But he can't. All he can offer is his sincere regret and the knowledge that this will stay with him forever." Ellis wiped a single tear from his eye.

The silence from the other end was broken by a guard barking orders in the background. "I hear you, son," Bobby replied. "There's been enough of us thrown away like garbage over things that were unintended. If you see that man again you tell him that I will forgive him someday. I don't know when it'll be, but it *will* happen."

"I'll pass the message on. I'm sure that he'd be grateful to hear that," Ellis said and cleared his throat.

"I don't suppose I'll hear from you again—" Bobby said before he was cut off. Ellis knew that the guard had probably killed his call for going over the allowed time.

He sat back in the wooden chair on the porch of his and Rose's newly acquired log cabin and looked at his daughter running around in the snow with Blackie. The dog had appeared on the side of the road one morning as they drove into town. He had been left in a box, unwanted by his previous owner and Rose took to him in an instant. Ellis smiled at the pair frolicking around and thought that the circle that life handed a person was certainly something to marvel at.

And here they were, the three who had returned after being discarded.

The End

Author's Note

Although the events in this story are not real, there are families like Ellis, Cynthia and Rose who deal with the struggles that were thrust upon these characters every day and in every country around the world.

When I first began to write The Discarded I didn't have much of an idea regarding the theme for the book. All I knew was that a snow-covered forest would feature heavily in the story.

As the characters developed and the story took its own direction, a strong message emerged from it that was not intentional or expected. What also took me by surprise was the desperation that came through from not only the victims of flawed justice systems but the damage that it could cause and how it reverberated through time and beyond the walls of correctional facilities.

Whichever way the events in this novel was interpreted by you, Dear Reader, one cannot disagree with the person that believes in the equalizing effects that different perspectives can bring to the world.

If we could all walk a mile...

Acknowledgements

It is never easy to put gratitude into words, but I will try my best.

Firstly, a huge thank you to the team at Kingsley Publishers for getting my story out there to see the light of day and for all the support. It means the world to me.

Thank you to my family, Liesl, Wehann, Jessie, Kayla and Amelie, who have supported me through the writing of this novel. Your words of encouragement and praise will forever be appreciated.

To my test readers—Ruelle and Ashleigh—your input and response were invaluable, and I am eternally grateful for your words of encouragement.

Thank you to my extended family—(Oom) John, (Antie) Sherril, Lauren, Ashleigh, Sean and the kids. Your words of praise and support were more than I could have hoped for.

Thank you to Mrs. Britz, my high school English teacher, who planted the creative writing seed within me many years ago. I apologize that it has taken so long to bloom, but without your words about my very first story, I wouldn't have ever considered doing this.

And finally, to my darling wife, Courtney. Without you, none of this would have been possible. Your belief in me is what keeps me going and I count my blessings every day that I get to have you by my side. Thank you for always backing me, even when I don't back myself, and for your constant love and support.

About the Author

Louis van Schalkwyk was born in South Africa and currently resides in Hong Kong. "The Discarded" is his debut novel, inspired by years honing his writing skills and drawing influence from his favorite authors. When Louis isn't writing he enjoys reading and sampling various cuisines with his wife, Courtney.

Connect with Louis on social media, he loves to connect with his readers.

Instagram: @louisvsauthor

Twitter: @louisvanschalk3

Website: louisvanschalkwyk.com

Printed in Great Britain
by Amazon

79392990R00181